Willa
of the
wood

Willa

e Wood

ROBERT BEATTY

DISNEY·HYPERION

LOS ANGELES NEW YORK

First Hardcover Edition, July 2018
First Paperback Edition, June 2019
3 5 7 9 10 8 6 4
FAC-026988-21320

Printed in the United States of America

This book is set in 12-pt Adobe Garamond Pro, Liam,
Qilin/Fontspring; Minister Std/Monotype
Designed by Maria Elias
Illustrations by Chi Birmingham

Library of Congress Cataloging-in-Publication Control Number
for Hardcover Edition: 2018013766
ISBN 978-1-368-00947-8

Visit www.DisneyBooks.com

**The Great Smoky Mountains**

1900

As Willa overheard the two day-folk men talking
about whether the earth was flat or round,
she shook her head. They were both wrong.
The world was neither flat nor round.
It was *mountains.*

Willa
of the
wood

Willa crept through the darkened forest, following the faint scent of chimney smoke on the midnight air. The silver strands of the clouds passing in front of the moon cloaked her movements in shadow, and she made little sound stepping across the cold, wet leaves she felt beneath her bare feet. All during the night she'd been moving down the slope of the mountain into the small valley where the homesteaders lived. When she came to the rocky edge of the river, she knew she was getting close to what she'd come for.

She didn't know the river's mood here, so she avoided the dark and dangerous currents by climbing up through the gnarled limbs of the craggy old trees and asking for their help. As the branches reached out over the water to hold her, they rustled in the wind, talking to one another, as if concerned about where she was going. Her tunic of woven green cane flexed with the movements of her body as she climbed, the branches of the trees holding her gently, intertwining wrist and arm, ankle and leg, then letting go in turn, helping her across with the care that they would give a sapling granddaughter. She made her way hand over hand above the misty breath of the tumbling river, then slithered down a trunk on the other side.

"Thank you," she whispered to the trees, touching one's bark with the palm of her hand as she left them behind her.

Passing a tranquil pool of starlit water among the stones at the river's edge, she glimpsed her reflection: a twelve-year-old willow wisp of a forest girl with long, dark hair, a rounded face with streaked and spotted skin, and emerald-green eyes. Unlike most of her clan, who coveted the glittering treasures of their enemies and even wore their deadened clothes, Willa wore no fabric or jewelry of any kind that might flash in the gloom. Wherever she went in the forest, her skin and hair and eyes took on the color and appearance of the green leaves around her. If she paused near the trunk of a tree, she turned so brown and barken that she became nearly invisible. And now, as she looked into the water, she saw her face for just a moment before it took on the color of the water and the nighttime sky above her and she disappeared, her dark blue cheeks dotted with glistening stars.

Continuing toward what she'd come for, Willa slunk low and quiet through the mountain laurel, up the gentle riverine slope, her heart beating slow and steady as she approached the homesteaders' lair.

She came from a clan of forest people that the Cherokee

called "the old ones" and told stories about around their campfires at night. The white-skinned homesteaders referred to her kind as *night-thieves*, or sometimes *night-spirits*, even though she was as flesh and blood as a deer, a fox, or any other creature of the forest. But she seldom heard the true name of her people. In the old language—which she only spoke with her grandmother now—her people were called the *Faeran*.

Willa stopped at the edge of the forest and blended her skin into the surrounding textures of green. Tendrils of leaves wrapped around her. She became all but invisible.

The soft sounds of the night's insects and frogs surrounded her. But she stayed alert, wary of beady-eyed dogs, hidden watchmen, and other dangers.

She gazed toward the lair of the homesteaders. They had built it with the cut-up carcasses of murdered trees nailed one to the other in long slabs. The bodies of the dead trees made flat walls with square corners, unlike anything else in the forest.

*Just get what you came for, Willa,* she told herself.

The lair had a high, slanted rooftop, a large railed porch that came around the front, and a chimney made of jagged rock the homesteaders had broken from the bones of the river. She saw no oil lamps or candlelight in the windows, but she knew from the thin line of gray smoke drifting from the chimney that the homesteaders—whom she sometimes called the *day-folk*, because they retreated into their lairs when the sun went down—were probably sleeping inside in their long, flat, pillowed beds.

She knew from experience that the homesteaders in this area locked the doors of their lairs at night, so she had to be clever.

Through an open window? Down the chimney? She studied the lair for a long time, looking for a way in. And then she saw it. In the lower part of the front door, the owner of the lair had fashioned a smaller door for his white-fanged companion to come and go.

And that was his mistake.

Her heart began to pound, for her body knew the time had come, and the leaves withdrew from around her. She emerged from the cover of the forest and quickly darted across the open grassy area that surrounded the lair. She hated open areas. Her legs felt strange and uneven as she ran across the unnaturally flat ground. She dashed up the steps to the wooden porch. Then she slipped down onto her hands and knees, pushed through the little door, and crawled into the darkened lair to begin the night's take.

Once inside the walls of the lair, Willa scurried out of the moonlight filtering in through the window. She hunkered down on the floor in the shadowed corner of the eating place, the small quills on the back of her neck rising up as her eyes scanned the darkness for danger.

*Where's the biting dog?* she wondered. *Are all the day-folk upstairs in their beds?*

Holding her breath, she slithered across the floor and looked out into the main room of the lair for attackers.

She waited, she watched, and she listened.

If they caught her here—actually *inside* their lair—they would kill her. They had hacked the trees of the forest and hunted the animals. They had murdered her mother, her father, her twin sister, and so many others of the Dead Hollow lair. The day-folk did not think. They did not hesitate. Whether it was the wolves who howled to find their loved ones in the night, or the great trees who raised their limbs to the sun, the day-folk killed whatever they did not understand. And they understood very little of the forest into which they had come.

As she pulled in a slow and steady, tightly controlled breath, she heard the sound of the small metal-wound machine ticking on the fireplace mantel and the slow hiss and crackle of the dying embers that had led her here to the lair.

The scent of something startlingly sweet reached her nose. She tried to ignore it, but her stomach growled. She turned to see a round, stonelike container sitting on a flat wooden surface above her. She knew she shouldn't let this distract her, but she'd been so hungry yesterday and all through the night.

She quickly rose up, lifted the container's lid, and gobbled down several of the small, crumbly lumps inside like a ravenous raccoon. As her mouth watered with the sweet flavor, she couldn't help but smile, but she was careful not to leave any crumbs that the day-folk might notice. She wanted to eat more of the lumps, but she stuffed half of what remained into her woven-reed satchel and hurried on her way.

As she snuck into the main room, she noticed a rectangle of tin with a mottled depiction of several of the day-folk, as though they had looked into their reflection in the pool beside the river and never escaped: a clean-shaven man, a dark-haired woman, two little ones maybe five and six years old, and a tiny crawler in the woman's arms. But Willa didn't look at them for long, because she didn't like to think about their souls inside the metal.

*Get what you came for,* she told herself again and pressed on.

Glancing nervously at the stairway as she worked, she quickly searched the main room for valuables. She found a small wooden box filled with a moist, brown substance that she was pretty sure was chewing tobacco. She stuffed half of it into her satchel. It wasn't the kind of takings she was keen for, but she knew the *padaran*, the leader of her clan, would be pleased by this special gift. She could see herself standing before his looming figure as she emptied her satchel in front of him, his eyes gleaming with approval.

Feeling pleased with herself, she continued on. In a very small, tightly enclosed room filled with nothing but clothing hanging down from strange, shoulder-like shapes, she found a long, dark overcoat with a leather wallet and coins in the pockets, and she smiled. She took half the bills and half the coins. These were the takings the padaran had trained her to find.

The padaran sent her and the other *jaetters*—the young hunter-thieves of the clan—out each night, and he gave his love to the ones who returned with their satchels full of coins or anything else of value.

She glanced at the stairway again, knowing that when danger came it would come down those stairs. She'd already had a good take, and she knew that a wise jaetter left when the leaving was good, but she wanted more.

When she'd returned to Dead Hollow the night before, her satchel had been light, and the padaran had struck her face so hard with the back of his hand that she'd fallen to the ground, astonished and ashamed to be wiping the blood from her mouth. Over the last few months, she'd thought that she had become his favorite, but now he had struck her, just as he did the other jaetters, and she still felt the fire of it on her cheek. Tonight she wanted more, more than she had ever taken before, to prove to the padaran and the rest of the clan what she could do.

Finally, she went over to the bottom of the stairs, cupped her hands behind her ears, and closed her eyes, listening to the rooms above. She heard a man snoring, and there were probably other day-folk up there, too, a little clutch of them, sleeping away the night.

*But where's the dog?* she wondered again. *The dog is death.* She'd run into trouble with the fanged beasts before, with their loud barking and their vicious, biting, scratching attacks. *I can smell the wretched creature around here someplace,* she thought. *I used its door to get in. But where is it? Why hasn't it come charging out at me with its snapping teeth?*

Most of her fellow jaetters stole things from unattended wagons, midnight yards, and dark-morning barns when there were no day-folk around. Very few ever dared to sneak into the day-folk lairs, and none would do it when the day-folk were actually inside. The jaetters had been trained to go out together in small groups, and to never take such risks. But she put her foot on the first step and began to creep up the creaky wooden staircase, treading as lightly as she could on the strangely flat surfaces, so unlike anything she encountered in the forest.

When she reached the top of the stairs, her legs trembled as she inched slowly through a narrow, cavelike tunnel toward the open doorway of the first room. In the forest she could use her camouflage and her other powers, but her powers didn't work in the inner world of the day-folk. Here she could be seen, she could be captured, she could be killed.

Her palms were sweating as she slowly peeked into the sleeping man's room.

She had noticed on her other takes that the day-folk seemed to sleep in twos. But this man was sleeping alone, on one side of the large bed, as if the one he slept with was gone. But there beside him was the biting dog she'd been looking for—a shaggy black-and-white fiend, lying fast asleep beside its master, its white fangs and sharp claws visible in the moonlight.

The man's face was bristled with whiskers and he was lying on top of the covers, his clothes torn and wrinkled, as if he had collapsed there in exhaustion. A chair and a small table and other day-folk things had been knocked to the floor as if there had been some sort of struggle. There was a wound on the man's head and a mat of dried blood on the dog's shoulder.

Seeing the blood, Willa's heart pounded heavily in her chest, and she swallowed hard. Had they attacked one of the animals of the forest and been entangled in a battle?

But then she frowned in confusion. If they had fought something in the forest, that wouldn't explain the knocked-over furniture in the room.

And then she saw it. Lying in the bed next to the man and his dog, there was a long piece of metal with a wooden stock and what looked like two iron pipes side by side.

*That's a killing-stick,* she thought, *right there beside them.* She drew in a ragged, unsteady breath and fought the urge to run.

Willa looked at the killing-stick with dread. She'd never seen one this close. She didn't know how they worked, but she'd watched enough hunters in her woods to know their wicked power. She'd seen deer struck dead from a distance, hawks killed in midair. During the previous winter, she'd found a wounded wolf lying on the forest floor and bandaged her wounds with healing leaves so that she could get back to her starving pups.

The man lay with his eyes closed in the bed. His hands moved restlessly beside his body, touching the killing-stick and the exhausted dog as he muttered in his troubled sleep.

Willa knew she should go, but she also knew that some of the most valuable things in the lair would be in this very room.

Into the room she crept, nothing but a shift of darkness moving through the shadows. Slipping over to the dresser, she quickly snatched half of the necklaces and earrings she found in the jewelry box, liking the weight of her satchel more and more.

The little ones in her clan who didn't steal, and steal well, didn't get fed. It was the way the padaran had run the clan since before she was born. If you didn't return to the lair with your satchel full, you didn't get dinner, and if it happened two nights in a row, you'd get worse than that. The padaran had told her many times that the day-folk were rich and didn't need their money or their belongings, and when she looked at everything the day-folk had, she thought it must be true. But she also thought maybe it was better to take only half of what she found and leave the rest behind, just in case the day-folk and their children were hungry, too.

She had stolen from many of the homesteads along this river. Stealing only half of what she found made her takings less noticeable. *Move without a sound. Steal without a trace.* That was what she had taught herself. If the day-folk were truly rich, then they wouldn't notice a few things missing come morning. Of course, she could never tell the padaran about her rule of halves—he'd thrash her until the stream that ran beneath their lair turned red—but she was very good at stealing, and he was usually well pleased with her take. She knew she was one of his favorites, and she was determined to keep it that way.

Her grandmother, her mamaw, whom she loved with all her heart, had told her that there had once been a time when the Faeran had lived in the forest desiring nothing but what the forest could provide them. But when the homesteaders came cutting with their axes and building their candlelit homes in the woods, the Faeran began to change—their words, their wants, their ways. Sometimes, when Willa was way out in the forest alone, apart from the rest of the clan, she felt the power of the forest and its creatures deep inside her, and she knew that her mamaw was telling her the truth. There had been a time before.

The man jerked in his sleep, snorted loudly, and took a sudden gasping breath. Willa leapt back in surprise, her limbs flooded cold with fear, but then the man mumbled something in the darkness as if he was fighting something in his dreams, the dog adjusted its position, and the two of them fell back to sleep.

When Willa started breathing again, she shook her head in mocking disbelief. That dog was *worthless*! It couldn't smell a thing! She was right here next to them, and it didn't even know.

Feeling more confident than ever, she searched the top of the dresser for more valuables. She noticed a closed black book with a long red tassel hanging down from the pages. The book had a short, single-word title that she could not read. Sitting on the book there was a gold ring. She picked up the ring and held it up in the moonlight that shone through the window. It was one of the most beautiful day-folk things she had ever seen. *What is this gleaming thing for?* she wondered. *What is its magic?*

Noticing a glint of light out of the corner of her eye, she looked over toward the bed. The sleeping man wore an identical gold ring on the third finger of his left hand.

She knew she should take the gold ring from the dresser and run as fast as she could. *Take it and leave!* she told herself. It had to be the most valuable thing in the lair, and it would definitely be the most valuable thing she'd ever brought back in her satchel. She could imagine the padaran's snarling grin as she set the shining gold ring in his awaiting hands. "This is a good take, girl," he'd rasp in pleasure, all the other jaetters ducking and sniveling around him, their jealousy writhing through them like poison as they snapped and hissed at her.

But as she held the golden ring in her hand, a sickening feeling crept through her. She tried to convince herself that taking one of the rings wasn't breaking her rule of halves, but there was something in her that felt strangely uncertain. Sometimes, two things weren't just two things; they were a pair, and a pair was a thing. Half wasn't always half, she thought. Sometimes half was whole.

She didn't know what the rings were for or what they meant, but it seemed wrong to take one, to separate it from the other—like tearing a wing from a swallowtail butterfly and telling herself it could still fly.

Before she could change her mind, she reluctantly set the ring back on top of the book where she'd found it, and crept out of the room of the snoring man and his dim-nosed, deaf dog.

She moved quickly toward the next room, determined to stay focused.

The next room was draped with dresses. Her heart quickened at the thought that she was going to see a day-folk girl up close. The girl's scent hung in the air, but there was no little girl sleeping in the room's bed. The fact that it was the middle of the night and the girl was gone seemed very strange. But Willa went over to the girl's dresser and took a shiny bracelet, a silver hairpin, several velvet ribbons, a tiny porcelain doll, and a locket.

As Willa darted down to the next room, it smelled immediately of boy. She knew it was a day-folk boy, but it was boy all the same. On a breezy day she could smell boys from across a meadow, whether they were day-folk or night. But the boy's bed was empty as well, the covers twisted onto the floor.

Willa's brows furrowed. *Where did the boy go? And where is the little sister-girl who should have been in the previous room? And why is the man sleeping with his killing-stick on his bed?*

*Get what you came for,* she told herself, shaking her head and continuing on. They were the words she used whenever she became ensnared in the bewildering details of the day-folk's lives. *Get what you came for and go, Willa.*

She hurriedly searched the boy's room for valuables.

The first thing she found looked like a large leather glove made for a giant hand. *The boy's hand must be grotesquely deformed and misshapen,* she thought. Beside the glove lay a white ball and a stout, wooden walking stick of some sort. *The boy's legs must be crooked as well.* She felt a little sorry for the poor, crippled creature, but she stuffed half of his coin collection and half of his Cherokee arrowheads into her satchel and dashed down the hall toward the fourth and final room. *Get what you came for.*

But then her ear twitched and the quills on the back of her neck stood on end.

The snoring had stopped.

The man had awoken.

She heard the muffled sound of movement, covers being pulled back. She felt the vibration as his feet hit the floor.

*"Get on up, boy,"* the man whispered urgently to his dog. *"They're back!"*

Willa exploded into motion. She sprinted down the length of the hallway, racing for the top of the stairs.

The man charged out of his bedroom with his killing-stick. Willa flashed by him, nothing but a dark streak.

He must have been as startled by her as she was by him, because he lurched back in surprise. She dove headlong down the darkened stairway, her feet barely touching the steps.

But the startled man raised his weapon and aimed blindly into the darkness.

A flash lit the air on fire, and the sound of it shook the world.

The blast struck her in the back. The force of it knocked her careening forward. She slammed into the wall at the turn in the stairway and tumbled down the rest of the stairs like a raccoon shot from a tree.

The lead shot ripped through her tunic and riddled her shoulder blade and arm, white-hot lightning piercing through her body as she crashed onto the floor at the bottom of the stairway.

The enraged man and his growling dog were charging down the stairway to finish her off.

*Get up,* she told herself, trying to find her way through the pain. *Get up, Willa. You've got to run!*

Willa lay crumpled on the floor at the bottom of the stairs, her right leg bent badly beneath her left, her arm twisted under the weight of her body. Her head lay flat against the boards, blood dripping down into her eyes as she gazed out at the dead furniture and murdered walls of the shadowed lair. She could see through her eyes, and she could hear the wheeze of the air moving in and out of her lungs, but she couldn't get her arms and legs to move. The only thing she could feel was the pain of the blast radiating through her shaking body. She lay helpless, stunned, and bleeding on the floor.

She felt the man's footsteps coming down the stairs behind her. His dog tore out in front of him, a blazing burst of growling teeth. The beast clamped onto her calf with its fangs, sending sharp bolts of new pain shooting through her limbs, jolting her alive. She spun around, screaming, and struck out with a quick jerking motion. The dog pulled back, trying to drag her with its teeth, but she wrested herself free. The snarling beast lunged in for a second bite, but Willa darted away.

The dog chased her, gnashing its teeth behind her as she scurried across the eating room floor. She dove through the dog door, scrambled across the porch, and ran, fleeing out into the night, desperate to reach the safety of the forest.

The man threw open the door and charged out, aiming his killing-stick into the darkness. Another shot exploded the world, shattering the night with a flash of light and a deafening roar, as Willa scrambled away.

"Get him, boy! Get him!" the man shouted, as the dog flew off the porch after her. "I'm going to kill you this time!" he screamed at her.

She knew that she'd been moving so fast through the darkness of his lair that he hadn't truly seen her, but he was angry, far angrier than she expected from a race of beings who were supposedly so rich that they didn't need most of their belongings.

*Get to the trees, get to the trees,* she thought frantically as she stumbled across the grass toward the forest. But she felt dizzy and disoriented, filled with nothing but pain and panic. Her head throbbed. When that first blast hit her, it had slammed her against the wall and then tumbled her down the stairs. Now the blood was oozing from her head down into her eyes, blurring her vision.

Running nearly blind, she ducked into the first cover she came to. She scrambled into a small, closed-in place, gasping for breath, and hoping the dog would pass her by.

All she wanted to do was close her eyes against the pain and curl up into a little ball, but she knew if she withered here she'd die. She wiped the blood from her eyes and tried to look around her. Had she crawled into a hollow log? Maybe she'd been lucky enough to find a fox den.

But then she smelled something. And it wasn't fox.

It was goat.

Her heart sank. She'd made it only as far as the homesteader's barn.

As she scuttled out of the pen, the startled goats ran bleating out into the yard and the chickens flew up in a squawking explosion of feathers. *Get to the forest!* her mind kept telling her, but she knew it was too late. She could hear the man and his dog charging toward the building. She scurried deeper into the shadows of the barn and hunkered down to hide.

A debilitating fear gripped her chest. "If they ever catch you alone in their world, they will kill you, Willa," the padaran had told her. "They cut down trees and burn with fire. They killed your sister and your parents!"

The barn door creaked slowly open.

The flickering light of the lantern entered first and then the gleaming double barrels of the killing-stick. The man came in slowly and cautiously. The day-folk were oddly blind at night. He held up his lantern, straining to see in the dim light, his weapon pointed in front of him.

Willa lay crumpled, curled up on the floor in the corner, wounded and bleeding, panting with an exhaustion so all-consuming that she couldn't move—like a fawn that had been shot through her heart and lay on the ground breathing her last breaths. Willa had the power of the forest animals within her, but none of her powers worked in this unnatural place.

She could tell by the man's careful movement that he couldn't quite make out what type of man or beast he'd shot in the darkness and cornered in his barn. It wasn't until he raised his lantern and peered at her at close range that he got his first good look at her.

She could just imagine what she must look like to him lying in the dirt like a trapped animal in the corner of his barn, shaking with fear, her greenish arms and legs pulled up to her chest, her chest moving up and down with fast, ragged breaths, and the blood dripping down her face between her emerald eyes.

When the man finally saw her, and she lifted her eyes and looked at him, his expression changed from grim determination to utter astonishment. The viciousness that had consumed him moments before disappeared as he tried to comprehend what he was seeing. She saw him realize, in the light of his lantern, that the thing he'd trapped in his barn wasn't a man or a beast.

"Wha . . ." he began to ask in confusion. "What are you?"

She could hear in the tremor of his voice the realization that he had shot some kind of strange little forest creature—not just a creature, but a girl. She didn't know what he was expecting, what type of enemy he thought had invaded his lair in the dead of night, but it was not this, it was not *her*.

Willa looked down the double barrels of the killing-stick pointed at her. This man could shoot her again right here and now and end it all. All he had to do was pull the trigger. Or he could strangle her with his bare hands or strike her in the head with a shovel. Without the powers of the forest, she could not defend herself from him. She was helpless. But as she looked into his face she saw something that she did not think was possible in a day-folk man: *kindness*.

"I . . . I don't understand," he said in bewilderment. "Where did you come from? Who are you?"

*I'm Willa,* she thought, but she did not answer his question out loud. The padaran had brought the Eng-lish sounds into their clan long before she was born, and she knew the sounds well enough to understand him. But whether she was using the old language or the new, Willa spoke to trees, not the men who killed them. How could day ever comprehend night? How could darkness ever know light? How could she say her name to a man such as this?

"Just hold on . . ." he said gently, watching her with steady eyes as he knelt beside her trembling body. He set the killing-stick and the lantern down onto the dirt floor of the barn. All the anger and fear that had consumed him moments before seemed to have disappeared from him now.

So wickedly fast these humans seemed to change their spirit.

"I'm going to take a look at the wound . . ." he said as he pulled a white cloth from his pocket and moved toward her as though he was going to try to stanch the bleeding.

But he was human. She knew she could not trust him.

She stayed perfectly still. She didn't move in any way as his hand came closer and closer.

Her heart pounded in her chest. The moment he touched

her, she sprang to her feet. Startled, he pulled back in surprise. She darted past him. The dog snapped at her but missed.

With her last burst of dying energy, she dashed through the doorway of the barn and out into the darkness. She ran across the grass. The moment she reached the edge of the forest, she blended into the night and disappeared.

The last thing she had heard him say as he grabbed his lantern and his killing-stick was, "Come on, boy. We're going after her."

Willa knew that the darkness of the forest would hinder the man and his dog for a few minutes, but not for long. The human would come trudging through the forest, lighting the way with his box of captured flame and carrying his killing metal, as all day-folk did. But what she was most worried about was the dog's speed through the underbrush and its powerful sense of smell, which she knew was akin to her own. She had foolishly scoffed at the dog when it had been fast asleep, but now that it had tasted her blood, it would be unstoppable. She had been hunted by dogs before. They were simple beasts, but relentless on a scent. She picked up a handful of dirt, raised it to her mouth, and filled it with her breath. Then she cast it wide behind her, dispersing the scent of the direction she'd taken.

She stumbled deeper into the forest, pushing through the spasms of pain from the lead shot that had struck the back of her shoulder and arm. She crunched leaves and broke small sticks beneath her treading feet, making noise that she wouldn't normally make, but she had to move fast. She had to escape.

Finally, she came to the reflecting pools at the rocky edge of the river. She didn't have the strength to climb up into the cradling arms of the trees and cross over the top as she had before, and she was far too weak to wade through the rapids, but she had to cross the water somehow to throw the dog off her trail. The dirt she'd cast behind her would confuse it for a little while, but when the dog came to the river it would run up and down the shoreline with blind, sniffing persistence until it found her scent again.

In the far distance behind her, she could hear the sound of the man's tromping feet coming in her direction.

She spotted the faint line of a deer trail that ran along the bank of the river. She knew that deer never crossed or even waded into fast-moving water, so she followed the trail hoping it would take her to what she needed.

When she reached a shallow riffle running over the small, rounded stones of the riverbed, she knew it was her only chance. She immediately started to cross, but even here the river dragged at her angrily, the white water bunching up like mountains around her knees, pulling at her, trying to drag her in. She fought against it, tried to keep pushing through it. But she finally lost her balance and collapsed down into the river, beset with pain, and the cold power of the water took hold of her and swept her away.

She kicked and she sputtered, gasping for air in the churning water, terrified that she was going to drown, but then the current pulled her quickly forward and slammed her against a rock. She grabbed hold. The raging water immediately wanted to tear her away, to pull her down into its darkest holes, but she gritted her teeth and held on to the cold, hard surface of the rock. She clung to it. *Climb it, Willa!* she told herself. *Climb it!*

She reached up her hand, found a crevice with her fingers, and pulled, dragging herself slowly out of the river.

The back of her shoulder throbbed. Her right arm, and that whole side of her body, felt numb, like all the blood had seeped out of it into the churning dark waters of the greedy river. She crouched down in between the large, jagged, broken boulders that crowded the river's edge and asked for their protection. The cracked, moss-covered rocks towered over her head, making caves between them where she could hide. She had always loved the feeling of climbing among rocks like these, and it gave her comfort to rest among them now, but she knew she couldn't stay here. The rush of the river was drowning out many sounds, but she knew that the man and his dog were still coming, still on her trail, and they would find her here. She had to keep going, but she was exhausted and bleeding.

Her lair and her clan were miles and miles up through the mountains beyond her reach. She could find no help from there.

But she could not let herself give up. She needed to find a way to escape.

She had lived in the forest all her life, and she had taken pride in helping the animals who needed her care. But she realized that this time, *she* was the one who needed help, or she was going to die.

She lifted her head, tilted her face toward the gleaming moon, and began to howl. It was a pitiful, soft little sound at first. She was weak, and not used to making any noise, especially when enemies were on her trail. But soon she pulled the pain of her wounds into her throat and she let out a long, plaintive howl. She howled in the way she had been taught, not by her mother who'd been killed years before, or even by her grandmother who'd raised her, but by a mother she'd befriended the winter before.

As the sound of her howl went out into the night air, she could imagine it drawing in predators from miles around, sharp-clawed creatures ready to prey on the weak and wounded thing she had become. And she could imagine the tracking dog and killing man raising their heads toward the sound and knowing they were getting close.

At first, all she could hear was the relentless, rushing voice of the river, but then she heard a faint sound in the distance. She stepped out from among the rocks toward the forest, cupped her hands behind her ears, and listened again.

*There,* she thought, *very far away.* It was another howl.

She howled again.

The returning howl sounded much closer now. Whatever it was, it was moving fast, coming at a run. Her heart began to thump in her chest. Even though she was the one who had started the howl, she couldn't help her legs from shaking. There was a part of her that was telling her that she had made a mistake, that she should run now, scurry quickly away, or duck back down into the rocks and hide.

She heard the beast pushing toward her through the undergrowth of the forest. She knew what she had done was dangerous, that it might get her killed.

Very close now, a pair of silvery, moonlit eyes peered at her from the darkness of the forest.

She took a long, deep breath, used her powers to consciously slow down her heart, and tried to stay calm. *You can't back out now,* she told herself. *You must finish what you started.*

But then thirty more pairs of eyes appeared in the forest, all gazing at her. Not just one had come, but *many.*

She looked toward the closest pair of eyes gazing at her from the darkness.

*"Un don natra dunum far,"* she whispered in the old Faeran language. *I need your help, my friend.*

But at that moment, the light of the man's flame came flickering through the trees.

A large wolf emerged from the forest a few feet in front of her, her silver-gray eyes studying Willa intently.

And then, behind the leader of the pack, she saw the others—the pale blue eyes of the younger wolves, and the gray and golden-brown eyes of the older wolves.

These were the great warriors of the forest, the clawers and the biters, and on any other night they might have tracked and taken down a little creature like her.

But Willa looked into the eyes of the leader of the pack, crouched down to the ground in front of her, and said the words to her again.

*"Un don natra dunum far."*

The leader of the pack stared at her. She was a beautiful animal, with a thick blackish-gray coat and the muscles of many hunts. She had a strong nose and mouth, and held her ears up high, alert for the coming danger—the man and his dog coming toward them through the forest. Wolves and the other animals of the forest didn't have names in the Eng-lish language of the day-folk, but in the old language, Willa knew her name was *Luthien*. She looked so different from the winter before, when Willa had met her and helped her, when the wolf had lain on the forest floor, shot by a hunter and torn by his hounds. And now, by the flow of time, all had come around.

Luthien lay down on her haunches so close at Willa's side that she could feel the warmth of the wolf's fur against her shoulder. Wincing in pain, but knowing that it was her only hope to live, Willa crawled onto the wolf's back.

The day-folk man had seen her in his lair and wounded her. She didn't understand why he had tried to help her in the barn, what kind of trick or twist of hatred had compelled him to such an act, but she knew she could not trust a human. And she knew that now that he had seen her, he would not let her go. He and his snarling dog and his clanking box of captured light and his killing metal were coming, moments away now, thrashing through the forest, trampling leaf and breaking branch, to capture her and pull her back into their world.

As Luthien rose to her feet, Willa wrapped her arms around the thick scruff of the wolf's neck.

"The dog in the man's pack has the nose to track us," Willa said in the old language, knowing the wolf would know what to do.

As the man and his dog came through the undergrowth of the forest, Luthien turned and looked at the other wolves of the pack. With a tilt of her head and a turn of her body, she gave the command. The other wolves turned and dashed in a dozen directions into the forest, yipping and yelping as they ran, as if inviting the coming enemy to pursue them.

The moment they were gone, Luthien lunged into the darkness and leapt into running speed. Suddenly, Willa was flying through the forest, her hair whipping behind her. Her shoulder burned with pain, and the blood from the cut on her head was dripping onto Luthien's thick coat, but Willa felt the joy of it, too, clinging to the wolf's back, tearing through the forest faster than she ever had gone. The trunks of the trees rushed past her. Great jutting rocks flashed by. The leaves of the bushes were but puffs of air swishing against her face. She felt the driving beat of the wolf's heart against her own, the air surging into the wolf's lungs, and the heat pouring out of the wolf's open mouth as she ran, her teeth gleaming in the moonlight.

Willa looked into the forest to their left and to their right to see two strong male wolves running with them, guarding their flanks. Craning her neck, she saw that two young wolf pups were following close behind.

She couldn't see the other wolves of the pack anymore, but she knew they were out there, running through the forest in opposite directions. There was no way for even the keenest tracking dog to follow them all.

"The wolves teach us how to work together," her mamaw had told her. "They hunt together, defend their territory together, play together, and raise their pups together. It's through their love for one another that they survive." Willa knew she wasn't a wolf and never could be, but it was the kind of kinship that she had always longed for.

Leaving the ravine of the river far behind them, Luthien climbed up through the rocky, forested ridges of the high ground, taking Willa up the slope of what the Faeran people called the Great Mountain. The Cherokee called it *Kuwa'hi*. But the day-folk called it Clingmans Dome on their maps, made from the ground-up flesh of trees. It seemed as if all the locations in her world had many names, old names and new, night names and day, as if the names, too, were fighting to possess these ancient places. It was seldom used anymore, but one of her favorite names for this place was the Smoky Mountain, for she had seen it say its name many times: in the waking dawn of each new morning, the white mist of the Smoky Mountain's breath floated near its rounded top and out across the world, flowing down into hidden coves and sweeping valleys, out to the other mountains and ridges, and down through the fog-shrouded trees and over the tumbling misty rivers, as if the Smoky Mountain itself breathed the life into the world each morning and took it back again each night.

Dead Hollow, the hidden lair of her people, was way up on the north slope of the Great Mountain, a place so treacherously remote, and so shadowed by thick trees and steep ridges, that no day-folk had ever trodden there.

But as she gazed around her through her blood-blurry eyes, she realized that wasn't the direction the wolves were going.

"Where are we going?" she tried to ask in the old language, but her voice was too thin and raspy to be heard.

As she clung to Luthien's back, she felt herself getting weaker and colder, the sticky blood oozing from her wound and down her side. She held on desperately to the warmth of Luthien's fur, but her eyes drifted shut and she began to slip away. All she could feel was the undulating motion of the running wolf.

When Willa opened her eyes again, she was still clinging to Luthien's back. She wasn't sure where they were or how much time had passed, other than that the sun was rising in the eastern sky, and the blood was still seeping from her aching body.

The wolves of the pack had come back together with her and Luthien on a rocky prominence that rose up from the surrounding terrain. All the wolves were looking in the same direction.

Wincing from the pain, Willa slowly lifted her head.

The wolves gazed out across a sweeping view of the mountains, the long blue ranges cascading one layer after another into the distance, the wispy white clouds hanging low in the valleys, with the dark peaks and ridges rising among them.

She knew that the wolves of a pack far from their den didn't just stare off into the distance for no reason. When wolves were far from home they acted with purpose. They ran with purpose, tracked with purpose. And now they waited with purpose.

They seemed to be watching for something in particular to happen, but Willa didn't know what it was.

Then she saw an old black bear trundling down the slope of the nearby hill.

All the wolves in the pack turned their heads in unison and looked at the bear.

This was what they had come for.

But they did not move.

They did not attack.

They waited and they watched.

The bear moved slowly, arduously, as if every step was painful to it as it made its way down the slope into the closest valley. It seemed gout-sick or wounded in some way.

*Were the wolves going to attack and kill the wounded bear?* she wondered, for the wolf and the bear were natural enemies.

But the wolves did not move forward. They stayed perfectly silent and perfectly still, watching the bear until it disappeared into the mist of the valley.

Luthien seemed to take note of exactly where the bear had gone out of sight. Then she looked at the other wolves in the pack and moved in that direction. Clearly understanding her, the other wolves slunk in close behind and followed her in single file.

As Willa glanced back, she could see that the two male wolves stayed closest to Luthien, right with her, strong and steady, their bodies hunched low, their muscles tight, and their eyes alert. The two pale-gazed young pups were slinking along behind them, wary and uncertain, one of them visibly shaking, his tail between his legs.

Willa did not know what kind of danger they were all going into, but she could feel her body responding to theirs, the hair on her arms rising up, her ears tingling, her temples pounding.

The wolves followed the trail of the sick bear into the white wall of thick fog and down into the valley. The colors of the forest faded into gray.

As the rocks and trees around them disappeared in the mist, Willa felt Luthien's muscles tensing, ready for the fight.

As the long, single file line of wolves moved through the fog, Willa couldn't see anything but white ahead, on either side, or behind her. She couldn't hold back the pang of fear. Where were the wolves taking her?

She held on to Luthien's neck as the wolf lowered her nose to the ground and followed the large tracks of the wounded bear.

Years before, when her mamaw could still walk, Willa remembered crouching down in the undergrowth of the forest with her twin sister, Alliw, the two of them watching their mamaw's wrinkled fingers tracing reverently over the tracks on the ground—the deer with their cloven hooves, the mountain lions and wolves with their four claws, and the massive bear tracks with five distinct claws on each foot.

Where the earth was soft, the prints were easy to see. But where the bear had crossed over rocky ground, the tracks faded and then disappeared. But Luthien kept her nose to the ground and followed the bear's scent. No animal in the forest other than the bear itself had a better sense of smell than the wolf.

A whirring, whistling noise passed overhead. Willa looked up, trying to figure out what it was, but the fog was too thick to see anything.

She glanced behind her and saw the two young pups looking timidly up into the fog; they didn't know what it was either.

When Luthien stopped, the other wolves gathered around her, the leader of the pack. And as the mist cleared, they all looked out in the same direction.

Willa lifted her eyes. She gazed in awe across a flat, silver-shimmering body of water, a vast lake that extended for as far as she could see before disappearing into the mist.

Water poured down from natural springs in the surrounding rocks, but the surface of the lake stayed perfectly smooth. As great flocks of mergansers, teals, and other ducks wheeled overhead, their whirling reflections were like dark, winged fish swimming in the smooth water below.

Willa looked at the serene water of the lake in astonishment. She had lived her whole life in a world of whispering streams, gushing rivers, and tumbling waterfalls—a place where water was *always* moving—but this flat, motionless lake was an amazement she had never seen before.

Noticing a dark shape moving down the slope, she turned to see the old, sickened bear making its way toward the sandy shore of the lake. The bear lumbered into the water, and then sunk its body down into it, grunting air through its nose in sounds of immense relief. The water seemed to soothe the pain of its aching body.

Willa looked along the edge of the lake. There were other bears, too, many of them brown or black, but others cinnamon or blue-gray, all up and down the shore, some of them swimming or wallowing in the water, others just sitting in the wet sand at the water's edge.

Luthien jolted in surprise when a massive white bear rose up in front of her roaring in anger. Willa pulled in a startled breath and clung tightly to Luthien's back, pressing her face into the thick fur of the wolf's neck. But instead of pulling back at the sight of the gigantic bear, Luthien leapt forward with her teeth snapping in a savage growl. The vibration of the wolf's growl reverberated through Willa's body. She pressed herself to Luthien as the bear stood on its hind legs and roared, outraged that the wolves had dared to come to this sacred place. The other wolves of the pack pulled back, and the whimpering pups scattered, but Luthien held her ground.

Willa could see that this bear was much larger and much older than any of the other bears. This was *his* lake, and he was going to protect it from intruders like these wolves. A single swipe of his enormous paw would easily kill a wolf or a Faeran girl.

But then to her surprise, she realized that the bear wasn't just looking at Luthien. He was looking at *her*.

Her skin and hair had reflexively blended into the color and texture of the wolf's fur. In all appearance, she had become part of the wolf.

But the bear appeared to be able to smell her, and its dark

eyes gazed in her direction. There was an uncertainty in the bear's expression, as if he thought he might know what she was, but he hadn't seen her kind in a long, long time.

As the white bear slowly stopped snarling, Luthien did the same.

The bear peered at Willa. She wanted to look away, to avert her eyes. She wanted to *run* away. But she held the bear's gaze.

Finally, the white bear dropped down onto all fours with a muffled grunt, and Willa let out a breath of relief.

"Thank you," she said in the old language, loud enough for the bear to hear. "My name is Willa. My grandmother told me about your strength and your wisdom. I am honored to meet you."

The white bear made a low guttural sound and turned his bead and his body toward the lake.

"He's letting us through," Willa whispered to Luthien.

As Luthien stepped slowly toward the water, the other wolves stayed where they were, even the two males who served as her guards. They seemed to understand that only Willa and Luthien were allowed to pass, and pressing the issue further would result in a battle that neither the wolves nor the bears wanted to fight.

As Willa and Luthien moved cautiously past the white bear, she could see that he was extremely old. He didn't appear weak or decrepit, but she could see the knowingness in his eyes and the gray streaks of time in his weathered face. She sensed that he had been living far longer than any Faeran or animal she had ever met.

For many years, her mamaw had taken her and her sister

Alliw through the cathedrals of the giant hemlocks, teaching them how to speak with trees more than five hundred years old. Willa knew that bears normally didn't live as long as Faeran, but she had a feeling that this particular bear had been a cub when those age-old trees had been saplings.

As Luthien took her down to the edge of the water, goose bumps rose on Willa's arms. She knew it was going to be cold. Every mountain stream she had ever entered had been shockingly, bracingly frigid, like melted snow.

But as Luthien lowered her slowly into the lake, Willa realized the water was warm and soothing. It felt as if the light of the sun had become liquid.

As she leaned back into the water with only her face above the surface, her body felt weightless, her arms rising buoyant at her side, her hair floating around her head.

She sighed in relief as slow, gentle waves rippled one after another through her body, lifting the pain away. She felt the torn skin of her wounds slowly coming back together, as if a month of healing had occurred in a few moments.

Her grandmother had told her and Alliw of a hidden lake that the Cherokee called *Atagahi* and a great white bear who protected it. From a distance, the lake looked like nothing more than one of the many mist-filled valleys, but hidden below the clouds was a powerful healing place where sick and wounded bears came for refuge. The great white bear encouraged his ursine kin to come to the sacred lake, but guarded it fiercely from all others.

As Willa floated in the water, letting its healing powers

move through her aching wounds, the white bear suddenly rose up onto his hind legs in alarm and looked toward the rim of the valley.

The quills on the back of Willa's neck went taut as she quickly got her legs beneath her and crouched down in the water.

She couldn't believe it. It was the man who had shot her! He was standing on the rocky ridge, holding his killing-stick as he stared out across the mist-filled valley. His dog stood at his side. It was clear that they had followed her here and they were still looking for her.

Luthien had carried her a great distance up through steep, rocky terrain that must have been exceedingly difficult for the man to climb. He must have run as fast as he could to chase her. What storm of dark anger and hatred had driven him to follow her so far?

Luthien stepped forward, growling and snarling, her shoulders bunched for the attack. The wolves of the pack maneuvered for battle. The white bear moaned a low and menacing growl, his teeth clacking as the other bears gathered to his side, ready to fight.

"Don't see us," Willa whispered as she gazed up at the man, her heart filling with dread, not just of the human and his dog, but of what would happen if they came down into the valley. "Don't see us," she said again.

She knew that if the man saw the wolves and bears, he'd become frightened, shooting his killing-stick this way and that, and they'd attack in return. The man and the dog, and many of the wolves and the bears, would die.

No day-folk man or woman had ever seen the healing lake of the bears. They might have heard about it from the stories of the Cherokee. They might have even searched for it. But none of them had ever lived to tell about it.

"Just turn away," Willa whispered as she gazed up through the fog toward the man. "Whoever you are, whatever you want with me, for your own sake, please just turn away."

When the man finally turned and headed in a different direction, Willa thought, *Yes, go. Take your killing-stick and your hatred away from here.*

Luthien's hackles lowered, and Willa sunk back down into the water.

The bears, too, returned to their wallowing in the nearby shallows as the white bear watched over them.

She liked how the white bear was older and stronger than the other bears, but he was *serving* them, *helping* them, *protecting* them. Her mamaw had told her stories about how it had once been the same with the Faeran, that all the members of the clan would work together, protect each other, take care of each other.

When the lake had finally stopped the bleeding and soothed

the pain of her wounds, Willa climbed back up onto Luthien's back.

"I wish I could stay here," Willa said in the old language, "but I need to get back to my clan. They're going to be looking for me."

Willa noticed the white bear watching her as Luthien carried her out of the water and up onto the shore. She knew that this bear had seen so many things with those eyes—the time of the first Cherokee long ago with their skin-piercing blow darts and their spear-slinging atlatls, then the homesteaders hacking their way through the wilderness with their sharpened blades and their killing-sticks, and now the newcomers with their smoking metal beasts. As the white bear looked at her, he seemed to be thinking, *And you see it, too, don't you, little one? You understand.*

As Luthien and Willa rejoined the pack, the wolves circled around them in greeting, and then they all headed off together, with Luthien leading the way.

They traveled for several hours, up into the dark realms of the Great Mountain, following secluded ravines along rivers that washed the stones bone gray, and up through chutes of ancient rock where once the water flowed.

Willa and the wolves came to a gorge where a gigantic skeleton of a dead tree hung upside down, wedged between two rock faces where a rushing flood had deposited it years before. Its roots reached up into the air and its branches hung down to the earth. The water had receded long ago, but the bare gray trunk and limbs of the tree remained. Her people called it the Watcher, for it loomed over the winding path that led up through the rocky gorge to the entrance of the Dead Hollow lair.

When Luthien came to a stop, Willa climbed reluctantly off the wolf's back.

Glancing up into the gorge in the direction of her clan's lair, Willa felt sick to her stomach. She didn't want to return to her clan. She wanted to go back to the lake of the bears. She wanted to stay with the wolves. She wanted to do anything other than return. But she knew she couldn't. A Faeran could only survive through her clan. The padaran had told them many times, "There is no *I*. There is only *we*." She belonged to her clan. And more than anything, she had to get back to her grandmother. Her mamaw needed her and she needed her mamaw. *There is no I, only we.*

As the wolves of the pack gathered around her to say goodbye, she knelt down in front of Luthien.

Willa knew that to be touched by a wolf was a privilege, but to actually be *carried* by a wolf like Luthien was a great honor. Luthien had saved her life, and risked her own life to do it.

Willa wrapped her arms around Luthien's neck and hugged her, feeling the thickness of the wolf's fur against her cheek.

When Luthien nuzzled up against her, Willa knew the wolf understood. Willa felt a loyalty toward her that she vowed to remember.

"I will never forget what you've done for me, Luthien," Willa said in the old language. "May your pack run strong."

In the moments that followed, she watched Luthien and the other wolves turn and slowly disappear into the forest.

When they were finally gone, she felt a lurch of loneliness in her chest. She didn't want to be left behind. She wanted to cry out to them, to raise her head up and howl for them to come back for her.

As she turned and looked toward the path that would take her back to Dead Hollow, the lair of the clan into which she had been born, she felt a lump of dark fear growing like black roots in the pit of her stomach.

Before she went home, there was one more thing she had to do.

When the jaetters went out thieving each night, they usually went out in small groups to keep an eye on one another, a rule the padaran had established long before she was born. Nothing in the clan was ever done alone. But more and more, she'd been sneaking out by herself, and the other jaetters didn't like it. They often lay in wait for her return.

She looked around at the surrounding forest to make sure she was alone, then went over to the Watcher, the tree wedged upside down in the gorge. She grabbed on to the lowest branches and started climbing, wincing from the pain in her shoulder. She knew that the movement of climbing might tear open the wound that the lake had soothed and begun to heal, but she had no choice.

She scaled the branches hand over hand, following the tree all the way up until she came to a large, oblong hole that had been dug into the trunk. Looking down inside the cavity, she saw the tiny, sharply angled faces of five baby pileated woodpeckers looking up at her.

"How are you this morning, my little ones?" she whispered.

But it was a careless mistake. As soon as she said hello, all the babies started squawking and cackling, excited to see her.

"Shh, shh, shh," she whispered. "Just soft now, don't give me away. I need you to hold on to something for me."

But as she pulled the satchel off her shoulder, the mother woodpecker came flying in with a burst of black and white feathers and clung to the trunk of the tree with her powerful claws. Willa was startled to see that something had happened to her since she saw her last. The area around her left eye was bleeding and her wing was badly bent, crumpled close to her body. It was a wonder that she could fly at all.

"Come here . . ." Willa said, clinging to the tree with her legs as she reached out and took the crow-sized bird into her hands. "Let me look at you."

The woodpecker knew she was trying to help her and did not fight her or try to fly away. A tangle of fibrous twine had wrapped tightly around the wing and body of the bird, biting cruelly into her skin and binding her movement. But as Willa investigated more closely, she could see that it wasn't just bits of string, it was pieces of a net of some kind.

"Oh my, who did this to you?" Willa said as she carefully unwrapped the bird's wing from the twisted fragments. It would have taken days to kill her, but the woodpecker would not have survived this, nor would her starving babies. "You must have fought very hard to get out of this net!" Willa said, the woodpecker watching her with its rapidly blinking eyes as she worked. "There you go, you're all clear now. I hope you feel better." The woodpecker bobbed its head, then tended to her babies.

*Why would someone be using a net in the forest?* Willa wondered. *Is this some kind of cruel new weapon or trap the day-folk are using?*

Knowing that she needed to get back to what she'd come for, Willa scanned the area below her one last time to make sure no one was watching. Then she stuffed her satchel into the cavity with the baby woodpeckers, careful not to block them or hurt them in any way.

"I know it's crowded in there," she told the little ones, "but I'll be back for it very soon. Don't worry."

Hiding valuables in trees was a trick she and her sister had learned from playing games with the ravens years before, but Willa was pleased with her cleverness. Even the mighty ravens wouldn't think of using an occupied woodpecker hole as a hiding spot.

What she was bringing back to the lair in her satchel was a good take, something she should be proud of, but she knew she was too tired to defend it from Gredic and her other jaetter rivals.

As she climbed down the tree, and the sunlight peaked into the gorge, her gut tightened with worry. If the sun was already in the ravine, that meant it was late in the morning. The padaran was going to be angry that she'd been gone all night and that she wasn't at the morning gathering. The other jaetters would come looking for her, sensing her weakness. She had to get back to the lair as soon as she could.

"What are you doing?" came a hissing voice from behind her, as soon as she stepped foot on the ground.

The quills on the back of Willa's neck went straight up as she spun around to defend herself.

Four jaetters surrounded her with their long sticks.

"Don't try to get away, Willa," Gredic hissed in the Eng-lish words, the only language he knew, as he shoved her hard up against the rocky wall of the ravine.

Years before, she and Gredic had been initiated into the jaetters at the same time, but he was a year older than her, and at least six inches taller than her now, with clawed, grasping fingers, and slimy, mottled gray skin. Like most of the Faeran of her clan, Gredic's skin didn't change color to match his surroundings. *Blending*—or *weaving*, as her mamaw called it—was a fading remnant of the past that had been dying out of the clan. Her mother, father, sister, and mamaw had it. And she had it. It ran strong in families. But few of the other Faeran had the ability. And the young jaetters of her clan never let her forget how different she was from the rest of them.

"Look at her, she's going all stony brown!" Gredic's twin brother chided her as he pushed her head against the stone. "Let's make her face change color, too!"

His name was Ciderg, and he was the largest and most brutal of the jaetters. The crooked nose and crushed cheekbones of Ciderg's mangled face were remnants of the savage fight the year before that defeated his brother's rival and put Gredic in charge of the jaetters.

But it was the nasty Kearnin and his brother, Ninraek, who scared Willa the most. "I think you're frightening her . . ." Kearnin rasped in snarling, fidgeting pleasure from behind the other two jaetters as he wiped his nose with the back of his gnarled hand. Kearnin and his brother were sniveling creatures with black, needy eyes that oozed a sticky, sap-like substance. Fascinated with everything Gredic did, they liked to watch, whether he was pulling the wings off a sparrow or pinning Willa against a rock and making her twist in pain.

Willa squirmed and tried to yank away, but Gredic gripped her arms with his clenching hands. It had always frustrated her that he was so much stronger than her.

"Where's your satchel, Willa?" he hissed, leaning his face so close to her that his foul-smelling breath crept into her nose like leeches.

"Yes, yes, where's your satchel?" Kearnin rasped from behind him, always repeating Gredic's words.

"Are you scared, Willa?" Gredic whispered into her face. "Can you feel your heart beating and your blood pumping?"

"Let's take her blood!" Kearnin shrieked.

"She's already bleeding!" Ciderg said, jabbing his stick at the wound on her back, as his brother held her.

Gredic wrenched her around by the arm and looked at her. "You're hurt . . ." he said in surprise, his eyes narrowing at her suspiciously.

"The little beastie is hurt . . ." Kearnin hissed.

When Gredic dug his probing fingers into the bloody wound, it sent sharp bolts of pain roiling through her back. She tried to squirm away from him, but he gripped her arm even tighter and shook her. "Where did you go, Willa? Tell me!"

"Leave me alone," she said, as she tried to pull away from him.

But he held her tight and his voice went quiet as he pushed against her. "What did you do, Willa?" he whispered. "What are you hiding?"

Gredic was far smarter than the other jaetters, and she could hear the fear seeping into his voice. He often used his anger as his power, shouting at her and the other jaetters to get what he wanted. But just as often, he was kind to her, almost gentle with her when he felt sorry for her, or was helping her—when his power was secure. But his kindness vanished when he thought she was slipping away from him in some way, or getting an edge on him. He knew that this wound from a different place meant that wherever she had gone that night, whatever she had done, she had done it without him. And this he would not allow.

She and Gredic had gone through the starving nights and beating blows of the jaetter initiation together, and in the years since, when the jaetters went out thieving, he had made sure the two of them were in the same group. *There is no I, only we.*

Gredic yanked her around to face him again and pressed her back against the wall with a harsh shove.

"Tell me what you did!" he demanded again, crushing her with his weight as he slipped his long, bony hands tightly around her neck.

She struggled against him, but Willa knew she couldn't fight Gredic. She couldn't overpower him. She couldn't strike him with a blow to defeat him. He was far too strong. And with his brutish brother, Ciderg, and the nasty Kearnin, and all the other jaetters who followed him, he had far too many allies.

As he pressed her up against the rock wall, the jagged edges of the stone jammed into her shoulder blades, driving a slash of pain into her wound. He pushed against her so hard that she could barely expand her chest enough to take a breath. But as the grip of Gredic's fingers slowly squeezed her throat shut, she pushed out a few last words.

"Let me speak, Gredic . . ." she wheezed.

Gredic leaned his face close to hers and looked into her eyes. "I'm warning you: no tricks, Willa. Don't try to run!"

"I will not run," she said, her voice thin and raspy through the grip of his fingers.

"Swear it!" he demanded.

"I swear that I will not run," she said.

Finally, Gredic loosened his grip on her throat and stepped back away from her.

"Now, tell me what happened to you last night. Where's your satchel?"

At that moment, Willa blended herself into the color and texture of the lichen that clung to the rock. She wove herself so completely into the world around her that she disappeared. Her skin, her eyes, her hair . . . she vanished.

Although they'd seen her do it before, the Faeran boys gasped, as much in anger as in surprise. Gredic immediately reached out to grab her again, but she had already dropped to the ground and curled into a little ball at the base of the rock.

"Where'd she go?" Ciderg shouted, sweeping his stick back and forth through the open air where he'd seen her last.

"She's tricked us!" Kearnin shrieked.

"Just find her!" Gredic screamed in frustration, as he searched the ground around him.

Willa had promised she wouldn't run.

And she didn't.

She *crawled* slowly and invisibly away from the jaetter boys.

They searched frantically for her, flailing their arms around them and poking with their sticks. They stabbed into the ground and jabbed into trees. They rustled bushes and kicked up dirt, but their efforts were useless. They couldn't find her.

Finally, Gredic said, "Come on. She'll have to come back to the lair sooner or later, and we'll catch her then."

"We'll catch her then," Kearnin repeated, dragging his hand across his nose as they headed off.

"The padaran's gonna be burnin' that she didn't come home last night," Ciderg said, seeming to relish the thought. "There's no slinkin' away from that."

"Maybe not," Gredic said. "But whatever we do, we need to get her satchel before she sees the padaran. She must have something good to be doing all this."

As the jaetter boys climbed up through the rocky gorge, following the path that led beneath the Watcher hanging between its stony walls, they finally disappeared into the distance, but she knew she hadn't seen the last of them. They'd be waiting, ready to filch her satchel and drag her empty-handed before the padaran in shame.

Her mamaw had told her that many of the jaetters had no parents or grandparents to raise them, and that they had lost their way. And just as with the humans, that which the jaetters did not understand, they destroyed. And that meant her.

When she was certain the jaetters were well gone, and she thought it was safe for her to come out of her hiding place, she climbed back up the giant tree and retrieved her satchel from the woodpecker's hole. She knew it was dangerous to carry it, but she realized now, more than ever, that she was going to need it as soon as she returned to Dead Hollow.

Just as she began to start her climb down, she heard voices

below her. She gazed from her bird's-eye view down into the gorge to see a band of the padaran's guards winding along the path and going out into the forest. They were moving quickly and with purpose, carrying their spears as well as other equipment she couldn't make out. She'd never seen anything like it. The guards seemed to be in some sort of hunting party, but Faeran didn't hunt the animals of the forest.

She knew she couldn't take the main path into the lair, so when she finally climbed down she took one of the side routes, then split off on her own through the steep and rocky forest.

She climbed up and over a thicket-strangled ridge, her arm and shoulder hurting all the way. The healing lake of the bears had stopped the bleeding and saved her life, but the jabbing sticks and probing fingers of the jaetter boys had reopened the wound. She could feel the sticky blood oozing down her back.

Finally, she could see the lair of her people. From a distance, the part of the Dead Hollow lair that was visible on the surface of the earth looked like a vast hornet's nest, with the same rough, gray-brown, irregular shape, but instead of being made from the hornet's sticky paper, the walls of the lair were made from a mesh of thousands of interwoven sticks. The walls had once been green and alive, woven together and sustained in life by the woodwitches of the Faeran past. They had used the same powerful woodcraft her mamaw had taught her, the same language she used to ask the trees to help her cross the river or intertwine around her when she needed to disappear. But the lair's walls were long dead now—dead for more than a hundred years, her mamaw said—the sticks twisted and rotting, blackened by age, their roots decayed, for the woodcraft needed to keep the walls alive had long faded from the ways of the Faeran. There just weren't enough woodwitches to keep the lair green and alive anymore. The very name *woodwitch* had become a title of scorn, even fear, to many in the clan, and the padaran had forbidden the old ways.

Willa climbed down into the gorge on the backside of the lair where few Faeran ever crept. She found the spot that her mamaw had told her about, where three large rocks had crashed down from the wall of the ravine and left a small triangular hole that looked like nothing more than a crack in the stone.

Getting down onto her hands and knees, she crawled inside. The crack became so tight that she had to get down onto her shoulder and wiggle her way along like a centipede.

When she finally reached the other side, she crawled out of the stone crack and found herself hunched in a small room enclosed with walls of twisting, wet, rotting sticks. She wrinkled her mouth in revulsion at the dank stench of decaying branches that filled the air. Putrid sludge dripped from the ceiling.

This area of the lair had been abandoned for decades, and had been strictly forbidden by the padaran, too dangerous for members of the clan to enter.

Anxious to get out of this wretched part of the lair, she followed a narrow tunnel. It turned, and then turned again, until she came to a split that led off into several different directions. She picked the one that led upward, and kept moving. She had to get home to her mamaw.

The inside of the Dead Hollow lair consisted of a maze of woven-stick tunnels, black and sticky from years of use, that wound through the gullet of the gorge into the small, darkened rooms and secluded caves of her people. It had once been home to many thousands of Faeran, but now only a few hundred remained, and there were many dark and empty places like this one left behind, old storage areas and dens where Faeran once lived, filled with nothing but the echoes of those who had come before. The tunnels of the lair connected one to the other like wormholes twisting and writhing through the earth.

As Willa tried to navigate her way back home, the wound on her shoulder began to throb. A wave of dizziness passed through her, and she nearly toppled to the floor. She clutched the wall to catch her balance and rest. When she touched her hand to the wound on her back, her fingers came back bright and slippery with fresh blood. Thanks to the healing lake of the bears, she felt a dull ache rather than a sharp pain, but her wound was bleeding again. If she couldn't find her way through these old tunnels, she was going to die here and no one would ever know. She had to continue on.

She came to a place where the tunnel split into three different directions, and she wasn't sure which way to go. She sniffed the air of each tunnel. In the tunnel on the left, she thought she could smell the distant scents of her clan. She hoped it led upward toward the more active parts of the lair. But then she heard a disturbing whimpering sound coming from the tunnel that led down to the right.

She stopped and stayed quiet as she tried to identify the

sound. It wasn't the wind howling wraithlike through the empty tunnels like it sometimes did. It sounded more like a wounded animal.

When she heard the sound again, fear seeped into her body. She wiped her dry lips with the back of her hand. There was something down that tunnel. She could *smell* it.

She wanted to go in the opposite direction. She wanted to get home. She *had* to get home. But the sound . . .

It wasn't a whimpering animal.

She heard it again.

It was a voice.

She took a few uncertain steps into the tunnel and cupped her hands behind her ears to focus the sound.

She heard something dragging across the woven-stick floor.

Then she heard something breathing.

Her chest began to rise and fall more heavily, pulling air into her lungs.

She tilted her head and sniffed. The smell was oddly familiar.

But it did not belong here.

Not *here*.

Her palms began to sweat.

It was the smell of a *human*.

*How is that possible?* she thought in confusion. *That can't be.*

She took a few more steps down the tunnel toward the noises she had heard. There were woven-stick doors on each side, with thorny vines binding them shut so that whatever was inside could not get out.

As she peered through the lattice of sticks, she realized that there wasn't an actual room on the other side of each door, but a small enclosure, some sort of prison cell.

Then she saw. Crammed into the hole—closed in by impenetrable, woven-stick walls—was a small Cherokee boy, about ten years old, staring out at her with wide, pleading eyes.

# 12

*This human boy should not be here,* Willa thought. The Faeran people did not attack humans. They did not capture humans and hold them prisoner.

She wanted to turn away from this. She wanted to run. She wasn't supposed to be here. This was the forbidden part of the lair. If the padaran's guards caught her here, she'd be in even worse trouble than she already was. And the wound on her back ached. Her arms and legs and her whole body felt weak and clammy from the loss of blood.

But she stayed perfectly still for several seconds, just trying to breathe, trying to understand, as the Cherokee boy's dark brown eyes stared out at her.

*Why is there a human here?* she thought. *What are they doing with it?*

She could see its little brown hands clinging to the door of sticks that imprisoned it. And as she peered deeper into its hole, she saw that it was thin and dirty and bleeding.

She felt the stab of a strange and unpleasant emotion twisting in her gut, but she quickly hardened her mind. If it had been an animal or a Faeran in this cell, she would have been right to feel sorry for it, but it wasn't. It was a *human*. Enemy of the clan. Murderer of her people. It wasn't a *him*. It was an *it*. And she was forbidden to have anything to do with it.

"Can you help me?" it whispered in a weak and desperate voice, wiping the long black hair from its face.

She stepped back, startled. She knew that the Cherokee spoke the Eng-lish words as well as their own, but the sound of its voice frightened her. She could hear the weakness, the fear, the starvation of it. She could hear it all. And she didn't want to hear it.

"Do you have food?" it asked.

*The creature is starving,* she thought in revulsion. It was as if someone had captured a wild bobcat and put it in a cage. No matter what you did with the bobcat, it was still a bobcat. It needed meat to survive.

Out in the world, down in the valleys of the day-folk, where she made her nightly takes, it would never even occur to her to help a human boy, to actually *feed* one. They were tree-killers. How could she help such a beastly little creature?

She could not give this boy food. She didn't have any human food to give it. She had never seen or heard of her people taking prisoners, but the padaran and his guards must have captured this human and put it here for a reason, something important to the clan. It would be an act of great disobedience to feed it without permission.

She knew all this! And she had no food. It was impossible.

"I'll eat anything," the boy begged her. "I'm just so hungry. Please!"

"Shut your mouth," she ordered it, her mind darting from one thought to another, trying to make sense of what was happening.

And then she remembered.

There was something in her satchel.

She looked down the corridor, first one way and then the other.

*This must be some sort of prison,* she thought, *hidden down here in the old part of the lair. But if it's a prison, there must be guards . . .*

She thought the guards might come down the corridor at any moment and find her here. And they'd punish her for her disobedience against the clan. They'd lock her in one of these slimy holes and bind the door shut like they had with the boy. She could *not* help this boy! It was impossible. *Get what you came for, Willa,* she told herself angrily. *Get yourself home.*

But it was no use. She knelt down on the floor.

"You must stay quiet!" she told the boy as she opened her satchel.

Watching her hands, the boy nodded obediently.

As its little fingers grasped the sticks that imprisoned it, she could see the brown under the fingernails where it had tried to scratch its way out. She could smell the sweat of its body and the blood of its wounds.

She reached into her satchel and pulled out one of the lumps she had stolen from the lair of the man. She pushed the crumbly food through the lattice of sticks that separated her from the boy.

The boy took the lump gratefully and shoved it in its mouth.

She fed it another lump, and it ate the lump even more quickly than the first one, for it had learned to trust her, to take whatever she gave it.

"These are so good, thank you," it said as it chomped the next lump down.

"Do not speak to me," she said fiercely, her face flaring with red as she suddenly remembered what a foolish thing she was doing.

The startled boy pulled back into its cell. "Why am I here?" he asked. "Why have you taken me?"

Willa's eyes widened in surprise.

"I haven't taken you!" she said.

And as soon as she said the words, she felt so out of place, so disobedient, to be defiantly separating herself from the clan in this way. *There is no I, only we.* There was the *clan*. There was the *us* and the *them*. There was no *I*. *I* was a person alone. *I* was an impossibility. *I* was something that shriveled alone and died. Only through the cooperation of the clan did a Faeran survive.

But she had said it, and she had said it strong. "I haven't taken you," she had said.

She knew she was part of the clan, but she wanted nothing to do with this. You run from humans. You hide from them. You steal from them. But you don't *hurt* them. You don't do *this* to them.

"If you're not one of them, then who are you?" the boy asked.

The question struck her mind like a blow. *Who are you?* It was the second time a human had asked her that question.

"My name is Willa," she said, unsure why she was allowing herself to talk to the human at all.

The Cherokee boy pressed its face against the lattice of sticks that formed the little window in the door. And now she could see it studying her, looking at the dirt on her arms and legs, and the smears of dried blood on her face.

"You look like you might be pretty hungry, too," it said. "You should eat some of the cookies."

"You eat them," she said, pushing the last two through the sticks at it. "I will have food soon enough when I get back home."

"Thank you," it said as it gratefully ate the last two lumps. "My name's Iska. What's going to happen to me? Why am I here? Please help m—"

The sound of approaching footsteps interrupted the boy's words. Willa jumped to her feet. The prison guards were coming.

# 13

The two guards spotted her in front of the boy's cell as they came around the corner. They were tall, gangly Faeran with grim, grayish faces, muscled arms and chests, and sharpened wooden spears.

"What are you doing down here?" one shouted at Willa. "Stop there!"

To disobey the commands of one of the padaran's guards was a great offense against the clan, but she was a rabbit under the claws of a swooping hawk. She fled, tearing down the corridor in the only direction she could go, deeper into the prison, every muscle in her body snapping with fear, her lungs sucking in air at a frantic pace.

The outraged guards chased after her, determined to catch her, to stab her with their spears. They'd drag her in shame before the padaran for her disobedience, or shove her into one of their black cells.

As she whipped around a corner, she heard the footfalls of the guards behind her, felt the vibration of their pounding, running steps on the woven-stick floor.

She threw herself against the wall and pinned herself flat. Her whole body buzzing, she closed her eyes and tried to blend into the wall.

*Stay still,* she told herself as she forced her heart to a slow and steady beat. *Just stay still.*

*I am the wall, I am the wall,* she repeated in her mind, and prayed that it would be enough.

As she quieted her heart and held her breath, the guards ran past her, one brushing by her so close that she felt the movement of the air on her cheek.

"What was that girl doing down here?" one of the guards asked the other as they ran by, his voice so loud in her quiet mind that it felt like it could knock her from the wall.

"Did you see her face?" the other asked.

"It looked like one of the jaetter girls."

"We've got to tell the padaran."

As the sound of the guards faded into the distance, Willa pulled in a much-needed breath and stepped away from the wall.

She immediately headed in the opposite direction from the guards, anxious to get out of the prison. But as she made her way up the corridor, she passed many cell doors and caught glimpses of faces in the woven-stick walls. They were strange white faces with blue eyes and brown eyes looking out at her as she passed, their spidery white fingers clinging to the sticks that bound them. Many more day-folk boys and girls had been trapped in tiny, dark prison holes. The faces were dirty with filth and gaunt with hunger. Some of them were bloody or disfigured by wounds. Her stomach churned with tight, twisting confusion as she pushed herself on.

She ran back up the tunnel in the direction she had come, desperate to get out of the prison and find her way up to the areas where she and the other members of the clan were allowed to be. She should have never entered the forbidden parts of the lair.

When she finally reached an active tunnel, her heart filled with gratitude. Most of the tunnels of Dead Hollow were empty and abandoned, but some were still used frequently by those few Faeran who still remained.

She spotted two Faeran adults walking ahead of her, both of them carrying bushels of leafy food gathered by the clan. She tried to look like a normal member of the clan going about her business, but it was difficult.

"Slow yourself down," one said to Willa as she hurried by with her head lowered.

Her mind kept trying to make sense of what she'd seen in the prison behind her, but she knew she had to block it out. It didn't belong to her. It didn't involve her. They were prisoners of the clan. They were *humans*. They were the enemy. Whatever was happening down there must be something the padaran wanted to be happening. She wasn't even supposed to be down there. And she vowed she'd never go into that horrible place again.

As she hurried through the tunnels of the lair, with other Faeran passing her this way and that, she kept to herself and she did not stop.

She longed to get home to her den, to her mamaw, just to see her, to fall into her gentle arms and her soothing words, to come back to the one person in the world who truly loved her.

But she knew that wouldn't be the end of it. A heaviness loomed in her chest, a dark sense of foreboding like she'd never felt before. She'd done too much this time. She hadn't meant to, but she'd *seen* too much. She'd been so disobedient in so many ways against the laws of the clan and the will of the padaran that she had no idea what was going to happen to her, except that it was going to be bad.

When Willa finally came to the tunnel that sloped down into the area of the lair she shared with her grandmother, a warm and gentle sense of relief poured through her body.

What she'd seen in the prison still haunted her, but the immediacy of her fear and confusion began to fade as she followed the familiar path home.

The walls on the way to her den weren't woven sticks like the rest of Dead Hollow, but a labyrinth of stone tunnels that had been bored and sculpted smooth by the flow of an ancient river.

Some of the tunnels led to small caves, others to dead ends. One of the tunnels, which her mamaw had warned her about many times, led to a drop-off into a black abyss. Some members of the clan believed that the dark hole of the abyss was the mouth of an ancient creature of the earth. Others believed that it was a bottomless pit that went on forever. She and her sister, Alliw, used to sneak away, crawl to the edge, and peer down into the hole. One time they dropped a rock into the darkness and waited. But they never heard it hit the bottom. The truth was, no one truly knew what was down there.

There were many pits and dangers in the labyrinth, but Willa knew the maze of winding, interconnecting stone tunnels better than anyone, because it was the only way to her den.

At long last, she came to the familiar tunnel close to home where the roof was permeated with smooth, round holes. River water had once poured through the holes, but now shafts of sunlight came filtering down instead, dappling the stone at her feet like rays of light shining through the leaves of great trees and touching the forest floor. This part of the labyrinth had once been inhabited by Faeran of old, and of all the places in the lair, these were the tunnels where she felt most at home.

The stone walls were covered with the charcoal drawings and colored paintings of the people who had lived here thousands of years before. On one wall were many sticklike figures with their arms and legs outstretched, swimming in rivers that were dry ravines now. Another wall showed crowds of people looking up in awe at a blazing sun blocked by a round shape, with stars and planets visible in the background. On a third wall, there were Faeran men and women and children standing among tall trees as they gazed upon herds of large, horned animals that no longer existed in the world.

But the most striking painting of all depicted what looked like a river that flowed along the length of one of the tunnel walls, but instead of curving lines of water, the River of Souls consisted of thousands of handprints, some large, some small, some put there a thousand years before, and others more recent.

"It's good to see you, sister," Willa whispered as she leaned down and pressed her open hands onto the two smallest and most recent pair of handprints on the wall. When she closed her eyes, she had a perfect memory of when she and Alliw were just five years old, her mamaw covering their hands with red paint, one sister's left hand and the other sister's right, and then, as if they had a single body, pressing their hands side by side into the ancient river of time.

"Never forget that you are forever among your people," her mamaw had told the two of them. "In the past, and in the present, and in the future to come."

The marks of her and Alliw's hands still remained, so small now compared to Willa's living hands, like ghosts of who she and her sister had been. But Willa knew that she and Alliw were still together in their souls, for among the Faeran, who were always born in twins, the relationship between two twins was sacred. Twins always took care of each other, protected each other. There was no more noble deed than to support a twin, and no fouler crime than to forsake one. It was the bond that could not be broken.

Whenever she came down this tunnel, it was like she was walking into a different time, a time long, long ago when the Faeran and the world were one, and true kinship held the clan together.

Willa had lived here alone with her grandmother for as long

as she could remember clearly in her mind. Everything else before was but a distant, clouded memory.

Her mother's twin sister, who would have normally helped raise her with her parents, had died of oak wilt before Willa was born. Her father, Cillian, and her mother, Nea, were slain by the day-folk when she was six. And the humans murdered Alliw that same night.

She remembered her distraught, grief-stricken grandmother stumbling into their den, taking her up into her arms, and whispering in the old language. "Your sister and your parents have passed away, my child," she had said. "You and I are all that's left now, and we need to take care of each other. You'll be my twin and I'll be yours."

Willa didn't know that night what those words meant, what it meant for someone to "pass away," and she didn't understand how her life would change, but she learned in the shadowed days that followed. It felt like something had been torn away from her, bleeding and raw. She kept looking for a sister who wasn't there. She kept trying to speak with a mother and a father who could no longer hear her. The anguish and loneliness she felt was one of her oldest and most powerful memories. For the rest of her life she had felt a dark hollowness in her soul, like something that should be there was missing.

She couldn't remember her parents very well anymore, and she still didn't understand how or where they had been killed, but the fleeting fragments of her life with her twin sister before she died haunted her like the sounds of children playing in the distance.

But her mamaw—her mother's mother—had been with her all her life. Her mamaw had been her teacher in the days before her parents and sister died, and her mamaw had cared for her on her own every day since. She had taught her how to speak, how to blend, and how to find her way among the trees.

As Willa walked through the doorway into the den, she knew that no matter what happened, no matter how she felt, no matter what she had done, she could count on one thing: that her mamaw would be there waiting for her.

# 15

"Come here, child," her grandmother whispered softly in the old language as Willa walked into their den. Her mamaw was a small, crumpled-up creature, unable to stand or walk, but Willa went to her immediately and wrapped her arms around her, knowing that she wasn't nearly as frail as she appeared.

Her grandmother was 137 years old, one of the oldest Faeran in the clan, and one of the last remaining old-time woodwitches. She had the most beautiful dark skin, marbled with streaks of brown, black, and white, and she was heavily spotted around her cheeks and eyes. Her skin was wrinkled and textured not just with age, but years of weaving into her surroundings. The strands of her long, finely braided hair were mostly black but intertwined with gray, brown, red, and gold, as if she had inside her the essence of every person who had ever lived.

"Where have you been all night?" her mamaw asked gently, the edges of her voice frayed with love and relief and admonishment all at the same time.

"I'm sorry, I was trying, but I couldn't get home, Mamaw," Willa whispered in the old words as she held her.

She and her mamaw always spoke in the Faeran language when they were alone within the smooth, curving stone walls of their den, but they were careful to never speak it in front of other members of the clan. The padaran had forbidden the use of the old language decades before Willa was born, insisting that everyone learn the ways of day-folk for the survival of the lair. But Faeran was the first language Willa had learned to speak from her parents and grandparents at home. The Eng-lish words, and some of the Cherokee words, that came to her ears later in her life had always been a struggle for her, always twisting on her tongue, which had made it even more difficult to fit in with the other jaetters.

"You're hurt," her mamaw said as her small, trembling hands passed over Willa's body. "Lie down here . . ." she whispered, patting the area beside her, and Willa immediately complied, laying herself in the cocoon of soft woven river cane that hung from the ceiling by vines.

When most of the members of the clan looked at her grandmother they saw a decrepit old woman who couldn't walk, but Willa knew her grandmother had once been a distant wayfarer of the mountains, a consummate weaver who could disappear into any background in an instant, and a friend to many of the most sacred animals of the forest. She carried the lore of the forest inside her—in her old body, in her mind, in her dreaming soul—and Willa had always been as greedy for that knowledge as a sapling was for light.

When her grandmother told long and winding stories of the past, the other members of the clan—especially the young jaetters—turned away in boredom, or even scoffed at her, but Willa wanted to hear her mamaw's stories. She wanted to be able to do what her mamaw had once done. She wanted to know what her mamaw knew.

But as Willa grew from sapling into tree, becoming stronger and stronger in her forest skills, her mamaw became weaker and weaker, her body sinking down to the ground like an old willow tree whose branches had become too weak for it to carry.

Most of the members of the clan ate the food that the foragers brought into the lair for them, but her mamaw had always foraged for her own food. When her mamaw could no longer go out into the forest and gather her own food, Willa went out and gathered it for her. When her mamaw lost the use of her legs, Willa made her a sling of woven reeds to keep her upright. When her mamaw's hands trembled, Willa steadied them in her own.

"Tell me what happened to you," her grandmother said as she examined Willa's wounds.

But Willa went quiet.

Her mamaw had told her many times how dangerous the day-folk could be. "I know the padaran expects you to steal from them," her mamaw had told her when she was ten, "but when you hear them coming, you must run. When you see them, you must hide. They are not of this world, so promise me that you will not go near them."

The last thing Willa wanted to do now was to tell her mamaw where she'd gone and what she'd done. She lay like an injured fawn curled up quietly as her grandmother worked on her wounds.

Needing supplies, her mamaw used the strength of her arms to drag herself over to a small niche in the stone wall where light filtered down through round holes in the ceiling onto a number of leafy plants and small trees that she had planted there years before. She had been caring for the plants ever since. As she approached them, the plants reached upward, not just toward the light of the sun, but to her nurturing hands and her murmuring voice, moving back and forth between her open fingers as if the leaves were being caressed by a gentle breeze.

One of the plants was a miniature tree growing out of a small stone bowl. It had fine tendrils of roots growing into the dirt, a bent little trunk, and a spread of delicate branches above that were covered in tiny bright green leaves.

"Thank you, my friend," her mamaw whispered as she carefully picked a single leaf from the tree and brought it over to Willa.

Willa had known this little tree all her life and had spoken with it many times. It had always been one of her closest friends. Her mamaw had told her that although it was small, this tree was more than six hundred years old and, in some ways, more powerful than the entirety of the lair above. She said that she'd been protecting it, hiding it, keeping it small, until one day it could come out into the light of the world and grow up into what it was meant to be.

Her mamaw put the tiny leaf into her own mouth for a moment, then brought it out again, crushed it between her fingers, and began to apply it bit by bit to Willa's wounds. The pain of the wound immediately began to subside. The lake of the bears had stanched the bleeding and saved her life, but now her mamaw continued the healing process.

This one room, this little den where she had grown up with her mamaw since her parents and sister died, was her protected place, her home. It was the one place that the outside world never came. It was the only place that she had ever felt truly safe and the only place she had ever felt truly loved.

But halfway through her work, her mamaw paused. Willa heard the sigh of her breath as she exhaled.

Willa winced a little as her grandmother's fingers pried carefully into the wound and pulled out a tiny piece of metal the size of a small pebble.

It was a piece of lead shot.

Her grandmother frowned.

"Willa," she said. "You must help me understand this. What am I seeing here? How were you hurt? Is there something you're not telling me?"

As she drew in a breath to speak, a bout of shame filled Willa's chest. "I was shot by a homesteader, Mamaw," she said, her voice cracking as her lip trembled.

"Ah, child . . ." her mamaw said as she wrapped her arms around her. "But how is it possible this wound is already healing?"

"I asked the wolves for help," Willa said.

"The wolves . . ." her mamaw said, her voice filled with a trace of respect.

"They took me to the lake of the bears."

"I see," her mamaw said, her eyebrows rising in surprise. "And the bears allowed . . ."

"The white bear was there, Mamaw, just like you said he was. He wasn't pleased about the wolves, but he let me go down to the lake."

"The white bear saved your life . . ." her mamaw said.

"And the wolf did as well. Her name is Luthien. We've become good friends."

When Willa looked into her mamaw's face, she could see the pride sparkling in her eyes, but then her grandmother's expression turned far more serious.

"But there is still one thing I don't understand," her grandmother said. "How did the man with the killing-stick see you well enough in the forest to shoot you?"

Willa's heart sank. This was one situation she couldn't blend her way out of.

"Don't tell me you went near one of their lairs . . ." her grandmother said, tilting her head and narrowing her eyes at her.

Willa didn't want to answer, but the reddened color of her skin answered for her. There were times when color was a curse.

"I went inside!" Willa blurted desperately. "I had to!"

"I've told you before that it's too dangerous!" her grandmother scolded her. Willa could see her mamaw moving her lips as she found the words. "You're not you in there," she said finally. "The old powers do not work in the lairs of the new ones. You know that!"

"I know I do," Willa pleaded.

"Then why did you do it, Willa? Why?"

"I wanted to prove to the padaran what I could do, that I could steal something good!"

"Aw, child," her grandmother said, shaking her head as she put her hand gently on Willa's arm. "The padaran doesn't deserve you."

Willa frowned in confusion and looked at her. "But he's the padaran."

"Yes, but don't let him control what's in here," her mamaw said, touching her fingers to Willa's chest. "I know you're trying to be part of the clan. That's good. It's an instinct of our people to stick together."

"But what?" Willa pressed her. "What did I do wrong? I don't understand."

"There are many dangers outside the lair," her mamaw said gravely, "but I'm afraid there are even more on the inside."

"What do you mean, Mamaw?" Willa asked. "I don't understand what's going on."

"The padaran is making changes in the lair," her mamaw said.

"I saw a band of guards leaving this morning," Willa said, "and I found a bird tangled in a net. Are the day-folk using the nets or our own people doing it? They're not trying to actually hurt birds and animals, are they?"

"You know that it is not the Faeran way to hurt any of the animals of the forest," her mamaw said.

Finally working up her courage, Willa decided to tell her grandmother everything she had seen. "On my way back home, when I was down in one of the abandoned parts of the lair, I saw human children in prison cells."

Her grandmother stopped what she was doing and went very still, as if she was trying to absorb what Willa had just told her. "Human children . . ." her mamaw whispered, as if even saying the words out loud might bring the padaran's guards rushing into the room.

"Why, Mamaw?" Willa asked. "Why are the guards imprisoning those humans?"

"I don't know," her mamaw said, "but I sense the decisions of a desperate mind."

*Whose desperate mind?* Willa wondered. "The padaran wouldn't order this, would he? The Faeran people don't harm day-folk. We don't harm anyone."

"Very little happens in Dead Hollow that the padaran doesn't control," her mamaw said. "You must be very careful, Willa, especially now. Too many of our people have been dying. Sometimes even *knowing* something brings death."

Willa was getting more and more frightened by her mamaw's words, and the tone of her voice. *Knowing brings death,* Willa kept thinking.

"The clan is restless," her mamaw warned.

"The foraging crews haven't been collecting enough food for everyone," Willa said. "They're angry and miserable. I don't understand why the padaran doesn't let more people go out into the forest and forage on their own."

"It is said to be too dangerous," her mamaw said.

"But is it truly too dangerous to even go out and forage in the forest for food? I go out thieving every night, either with the other jaetters or on my own. Didn't all the Faeran of old forage in the forest?"

"I've tried to teach you in the old ways, so that you wouldn't be beholden to anyone," her mamaw said. "But most of the members of our clan no longer have the skills to survive in the forest."

Willa remembered what had happened with her friend Gillen, a fellow jaetter whom she often went out thieving with. Gillen was one of the toughest jaetters she knew, fast and strong. But one night Willa took Gillen out into the forest with her to forage for food. Willa found some blackberries and started eating them, but when she glanced over to Gillen, she saw that the girl had picked up a beautiful white mushroom instead. Willa leapt at her, pushed her fingers into her mouth, and pulled the mushroom out by force. "Spit it out! Spit it out!" she had screamed.

The mushroom Gillen had chosen had been a Death Cap. A single swallow would have killed her.

Willa looked at her mamaw. "Do you remember the time I took Gillen out foraging with me?"

"Gillen doesn't have a mother to teach her," her mamaw said.

"Or a grandmother," Willa said, smiling at her mamaw.

"Or a grandmother," her mamaw said, smiling in return.

"I taught Gillen how to tell the difference between the good ones and the bad ones in that particular patch," Willa said. "But they were all growing in that same area and many of them looked very similar."

"There is much to teach, isn't there?" her mamaw said gently, and Willa had a feeling she wasn't just talking about Gillen.

Willa had been learning from her mamaw all her life, but she knew there was still much for her to learn. Her grandmother had always been careful to only teach her what she thought she could truly understand and use wisely. “A tree must grow to reach the sky,” she would often say.

Willa’s thoughts turned back to Gillen. Her friend lived in a distant part of the lair, where many of the jaetters slept huddled together in tight pockets, shivering together through the cold winter nights, generating the heat that kept them warm enough to survive. *There is no I, only we.*

“Did you and my parents ever live in the upper parts of the lair, Mamaw?” she asked.

“You and your parents and your sister lived down here in the labyrinth with me and many of the older families, including my own twin sister, and my husband, and many others who have passed.”

Her mamaw had warned her not to ask too many questions about how people had passed, especially her parents and sister, lest her heart become too entangled in things she couldn’t control, but she couldn’t help it. “Did the humans discover the Dead Hollow lair and attack it? Is that what happened? Is that how my sister and parents were killed?”

Her mamaw gazed at her but did not speak. It was as if her grandmother had no idea how she could possibly answer her question, as if she knew that the answer itself would lead to a series of consequences too awful to think about.

“Did you see it happen?” Willa whispered, her chest tightening as she leaned toward her mamaw. “What did the padaran and the guards do when the day-folk attacked? How did they defend the lair?”

"I did not see your parents and sister die, Willa," her grandmother said.

"But you had to have been there . . ." Willa said.

"There was a gathering of the clan in the great hall that night," her mamaw said. "And everyone was there. Your father was one of the most respected elders of the clan, a guardian of old ways. Immediately after the gathering, your mother, father, and sister left the lair through the main entrance that leads beneath the Watcher."

"Where were they going?" Willa asked, anger leaking into her voice. "Why wasn't I with them? Why would I be separated from Alliw?"

"You were here, with me," her mamaw said gently. "I had decided that the time had come for you to learn the song of the little tree."

Willa glanced over at the tree sitting in the stone niche, with the sunlight coming down from the hole above. The Faeran of old had used words to talk with and persuade the ancient guardians of the forest, but songs sung in the Faeran language were even more powerful. It was so long ago that she had forgotten, but Willa suddenly remembered fragments of the song her mamaw had taught her for the little tree, a soft and beautiful melody, but the bile rose in Willa's throat as it came into her mind. She had gained a song, and lost a sister.

"Do you remember now?" her mamaw asked gently.

"Yes," Willa said, her voice cracking as she wiped the tears from her eyes. She didn't want to cry right now. She wanted answers from her mamaw.

"I'm sorry, Willa," her mamaw said. "I'm sorry about everything that happened that night. The three of them went out into the forest, but they never returned."

Willa looked up at her. "But what happened to them?"

"The day-folk caught them and killed them."

"But how?" Willa asked. "They could all blend."

"I don't know," her mamaw said. "You know that I taught your mother myself, and I taught Alliw as well. If enemies came, they should have been able to hide themselves—"

Her grandmother stopped abruptly, unable to continue. Willa could suddenly see the pain that had been living inside her all these years, the tremble in her hand.

"And then I became a jaetter . . ." Willa whispered, to herself as much as to her grandmother.

She couldn't remember all the details of that part of her life, other than the living nightmare of the initiation—the pleading, the isolation, the starvation, the long training through the night.

"It is the padaran's law that all the children of the clan become jaetters," her mamaw said in a low voice, looking into her eyes. "I tried to tell them that it was too soon for you, that you were too young, that you needed time to grieve. Your father would have never allowed you to be a jaetter if he'd still been alive. But your initiation started the day after your parents died . . . You were just six years old . . ." Her voice trailed off, and for a moment her eyes closed and her lips pressed together. When she opened her eyes again, she said, "You were the last jaetter to be initiated in the Dead Hollow clan."

"Me and Gredic."

"Yes," her mamaw said, "the young boy as well."

"At least Alliw didn't have to go through it," Willa said. "That would have broken my heart."

Despite everything that had happened, and the sadness she felt, Willa knew that she wasn't the only one who had suffered in their lair. The Dead Hollow clan was dying. It had been withering for decades. From the murderous day-folk, from the predators of the forest, from starvation, from eating poisonous foods, from oak wilt and other diseases, from a thousand causes, they had been dying. The empty corridors and shadowed rooms of the vast Dead Hollow lair were a constant reminder. Willa, Gredic, and the other jaetters were the youngest Faeran in the clan. The few pairs of babies that had been born in the last dozen years had been small and sickly creatures that did not survive. Willa had never even seen a baby with her own eyes, and she'd never heard one laugh or cry.

Filled with too many thoughts, she looked up at her mamaw. "Do you think the padaran can save us?"

She knew it was a foolish question.

Of course the answer was yes.

The answer *had* to be yes.

Gazing at her with steady eyes, her mamaw paused, and she said, very quietly, "No, I don't."

"But . . ." Willa said, wanting to argue.

"The padaran cannot save us," her mamaw whispered. "But you must never speak of this. You must not even think it. Knowing brings death. Do you understand?"

Willa didn't understand, and she started to ask another question, but she was interrupted by a faint sound in the distance.

She rose quickly to her feet.

It was the sound of many footsteps coming through the labyrinth of corridors toward their den.

"What is that?" her mamaw asked. "Who's coming?"

"They're coming for me, mamaw," Willa said, her voice filled with dread.

"What's happened, Willa?" her mamaw asked in dismay. "Where did you go last night? What have you done?"

The strained and fearful sound of her mamaw's voice made Willa want to cry, but she didn't have time for that.

"They're going to take me to the padaran," she said as she quickly dumped out one of her grandmother's old medicine bags and filled it with the contents of her satchel. All she left in the satchel were two copper pennies that she stuffed deep inside its inner pocket.

"But what have you done?" her grandmother asked again.

"Too much," Willa said.

Her grandmother reached forward and pulled her behind her, physically protecting her with her own crippled body. "Remember: speak only Eng-lish!"

"I will, Mamaw," Willa said, switching to the Eng-lish words.

Gredic and Ciderg stormed into the room, hissing and snarling. Four of the padaran's guards followed close behind them.

"There she is!" Gredic shouted, pointing a clawed finger at Willa.

As the guards reached for her, her grandmother quickly moved in their way and tried to block them.

"Don't hurt her!" her mamaw cried, but they shoved her aside and knocked her to the woven-stick floor.

They were the last words Willa heard her mamaw speak as the storming guards and hissing jaetters grabbed her with their bony, clutching hands and dragged her down the tunnel toward the Hall of the Padaran.

The guards hauled her across the floor on her knees into the cavernous central hall of the Dead Hollow lair. For as long as she could remember, entering this place had filled her with dread, whether her satchel was full or not. It was as if she had always known that one day it would come to this.

They dragged her through the seething crowd of Faeran—the throng of jaetters, guards, and hundreds of clan members—and hurled her to the floor in shame in front of the padaran's empty, waiting throne.

Gredic, Ciderg, and two of the guards held her down to the floor. The sniveling Kearnin wiped the sticky ooze dripping from the corner of his mouth with his gnarled hand as his brother chattered his small, sharp teeth and jabbed at her with his stick.

Her cheeks burned with humiliation as she looked up at the

crowd of Faeran, all peering at her now, pressing around her, gathering for the spectacle of her punishment and disgrace.

The faces in the crowd were mostly middle-aged Faeran, with few grandmothers and grandfathers among them, for many of the elders had passed away in the last few years, and there were no children other than the hissing jaetters. Having spent most of their living hours in the torchlit shadowed walls of the decaying lair rather than the moonlit meadows of the forest, many of the Faeran had mottled dark gray skin, sticky and muculent like slimy toads, and their hair fell gray and straggly from their heads. Others had greenish skin similar to her own.

Most of the Faeran in the crowd stared at her with scowling faces, anxious to see her fall. Others watched with despairing, fearful eyes filled with sadness. The people came because they had to come. They watched because they had to watch. They had to be part of the clan, no matter what it was doing. If the clan was cheering, everyone had to cheer. If the clan was hissing, everyone had to hiss. There was no choice in this—no standing against the commands of the padaran or the will of the clan. *There is no I, only we.*

Many of them didn't know the reason she had been brought there, but they still snapped and sneered, for the padaran and his most ardent followers had shown them year after year that to be weak, to be dragged, to be down, was itself deserving of shame in the lair's eyes.

"It's one of the jaetters!" a Faeran in the crowd murmured to the one next to him.

"It's the little woodwitch," one of the others said. "Look at her! They've really got her."

"What'd she do?"

"She went missing during the night."

"She shouldn't be sneaking out on her own."

"It's that old witch that teaches her."

"The padaran sent out search parties during the night."

"I heard she was dead."

*But here I am,* Willa thought, beneath the cuts and blows of the grasping hands and the whispering words, wounded and weak, held by force in the center of the room for all to see, surrounded by the scolding, murmuring crowd, as they all waited for the padaran to arrive.

Willa looked around at the grimacing faces for anyone who might defend her, anyone who might remind the others of her loyalty to the clan or beg the guards to show her mercy. She spotted her friend Gillen. She was sure Gillen would rush forward to the front of the crowd, push Gredic away from her, and talk to the guards on her behalf. But Gillen was standing there, just watching, too frightened to move.

"Gillen," Willa said, looking toward her.

Gillen held her gaze for a moment, her eyes pleading for Willa to understand, and then looked away in shame.

Willa's mind filled with despair. Not even Gillen was going to help her.

Willa lowered her head and peered down through the floor of meshed sticks, down to the creek that ran below, wondering if she could somehow escape into the dark spaces beneath the lair, slip into the stream, and let it carry her away from this wretched place.

But she knew there was no escape. There never had been and there never would be. She was part of this clan, and it was part of her, as inextricable as root and soil. Willa looked up, beyond the throng of the Faeran that surrounded her, toward the ceiling. The hall had been built for many thousands of people to gather here, but far fewer than that remained. The walls of the great hall rose up all around, vast expanses of dark brown woven sticks reaching to a large gaping hole broken to the sky above. What was left of the decaying ceiling and walls was held aloft by the ancient, massive woven-stick sculptures of giant trees, the columns of their trunks soaring upward to spreading canopies above. Thousands of hand-curled leaves glimmered with emerald green, and brilliant kaleidoscopes of ornately woven birds of all shapes and sizes and colors seemed to be flying through the branches of the trees. The name had been changed to the Hall of the Padaran decades before, but in the old language the great hall had once been called the Hall of the Glittering Birds. The walls of the great hall were ragged with rot now, the woodwitches who made them long dead, and many of the sculptures of the birds had disintegrated. The only birds that remained undamaged by time weren't the sculptures, but actual living birds—carrion-eating black vultures circling in the hole above, floating on the smoky, steaming heat of the rising air, waiting for another Faeran body.

As Willa's eyes drifted down from the vultures, she noticed a pile of tattered brown rags lying on the floor near the base of one of the woven-stick trees. But then she realized it wasn't just a pile of rags. When she looked more carefully, she saw the long blackish hair and the dark brown skin matching the color and texture of what was around it. It was a very old Faeran woman crumpled on the floor, and she was *blending.*

*Mamaw,* Willa thought, her heart leaping.

Somehow, her grandmother had pulled herself along the floor with her arms, dragging her useless legs behind her, and made it all the way to the hall, her ragged medicine bag slung over her shoulder.

To the rest of the clan, she was a craggy old stump of a woman, too rough and gnarled to care about or even notice, but to Willa, she was a tendril of bright green hope.

*"Thank you, Mamaw,"* Willa said softly.

At that moment, the room shifted. All the faces in the crowd blanched with dread. Hundreds of pairs of eyes widened. Bodies went still. Whispers went silent.

Willa turned to see the padaran emerging from a passageway behind the throne.

The padaran moved with commanding ease, hunched with massive shoulders, his arms and legs stout with muscles, and the quills on the back of his bulging neck as thick and sharp as a porcupine's. His skin wasn't gray like many of the others, or streaked and spotted green like hers, but a woody bronze. As the crowd looked up at him in awe, his face seemed to almost glisten with color, shimmering like the reflection of moving water in the morning sun. He was the god of the clan, their sacred leader, their padaran.

Willa had never seen or even heard of another Faeran like him. He was said to be very old, but he did not look old. He was the strongest and most vibrant Faeran she knew. Some believed him to be what Faeran used to be. Others said he was what Faeran would someday become. But no one still alive seemed to know, or at least be willing to talk about, who or what he truly was. To the inhabitants of the lair, the padaran was not a mortal being. It was said that he had never been a boy, never been a normal Faeran. He had no wife, no children, no twin brother, no name. He had come down from the Great Mountain to lead them, and he held the clan together with absolute power.

The padaran's guards stood ready for his orders, and his pack of sniveling jaetters swarmed around him, but he ignored them all. As he sat on his throne of blackened, twisted, rotting sticks, it creaked beneath his weight. He gestured toward Willa with a flick of his clawed finger. Gredic and the guards immediately dragged her forward and hurled her to the floor at the padaran's feet.

As the padaran stared down at her with his searing glare, Willa wanted to wither into a little ball.

The god of the clan leaned forward, looming over her with his long, square, protruding face and his massive biting jaws.

"Why have my guards brought you before me in this way?" he snarled. "Where have you been, jaetter?"

Willa wanted to stay strong. She wanted to be brave, to stand up to him, but she couldn't keep her body from shaking. The menacing stare of the padaran was too much to bear.

"What have you done, jaetter?" he asked her, his voice low and growling.

She knew he was already aware of much of what she had done. He wanted her to explain herself, to beg him for forgiveness, but even lying on the floor before him, under the looming threat of his presence, she couldn't find the dark and murky pit in herself to say the words he wanted to hear.

"I don't know why your guards brought me here," she said sullenly. "I am a loyal member of the clan."

The crowd gasped at her insolence. Nothing but subservience and apology was ever allowed at the feet of the padaran.

Gredic darted in and jabbed her with his stick, outraged that she wasn't whimpering in submission.

The whole room began to erupt, but the padaran raised his open hand and closed his clawed fingers into a fist, bringing the room to immediate silence.

The padaran picked up his long, steel spear in his right hand. The jaetters, and the guards, and everyone in the crowd had seen him use the spear of power many times to kill the Faeran who had committed crimes or gone against the will of the clan. The padaran's spear was the only metal allowed in Dead Hollow other than what the jaetters brought back in their satchels, and each jaetter's take must always be given to the padaran the moment the jaetter returned.

Still holding his spear, the padaran peered down at Willa lying on the floor in front of him.

"I will tell you why you are here," he said, his voice filled with a dark and scathing tone, his eyes flicking out across the watching crowd. "Last night you crept past the Watcher. The Watcher sees all, and so do I. Not only did you leave the lair without my instruction or my permission, you left without the other jaetters. You went out thieving on your own."

The padaran's eyes shifted back and forth across the faces of the crowd, gauging their reaction as he spoke.

"And when you finally returned, you slithered back into the lair like a rat, without making yourself known to me or my guards. You entered places in the lair that you knew you were not allowed and you did things you knew were wrong."

By the time he came to the last of her crimes, his voice had become a vicious roar. "What is the meaning of this behavior, jaetter?"

The walls of the hall seemed to vibrate with the power of his voice, and the people hunkered down in fear.

Willa wanted to scream up at him that she'd been hurt and needed his help. But she knew he wouldn't care, and if he found out that she'd been shot by a homesteader, it would make him even angrier.

She could hear the murmurs of hostility toward her spreading through the crowd, and the padaran seemed to sense it, too. He leaned down toward her and shouted, "This is your clan, jaetter! These are your people! Everything you do must be for the others! Do you understand the harm you cause them when you split away from me and the other members of the clan, when you do these things on your own? The members of a clan must stick together. We must fight for each other! Care for each other! There is no I, only we."

As he said these words, his voice soared and his skin glistened, and the people looked up at him with adoration in their eyes.

When he rose once again to his full height and stepped toward her with his spear in his hand, the swarm of the crowd shrunk back in fear. The jaetters cowered. Willa's heart pounded in her chest. He was going to thrust the point of the steel spear into her body at any moment.

"Do you wish to die, is that it?" he asked her. "And after all that you did wrong, you didn't come to me when you returned to the lair. You were pulled to my throne against your will by my guards. And you appear to have come empty-handed. You have *nothing*! You were a good jaetter once, but now I see nothing before me but a creature without a clan."

They were the harshest of words. A Faeran without a clan did not survive. And the padaran's words weren't just a punishment or a reprimand. They were a threat. With a thrust of his spear, he could kill her, but with the roar of a command, he could cast her out, a fate that most Faeran considered more cruel than death itself.

"Do you wish to starve, is that it?" he asked. "Do you wish to freeze alone in the winter cold?" he asked, raising his voice as the surrounding swarm hissed and jeered at her. "You're acting like a girl who doesn't understand the value of the clan that protects her!"

Seeing that there was no way for her to defend herself, Gredic rushed in and grabbed her satchel. He tried to yank it away, but she'd been expecting his attack. She leapt to her feet and clutched the satchel to her side. The padaran stepped back to let the two jaetters fight it out, one against the other. But Gredic's brother, Ciderg, charged in. He struck her so hard that she hit the ground, gasping for air, her ribs burning. Ciderg ripped the satchel away from her hands and handed it to his brother.

Gredic held the satchel up for all to see. "It feels very light!" he shouted triumphantly as the crowd hooted and hollered in return. They'd been watching the rivalry between the jaetters for years, with all their tricks and takes, their rises and their falls.

But as Gredic pawed through the satchel, it became clear by

the grim expression on his face that something was wrong. "It can't be empty," he grumbled in confusion. "It can't be . . ."

But then he hissed with pleasure.

"The sneaky little beast has hidden something in a concealed pocket . . . She's trying keep her take for herself! She's trying to steal from the clan!"

Then Gredic went silent.

His expression changed.

It was clear to everyone that he had discovered something in the satchel so deliciously wicked that even he couldn't believe his luck.

He lifted two small brown coins above his head. "After all the trouble she's caused, all Willa got last night were these two copper pennies!" he called out above the rising clamor of the crowd. "Two copper pennies! That's all she got!"

As Willa gathered herself slowly, painfully, up onto her knees, and then up onto her feet, the padaran moved toward her with his spear.

Standing before him, she did not look away as others always did. She stared right back at him.

*My name is Willa,* she thought defiantly.

But as the padaran studied her, the malice in his expression slowly changed to something else, something more wary and uncertain than simply angry. And that was her only hope now.

She had snuck into the homesteader's house and stolen his belongings to get the padaran's attention, to earn his praise. But now that the sun had risen and the harsh light of the padaran's gaze was on her, her heart pounded in her chest.

Would there be praise or punishment?

The bronze skin of the padaran's face seemed to glimmer as he turned toward Gredic. He looked at the two pennies in Gredic's hand, then out at the crowd. And then finally, his eyes came back to her.

"Is this truly what you've brought me?" the padaran asked. "You've been a strong and effective jaetter for this clan, quick of hand and deft of thought. But two nights ago, you failed me with an empty satchel. And the night before that your satchel was light as well. And now this . . . Is this the take you have brought to your padaran?"

Willa met his eyes, and held his gaze as steady as she could, but she did not speak.

"Answer me," he demanded in a growl. "Is this what you have brought me, Willa?"

"No, my padaran," Willa said finally, her tone soft and filled with respect. But then her voice took on a sharper edge. "This is what I brought for Gredic."

Gredic hissed and moved toward her, but the padaran pointed his clawed finger at the jaetter. "You stay right there," he snarled, and Gredic stopped dead in his tracks, too frightened to move another step.

When the padaran looked at Willa, a knowing expression slowly inched across his face. "Gredic and the other jaetters have been stealing your take from you . . ."

Willa nodded. "Yes, my padaran. He got his two cents this time, just as I knew he would."

"It's a lie!" Gredic screamed. "I bring home a good take every night! You know I do! The little beast is lying!"

"If I may, my padaran," Willa said, "I would like your

permission to walk over to that tree over there so that I can show you something."

The padaran glanced toward the woven-stick column, and then looked back at Willa, his eyes narrowing in curiosity. "You may go," he said.

Willa noticed the padaran's eyes shift across the room. She couldn't be sure, but it was almost as if he was trying to gauge the crowd's reaction to what was happening. She had noticed in the past that although he was the great leader of the clan, he seemed to live in worry of what his subjects were seeing when they looked at him, what they were thinking at that moment.

As she walked over to the woven-stick tree, she felt and heard the moment the people in the crowd behind her realized there was actually an old woman lying on the floor at the base of the tree.

"May I borrow your bag, Grandmother?" Willa asked, using the most formal title she could for her mamaw, reminding people in a small, quiet way that she herself was just a girl, with a grandmother and a clan, respectful of the old ways of her people. Willa knew from watching the padaran that words had power, the power to persuade and the power to deceive.

As her mamaw handed her the old, tattered bag, she looked up at Willa and their eyes met. *Be careful, my child,* she seemed to be saying.

"Thank you, Grandmother," Willa said.

"What kind of trick is this?" Gredic hissed in protest as Willa returned with her mamaw's medicine bag and set it before the throne. "I have brought this for you, my padaran . . ."

"And what is it?" the padaran asked.

Taking that as her cue, Willa stepped forward and reached into the bag.

"My padaran, will you please . . ." she asked softly, and then, as the crowd looked on, Willa poured a waterfall of silver coins out of the bag into the padaran's cupped hands.

Gredic writhed in anguish. "It's one of the little beast's dirty tricks!"

"You have done very well, little one," the padaran said, using the term "little one" for Willa as if she wasn't just a thieving jaetter, but once again a child of the clan, to be protected and honored. *Words have power,* Willa thought again. He knew it. And she knew it.

"But this is not all, my padaran . . ." she said as she pulled wads of crumpled green bills from the bag and put them in his hands.

The crowd erupted with pleasing sounds at the riches she had brought. Then she pulled out the Cherokee arrowheads, which were highly prized in the clan, for they could be used on the tips of their spears.

"You have pleased the padaran, my child," the god of the clan said as she filled his hands with treasure, the praise pouring out of him like poison from a festering wound.

Willa could see her grandmother watching her and the padaran with steady eyes, as if she was seeing the plot of a play unfold.

"But that is not all . . ." Willa said again.

As she slowly pulled out the glittering silver jewelry she'd stolen from the man's lair and laid it in the padaran's hands, his eyes widened and whispers of approval ran through the crowd.

There was no doubt now. It was a large and bountiful take, but it wasn't important just because the padaran and his guards could sell and trade these goods for the benefit of the clan. It wasn't just about the money and the valuables. The size and tradition of a jaetter's take was a symbol of his or her loyalty to the padaran, her embrace and acceptance of everything that held the clan together.

But as the padaran and the jaetters and everyone in the crowd gazed upon her take with gleaming eyes, Willa felt a strange and lingering shame.

So much had come to depend on her take each night—whether it was more than Gredic's or less, whether the padaran was pleased or angry—but deep down, she couldn't help herself from wondering what difference it all made to her and her people and the forest in which they all lived.

Gredic groveled low to the floor as he crept toward the padaran like a slithering creature. "You know I am your loyal servant, my padaran . . ."

Willa watched as the padaran's eyes slid reluctantly over to Gredic.

"You know you can trust me . . ." Gredic said.

"Speak what's on your mind," the padaran said gruffly.

"What the little beast said isn't true. We haven't been stealing her take. She's been stealing ours. This take is ours, ours to give to the padaran. She stole it from us and hid it with the old witch. We all know the little beast is a woodwitch, too. She can't hide it."

As the gang of jaetters surrounded her and started a slow and steady hiss in unison with Gredic's charges against her, Willa's heart began to sink. She knew that no matter what she said or did now, most of them were going to support Gredic's claim against her.

Willa glanced over at Gillen. Her friend's eyes blazed with anger at the way the jaetters were turning on her. But when Gillen moved forward to stand in her defense, Kearnin and the other jaetters shoved her back. Willa looked over at her mamaw, but what could her mamaw do for her? How could she save her?

The padaran turned to Willa, his eyes moving from her streaked and spotted face to the leaf-colored skin of her arms and legs to her head of long, dark hair.

"Your fellow jaetter has made a charge against you," the padaran said. "Can you prove that this was your take? Can you prove that you didn't steal this from Gredic?"

Willa met the padaran's eyes. She knew he was far smarter than the other people in the room, far smarter than even Gredic, and he already knew the answer to all his questions. He knew this was her take. He knew she had tricked Gredic. But he wanted to watch her confront this new challenge.

Willa held the padaran's gaze in silence for several seconds, her chest tightening with frustration. Now she had to prove it. Not just venture down into the valley miles away and sneak into a killing man's lair. Not just get shot and crawl back into Dead Hollow on her belly, and fight and hide and blend and run. She felt it boiling up inside her. Now she had *prove* it, *prove* that she had actually stolen these things, *prove* that she was loyal to the clan, *prove* that she was loyal to the padaran.

She looked at Gredic and the other jaetters, and out across the crowd of Faeran waiting for her answer. Then she looked over at her grandmother, who was watching her and the padaran.

Finally, she nodded. "Yes, I think I can," she said.

She lifted the bag and held it above her head.

"If what you say is true, Gredic, that I stole this take from you, then you should have no trouble telling everyone here what remains inside this bag."

She could see Gredic furiously trying to figure out what she was doing. She could see him trying to think it through. She had put so much treasure into the padaran's hands. How could there possibly be more still in the bag?

Gredic's face grimaced with uncertainty. "It's another trick!" he declared.

"You claim that it was your take," she said for all to hear. "So is there something still left in the bag, or is it empty now?"

# 21

Gredic studied her with his narrow eyes, his face contorting as he grappled with her question. He looked at the deflated bag, then back at her.

"It's empty," he said. "There's nothing left of value in there."

"Gredic is right," Willa said loudly, nodding as she looked around at the faces in the crowd.

But then she turned and looked at the padaran. "He's right that what is left in the bag is of little monetary value, certainly no value at all to *him*. It's a personal gift from me to the padaran to thank him for all he's done for me, and for our people."

Everyone watched as Willa reached her hand into the bag and pulled out a small pouch of brown material. She bowed her head in a gesture of honor and handed the padaran the chewing tobacco she had stolen from the lair of the day-folk man.

She knew that the tobacco that the humans used was one of

the padaran's most private and beloved pleasures. The padaran's shoulders rolled with seething anticipation as he pulled the tobacco into his covetous hands, not just because he was pleased with her gift, or because her words had touched his heart, but because he loved the conniving way she had tricked her rivals. He was the god of the clan, but she knew that deep down he would suck delight from the thought that she had learned the power of deceit from him. And the truth was, she had. She'd been watching him all her life, learning how to gain his smiles and avoid his strikes, how to not just persevere but to prevail in the world he'd created.

"This is a very good take, Willa," he said, using her name in the most powerful way.

Gredic and the other jaetters exploded in contempt, hissing and snarling. They swayed their bodies and gnashed their sharp little teeth. Despite all the wrong she'd done against the clan, she had once again shifted her colors and slipped away. She was the mouse that always squirmed out of their grasp!

And the jaetters knew that her words to the padaran were all part of her trickery. *They* were the loyal ones, not her!

But worst of all, Gredic and Ciderg and Kearnin and the others knew that Gredic's time as the leader of the jaetters was waning.

But Willa, despite all her victories, couldn't feel the glory of her moment the way she thought she would. Deep down, the actions she performed and the words she said left her cold and empty. She had brought her satchel home fuller than it had ever been, she was surrounded by her clan, and praised by the padaran. This was what she had always wanted. But the only thing she could think of—the only sensation she wanted to feel—was the friendship of the wolves, the acceptance of the bears, and the sight of the glistening lake. And then—to her surprise—she thought about what the human boy had called "cookies." Those peculiar little lumps she had passed through the mesh of the prison cell.

For some reason, it felt like *that*—helping the human boy trapped in the dark prisons of her clan—that strange and dangerous thing that came from the *I* deep inside her instead of the *we* of the clan, had been her most satisfying reward for coming home with her satchel full.

Her mind kept returning to one thing: the way the man with his killing-stick had looked at her when he found her wounded in his barn. She remembered the way he had spoken to her in soft tones and found a cloth to tend to her wound. All the other thoughts slipped away into a murky, muddled nothingness, but that one act of kindness dwelled in her mind and her heart like nothing ever had before.

As the jaetters jeered at her, the padaran looked upon her, and the rest of the clan watched it all, Willa turned to her grandmother at the edge of the room.

Her grandmother's eyes were looking at her, holding on to Willa with everything she could. But her mamaw's eyes weren't filled with pride or happiness or even relief in her accomplishments. They were filled with worry. It seemed as if her mamaw was thinking, *You're blending in a way that I never taught you. But it's keeping us both alive.*

When Willa turned back to look at the padaran, she was startled to see that he wasn't looking at the crowd like he normally did, or even at her, but across the room at her grandmother.

Willa knew that her grandmother had lived a quiet, peaceful life for many years, blending into the rest of the clan, nurturing the plants in her den, and raising her granddaughter. But now the padaran's eyes were studying her grandmother as if he was wondering just what kind of trickery the old woman had brought into his hall.

Then he turned slowly back toward Willa.

"Come here, Willa," he ordered, his tone filled with a commanding tone that turned her blood ice-cold.

With those simple, blunt words, the room went silent. Willa's chest tightened.

Having no other choice, she stepped toward the looming presence of the great leader.

"I want you to tell me where you got this take," he said.

"I stole it, my padaran," she said, trying to sound proud, but her voice was trembling. It was a truth she knew she should be proud of in his eyes. He had been the one who taught her how to steal, how to deceive. But she felt the heat rising to her cheeks. He had seen something. He had *sensed* something.

"Where did you steal it?" he asked.

Knowing that it would anger him if he knew she had risked creeping into a homesteader's lair, she didn't answer.

"Where did you get all this, Willa?"

The padaran knew she didn't want to divulge her secrets to her jaetter rivals, but he pressed her anyway. He seemed to sense that she'd seen something or done something out there in the world that had changed her in some way.

When he stepped closer to her, a drop of sweat dripped from his face and fell into her hair. He was so close that she could smell the musk of his body. She desperately wanted to shrink away from him. But she knew she couldn't.

He leaned his face to her neck and sniffed. "What is it that I smell on you?" he asked her.

"Nothing, my padaran," she said as quickly as she could.

"Have you been touching some sort of"—he paused and tilted his head and sniffed again—"some sort of animal? What kind of animal is that I smell?"

"Nothing, my padaran," she said again.

He clamped onto her shoulder with a crushing hand. "You will come with me."

The padaran had commanded it, so Willa had no choice but to follow him. The god of the clan pulled her behind the throne and through a woven-stick archway that led into a narrow passage.

She tried to wipe down the quills on the back of her neck with the cup of her hand, worrying that they'd betray the increasing sense of dread churning through her body.

Still carrying the spear of power, the padaran led her into the inner sanctuary of his private den, a heavily protected part of the lair that she and the other members of the clan were never allowed to enter. It was a great honor, but she couldn't help but realize that she wasn't being invited. She was being brought by force.

Every instinct in her body was telling her to run, to get away from him. But the padaran walked fast and hard, pulling her along with the dark and invisible force of his will.

Two guards pushed her from behind with their sharpened spears pointed at her back. One of them was Lorcan, the commander of the padaran's guards.

Lorcan was the tallest Faeran guard she had ever seen, with long, gangly arms and legs. He had a mash of hair the color of rotting twigs, a high forehead like a jutting boulder, and black, bulging eyes. He'd been serving the padaran since long before she was born.

Wedged between the padaran ahead of her and the two guards behind her, she climbed her way up the narrow, winding woven-stick tunnel, which was so tight that the padaran's shoulders scraped the walls, and so steep that her calves burned. When they finally reached the room at the top, she gasped at what she saw.

The room glowed with the orange blazing light of many burning torches. And it was stacked from floor to ceiling with hundreds of day-folk objects, from the tools she'd seen in homesteader barns to strange mechanical instruments of all shapes and sizes. She had no idea what all these bewildering things were for, or why they were here.

She had always thought the padaran sold and traded their takes to the day-folk for food and other necessities for the clan. But now she saw that he'd been acquiring these objects year after year, hiding them all this time.

"If we are going to survive," the padaran said, "then we must understand the tools and weapons of our enemy."

She reached toward a complicated-looking brass device with spoked metal circles and many levers, dials, and thumbscrews.

"The newcomers use it to look at the terrain of the earth and plan out the paths of the roads they build," he said. "Humans do not seem to be able to understand the world, or even find their way through it, until they have measured it and marked it on their maps."

As he spoke, the padaran's long, clawed fingers caressed the device's wheels and knobs possessively. He did not appear to know how to use the machine, but he held it as if he owned and controlled its inner power.

Then the padaran walked over to a collection of hammers, spikes, and other iron accoutrements. "The clanging men use these to lay down the long steel rails that the steaming beasts follow into the forest," he said, picking up one of the iron spikes. "This is the future," he declared, looking at the metal object with true reverence in his eyes.

It was hard not to let his confidence, and his knowledge of the outside world, draw her in, but she didn't understand. Did he mean that the future belonged to those who controlled the metal? Or that more of these things he called the steaming beasts were coming? Or that iron was the direction he was going to take the Dead Hollow clan? Or that the spike itself possessed some sort of magical power?

But the most disturbing thing was that she wasn't even sure *he* knew the answer. He seemed convinced that the power of the humans lay in these strange metal objects, but he didn't seem to truly understand the purpose of the devices or how to use most of them. It was as if he thought that by simply possessing them or being near them he would somehow gain their power.

She had watched the padaran all her life. He was the closest thing she had to a father. He'd always been a strong and forceful leader for the clan, someone she looked up to, someone she feared. But it seemed as if he had spent countless hours in this room, holding these objects in his hands, studying them, trying to divine their hidden secrets. They had become a festering obsession in his mind.

When her eyes were drawn to a long, gleaming brass tube mounted on a three-legged stand, he said, "Step forward and look through it." It appeared to be one of the few devices he had actually figured out how to use.

She studied the contraption uncertainly, wondering if its purpose was to rip out little girls' eyeballs when they went against the will of the clan.

Seeing her timidness, he put his hand on the device to steady it, to hold it in his control, as if to make it clear that only through him was it safe for her to use.

Quieting her breathing as best she could, she stepped closer, leaned slowly forward, and put her eye up to the end of the long tube. When she blinked, the flash of her eyelash startled her so severely that she leapt back in surprise.

"Now conquer your fear and try again," he said. "Close your left eye and look through with your right."

As she leaned forward, she squinted her eye one way and then the other until she began to see light coming through the tube. Then she caught a glimpse of several Faeran standing together talking among themselves. She pulled back in astonishment. There were no such people in the room, and yet she saw them quite clearly!

"The humans call this a telescope," he said, showing her a small opening in the wall through which the tube was pointed. When she peered through the hole, Willa saw the Faeran gathered in the Hall of the Padaran far below them, like bees in a crowded hive. From this vantage point, the padaran could spy on all the Faeran in the great hall, but other uses for the device immediately sprang into her mind as well.

Watching her, the padaran asked, "Do you understand the device's power?"

"Yes," she said excitedly. "If you took it to the top of the Great Mountain and pointed it outward, you could see to the edge of the world."

The padaran's eyes widened ever so slightly. She could see that it wasn't an idea that had occurred to him.

"Now follow me," he said, dragging her by the arm as the two guards followed close behind them.

As they left the padaran's hoard of human-made objects behind them, they crossed through a series of dark, empty rooms with crumbling ceilings and disintegrating walls, one room interconnected to the other, a vast hive of hundreds of abandoned Faeran dens. The murky world of the hollow, dripping rooms had once been the most luxurious chambers of the Faeran of old, but they had come to stink of black and seeping mold.

When she glanced behind her, the guards seemed just as anxious to leave this decaying place as she was.

The padaran moved quickly through the abandoned dens, intent on reaching some distant point on the other side.

Finally, they came to an area where the walls of the rooms and corridors were mostly still intact and a little bit of light filtered down through small holes in the woven-stick ceiling. They crossed through a den that looked different from any Faeran room she had ever seen. Clean and dry, it was adorned with human furniture—a table, a chair, a mirror, a wax candleholder, a small decorative box for holding tobacco, even pillows and woolen blankets. It startled Willa to see what looked like a human's bedroom inside the lair of Dead Hollow.

But the room didn't smell of humans.

It smelled like the padaran.

It was the padaran's private den. But what astounded her was that there wasn't a cocoon of woven reeds like her and the other Faeran slept in. The padaran appeared to sleep in a large, wooden day-folk bed!

"Come this way," he said, pulling her through the room and into the next.

They reached a narrow passage and went up a winding tunnel toward what smelled like fresh air, but Willa's mind couldn't let go of what she had just seen.

*The padaran's collection of day-folk objects . . . The human bed in his den . . . Why does he think I won't tell anyone about what I'm seeing here?* she wondered. *Where is he taking me?*

*Knowing brings death.* Her grandmother's words slipped into her thoughts.

The padaran pushed open a woven-stick door with his steel spear and pulled her outside, into a dense and secluded area of forest. Lorcan and the other guard came up close behind her with their spears as the padaran led her along a narrow trail, crowded with the bent and twisted limbs of blackened trees.

Looking around her, Willa could see that they had come out somewhere on the upper side of the Great Mountain, just above the lair, but she'd never been to this area of the forest before. On both sides of the path, she saw what looked like white bones and rotting brown heaps lying in the leaves.

A sickening feeling crept into Willa's stomach.

*Where are they taking me?* she thought again. *And why is the padaran still carrying his spear?*

"Back in my rooms, you saw the machines of the humans," the padaran said as they walked.

"Yes, my padaran," she said, glancing behind her at Lorcan and the other guard, wondering if she could outrun them. Her chest started pulling more air into her lungs, getting her ready.

"And you understand who I am," the padaran said.

"You're the sacred leader of our clan, my padaran," she said, as her eyes scanned the forest around them. Her skin was beginning to crawl. The truth was, she had no idea who he was, where he came from, or how he had come to wield such dominion over the clan.

"You see now that I can give you anything you can imagine from the day-folk world," he said.

"Yes, my padaran," she said, her throat feeling tighter and

tighter. She had no idea why she would want something from the day-folk world, but this appeared to be an offer of great significance to him, intended to impress her and draw her in.

"And I can give you more power in the clan than you ever imagined possible."

"Yes, my padaran," she said, the muscles in her legs beginning to twitch.

"If Gredic and the others are bothering you, then I can eliminate them, get them out of your way."

"Yes, my padaran," she said, her breaths getting shorter. Now *this* was something she understood.

"If I wish, I can make you the leader of the jaetters."

"Yes, my padaran," she said. But why was he telling her this here in the middle of the forest?

Finally, the padaran stopped. When he turned and peered into her eyes, she couldn't help but shrink back from the long, sharp tip of his steel spear. With his voice low and menacing, he said, "But if you lie to me, Willa, if you try to deceive me in any way . . ."

"No, my padaran, I wouldn't do that," she said, trying to back up but feeling the point of Lorcan's spear against her spine.

"If you try to go against me, then I will hurt you," the padaran said. "And I'll hurt everything you love. Do you understand?"

"I haven't been going against you, my padaran," she said, her voice shaking.

"Do you know why I've brought you out here?" he asked.

"No, my padaran," she answered. "I do not."

"The world is changing," the padaran said, as they continued down the path through the forest, leaving the heaps and bones behind them. "If we are to survive, we must change with it. The day-folk homesteaders have been living in these mountains for a hundred years, and now the newcomers are pouring in with their iron machines. We cannot stop them."

"But where are they all coming from?" she asked him. She still didn't understand why he had brought her into this part of the forest, but the questions burned in her mind. "Are they coming from the other side of the Great Mountain? Or the ridges that we see in the distance?"

"No," he said, shaking his head. "They come from a place where the land is flat."

"Flat?" Willa said. "I don't understand. What about the mountains?"

"Beyond the mountains, beyond the valleys, beyond the towns at the edge of our world, beyond all that you can see, the land is flat. To get to that land, they crossed a stationary river so wide that it took sixty phases of the moon to travel across it."

Willa took a breath in astonishment. "How could that be possible?"

"They floated on the water in the carcasses of trees that they cut down in the world they came from. The day-folk are cutters, builders, conquerors, spreading from place to place."

The skin on the side of Willa's neck tingled with fear. She didn't know what all those words meant, but she knew it wasn't good. When she listened to the padaran, the threat of the invading day-folk seemed more looming and horrible than ever before.

"We must learn their ways, their language, and their skills, Willa," he told her. "We must master their tools and their weapons and their way of life, or our clan will die. Do you understand?"

"Yes, my padaran," she said, marveling at how much he seemed to understand the way the world worked.

"The day-folk are a violent and hateful people," he continued, "filled with capabilities beyond our imagining. But they are driven by greed. That's why we steal from them, for without their money, we have nothing. We need their tools, their weapons, but even beyond their greed, they are consumed with fears and superstitions."

"What do they fear?" she asked in amazement.

"They kill the things that they think might do them or their children harm: bears, mountain lions, deep forests—they fear anything that is different from the place they came from. And that is where we will gain an advantage, for we know these forests and these mountains far better than they do. The money the day-folk pay is called a bounty. They will pay us to kill the things they fear, and to bring them the meat and fur. That is why I am selecting a few of my best jaetters to begin collecting a very special kind of take."

Far from the lair now, they had reached a deeply shadowed area of the forest, and the padaran turned to Lorcan and said, "Bring it to me."

Lorcan and the other guard walked into the forest, did something on the ground with their hands, and then returned with what looked like the jaws of a large fanged animal. But the jaws weren't old white bone. They were gleaming, bluish-black steel, and they were lined with many sharp teeth.

"The newcomers call it a leghold trap," the padaran explained. "It's one of the ways they capture and kill the animals of the forest."

Willa stepped away from the trap in revulsion, finding it almost too horrible to believe that even the newcomers would attack animals in such a cruel and vicious way.

"But why do they do this?" she asked.

She could imagine the snapping steel jaws of the trap clamping onto the leg of an animal, the poor creature trying desperately to get away, days upon days terrified and starving, its bloody leg caught in the trap until its enemy finally arrived to kill it.

"Come this way," the padaran said, leading them down a path

that wound through the forest. "You must be careful here, for beneath the leaves we have set traps all along this trail. Place your feet exactly where I place mine. You must follow in my footsteps."

Her stomach churned.

That was why he'd brought her here, to join him, to follow him, to bond herself to him even more profoundly than she already was. He wanted her, with all her forest skills and wily ways, to be the leader of his new force of animal-killing jaetters.

As she walked behind the padaran, carefully putting her feet where he put his, her heart beat heavily in her chest. If she put her foot in the wrong spot, the snap of the trap's jaws would clamp onto her ankle and crush her leg like a twig. She tried to look ahead, tried to see where the traps were before she came to them, but they were hidden beneath the leaves.

"How do you know where to step, my padaran?" she asked as she followed him along the path.

"We've put a stone next to each trap to show us its location. We know to look for the stones, and avoid the leaves next to them, but the animals do not."

Willa marveled at the cruel effectiveness of this trail of death that the padaran and his men had laid.

"This way," the padaran whispered to her as he moved quietly along the path. "Now look ahead. This is where we found the den."

*The den?* Willa thought in sudden shock. *Whose den?*

Finally, the padaran crouched down with his spear at his side, and Willa crouched with him. The padaran pointed to a gnarly old cedar tree in the distance, its base nearly eight feet across and its thick, red, shaggy bark covered with bright green moss. It appeared as if lightning had struck the tree, scorched it black, and left a long, twisting crevice that now led to what looked like a small cave inside the hollow of its trunk.

Fear crept up Willa's spine.

"What's inside the cave?" she whispered, but she didn't want to know the answer. She didn't want to be there. She didn't want to think about what was going to happen. There were stones all along the path to the cedar tree. The jaws of the traps were open and waiting, their springs coiled tight and ready to snap.

Suddenly, she heard a soft whining noise coming from the direction of the tree. She sniffed the air to see if she could pick up the scent, and then she heard the whining again.

It took her several seconds, but then she closed her eyes and pulled in a lungful of air in despair.

She knew what it was.

There was a litter of wolf pups in the hollowed-out base of the cedar tree.

*No,* Willa thought.

The pups were hungry and whimpering. They could sense their mother drawing near.

*No.*

Willa's heart wrenched when she heard the soft padding of trotting footsteps.

*No.*

The mother wolf was coming down the path toward her den of pups.

It was Luthien.

"No, no, no," she whispered desperately as she watched the wolf trotting down the path of traps toward the den.

She knew now that the padaran hadn't brought her here just because he was pleased with her take. He had brought here because he had sensed her pulling away from him, her loyalty shifting. If she was to truly join him, if she was to be the leader of his new band of jaetters, then he had to be absolutely certain of her loyalty—not to the wolves or to the forest or to the old ways of her grandmother—but to *him* and only him.

"The day-folk are the enemy of our people," he had told her many times. "If they catch you in their valleys, they will kill you. You're only safe with the clan."

Willa had nodded her head obediently whenever she heard the padaran say these words. They went into her mind as readily as water running down into a hole. There was a part of her that found the familiarity of the words to be reassuring, to know that what she'd known all her life was true. There was a deep satisfaction and sense of well-being in the comfort of knowing who to hate.

But the padaran had said, *If they catch you, they will kill you.* And that was where the problem lay.

She kept remembering the man with the killing-stick who had cornered her in his barn. He could have shot her again. He could have hurt her or killed her in so many different ways.

*But he didn't.*

After that man saw who and what she was, he did not try to harm her. He tried to *help* her.

She had been caught, and she hadn't been killed.

But if the padaran was the god of the clan, how could he be wrong?

And if he was wrong about this, then could he be wrong about other things, things he'd been telling her all her life?

Was it possible that her own thoughts and her own feelings could be as good or even better than his?

Was it possible that she could be more Faeran in her heart than the god of the Faeran clan?

It was clear that the padaran saw the mother wolf as expendable, as worth the bounty he would earn from the newcomers when he brought them her pelt. He had learned the language of the day-folk, but he had forgotten the language of the wolves. Did that make him a supreme being? Or a lesser one?

As Willa looked at all the steel traps lying beneath the leaves, and watched Luthien coming down the path toward her den of pups, dismay poured through her. She knew she was supposed to stay at the padaran's side and watch the trap spring. She knew she was supposed to watch the wolf die. She *knew* that was what her padaran and her clan demanded of her. And through all this, she kept remembering the look in her mamaw's eyes, the way her mamaw seemed to be thinking, *You're blending in a way that I never taught you. But it's keeping us both alive.*

But the thought of the steel trap crushing Luthien's leg, holding her there as she tried frantically to tear her leg away and save her pups, was more than she could bear.

Willa grabbed the spear of power out of the startled padaran's hand and leapt to her feet. She felt the press of the spear's cold steel shaft in her grip and the weight of it in the muscles of her arm. Then, as the mother wolf ran toward her pups, Willa gathered all her strength, pulled back her arm, and hurled the spear in the direction of the coming wolf.

As the spear soared through the air, it looked like it was going to strike the wolf. Everything seemed to be moving so slowly—the shocked look on the padaran's face, the running wolf, the spear arcing through the sky—it almost felt as if she could stop it, reverse it, pull it back. But she knew she couldn't. She'd already grabbed the spear. She'd already thrown it. It was far too late. There was nothing she could do to change the spear's path now. Or hers.

"Luthien!" Willa shouted a warning.

The wolf dodged out of the way just in time and the spear struck the trap. The trap snapped shut with a sudden jerk.

"The traps are all over the path!" Willa shouted to Luthien in the old language. "Get your pups and flee!"

"You little fool!" the padaran shouted at her.

"Better a fool than a traitor!" Willa shouted back at him in the old language.

"Kill her!" the padaran ordered his guards.

Lorcan thrust his spear straight at her chest. Willa dodged the attack, but the other guard lunged forward and clutched her with a bony hand. Willa flipped wildly upside down, kicking like a panicking rabbit, and tore herself from his grip as she hit the ground. Then she scurried rapidly across the forest floor like a wiggling salamander, blending as she went, Lorcan stabbing and then stabbing again, until she sprang to her feet and ran.

She sprinted down the killing path where the traps had been laid, her legs exploding with strength and propelling her forward.

Her chest pumped with fast, shallow breaths as she ran down the path, frantically avoiding the leaves next to the marking stones. One wrong step and she'd suffer the pain of the clamping teeth, and then feel the thrusts of her enemies' spears.

When she glanced behind her, she thought she had put a good distance between her and her enemies, but the padaran and his men were in close pursuit, charging after her. They were fast runners. They were gaining on her. And she knew they weren't going to give up. There was no way to escape them, no way to slow them down.

Then she had an idea.

She dove to the ground and draped her body over one of the stones that marked the location of a trap. Then she blended herself into the leaves.

The padaran came running down the path. "I want her

dead!" he screamed to his guards as he ran. "Find her and kill her!"

He saw only leaves.

The trap snapped shut with a sudden, violent jump. The steel teeth cracked against the bone. The padaran shrieked in pain and tried to leap away, but the trap had clamped onto his leg, driving its teeth into his shin. He roared in agony as he crumpled helplessly to the ground, his bloody hands trying to pry the trap from his leg.

Lorcan and the other guard stopped to help the padaran, pulling desperately at the closed trap, but it was jammed into place.

"Get it off!" the padaran howled as they frantically tried to pry it open with their hands.

Willa leapt to her feet and ran. When she glanced back, she was expecting to see the padaran on the ground screaming in misery, but she saw an even more startling sight. The padaran's skin had actually changed from radiant bronze to splotched and wrinkled gray, like many of the oldest Faeran in the clan. Slimy sweat dripped from all over his shriveled face and arms and legs. A dark fluid oozed from the corner of a clouded eye, and his hair hung loose and straggly around his old, withered head.

As she ran down the trail back toward Dead Hollow, the wailing screams of the padaran rose up behind her like the screeches of a ghoul.

Willa didn't understand what she'd just seen, but she had to keep running. She didn't look back again and she didn't slow down. Even after she had gone far enough to leave the screams behind her, she kept going. She had harmed the padaran. She had betrayed the clan. As soon as the guards freed him from the trap, they'd return to the lair. The padaran would instruct his stabbing guards and hissing jaetters to rain violence upon her world. When the members of the clan learned of her betrayal, the entire clan was going to swarm against her. They'd destroy her den. They'd destroy her. But worst of all, they'd destroy her grandmother.

She heard the screaming first. And then the shouts and footfalls of jaetters and guards and other Faeran running all through the Dead Hollow lair. It was as if they had already heard about what she did, but that wasn't possible. She had run back to the lair and arrived before the padaran and his guards. Something else had happened.

A new fear seized Willa's chest. Her heart pounded as she sprinted down the tunnel toward her den. When she came through the door, she immediately screamed out and averted her eyes from what she saw.

"Mamaw!" she cried as she collapsed to the floor a few feet away from her, too frightened to get closer.

"Gredic came . . ." her grandmother rasped in the old language, her voice ragged and weak, so low that it sounded like the flow of a stream.

Willa couldn't bear to raise her eyes and look at what they had done to her, but she crawled and slid her hand slowly forward across the floor, until she reached her mamaw's tiny hand and held it in hers.

"Tell me what to do to save you," she whimpered, pressing her face to the floor as she said the words, but she already knew it was too late. She felt so powerless, like the entire world was ending.

"You are the last, Willa," her grandmother whispered.

"I don't understand," Willa said, crawling forward on her belly, closer to her mamaw, as she gripped her mamaw's limp and slippery hand.

"It's time for me to go," her grandmother said.

"Please, Mamaw! Tell me what I need to do to save you!"

"Protect it, hold on to it," her mamaw said. "It's the most precious thing we have."

"I don't understand. Protect what, Mamaw? How can I protect anything?"

Willa clung to her mamaw with both her arms, curled up on the floor, feeling the warm liquid oozing all around her.

"Please, Mamaw! Don't leave me!" she cried.

*"Naillic,"* her mamaw whispered.

"What?" Willa asked. "What does it mean?"

"I didn't want to tell you this until you were ready to understand, but we are out of time. Do not say it out loud until you wish to destroy everything and everyone, including yourself. *Knowing brings death.*"

Willa didn't understand. What was she talking about?

Wild screams and angry shouts erupted someplace in the lair above them. The wounded and enraged padaran and his guards had arrived. Now everyone in the clan knew what she had done. They knew she had hurt the padaran. There was no doubt in her mind now: her clan was going to find her.

Her mamaw squeezed her hand. "You have to go, Willa. You must leave this place. Follow the blood . . ."

The sound of shouting and rushing footsteps came pouring down the tunnel. The hissing jaetters and the stabbing guards were going to tear her apart.

When Willa finally gathered herself up, she didn't look. She didn't look at her mamaw's arms. She didn't look at her legs. She didn't look at her chest, or her neck, or her face. She looked only into her mamaw's eyes.

As her mamaw looked back at her, Willa could see her remembering all their time together, their sunlit mornings walking among the trees of the forest, the eagles they had seen together flying in the sky, their nights in their den with the moonlight filtering down. And then her mamaw's eyes finally closed, and the long, last breath came from her body.

"Don't leave me, Mamaw," Willa sobbed as she pressed herself to her grandmother. "Please don't leave me!"

But she felt her mamaw's spirit leave her body and rise up through her own, into her arms and her legs, into her chest and her heart. Where does a spirit go? Where does the new world begin? Into the boughs of the trees? Into the stone of the earth? Into the flow of the river? Into the ether of the air? It passes from one person to another, each into the other.

All Willa could do was cling to her mamaw and breathe.

Willa heard the jaetters and the guards coming down through the tunnels that led to the den, at least fifty of them, hissing and gnashing their teeth, brandishing clubs and their sticks and their sharpened spears.

All she could do was breathe.

She could weave herself into one of the walls and hide, but they'd block off the door, close in the room, and stab with their spears until they found her.

All she could do was breathe.

The coming mob was filled with a screeching violence more terrible than anything she had ever heard.

All she could do was breathe.

She was trapped.

There was no way out.

Then she looked down at the woven-stick floor.

*Follow the blood.*

Willa reached down and touched the woven-stick floor with the tips of her bare fingers, feeling the woody texture of it. Living here in this room with her grandmother, she had crawled on this floor, walked on this floor, grown up on this floor. She had never thought of it as anything other than a floor. Unmoving. *Unmovable.*

But now, her hands trembling and her eyes blurry with tears, she gripped one of the sticks, broke it, and pulled it away.

Then she pulled out another and another.

Soon she was tearing the sticks away as fast as she could, scratching at the floor like a clawing animal. Down on her hands and knees, she bit at the sticks with her teeth, biting them away, ripping at the sticks with her hands. Her fingertips bled. Her fingernails tore. But it didn't matter. She had to keep clawing.

As soon as she made the hole large enough to fit through, she scurried down inside and tucked herself below. But she couldn't leave a gaping hole in the floor. Gredic and the other jaetters would follow right after her.

She pressed her fingers against the stick-frayed edge of the hole. If the sticks had still been green and alive, she could use her woodcraft to re-intertwine them, but these sticks had been dead for a hundred years. There was no life in them, no moisture, no soul.

*I don't want to do it,* she thought. *Not here, not like this. Not ever!*

But the truth was, her mamaw had taught her what she needed to do. Her mamaw had shown her how to inspirit the dead when she was seven. But Willa had frightened herself so badly she never did it again.

*But you have to, Willa. You have to escape this place!*

She pressed her bleeding fingers to the sticks and began to push them and pull them into motion, infusing them with her own life. The moisture and blood of her fingers seeped into them. She felt the dead sticks sucking the spirit and nutrients from her body, white, cold pain tearing through the skin of her fingers, then radiating up into her hands. She pulled in a sudden breath of revulsion when the sticks started creaking and cracking with their own twisting, crawling movements like writhing black worms. The sticks were pulling her life out through her pulsing fingertips, draining her of the inner forces that kept her alive, like roots pulling water from the ground. Finally, she yanked her fingers away before it was too late. A few seconds too long, and she'd be dead.

Asking the living trees to help her cross a river felt as natural to her as having a conversation with old friends, but bringing back the dead was woodcraft in its darkest form. And she knew it would leave her a dried husk if she wasn't careful.

Putting her dry, skin-cracked, ice-cold fingers into her mouth to warm them, she looked up at the place where the hole had been and saw that she had succeeded in weaving the sticks together and closing the hole.

Blending her colors, whispering with wolves, running through the limbs of the tallest trees—her grandmother had taught her so many things, the brightest and the darkest lore of the forest. She couldn't even imagine living without her mamaw. What was she going to do? Where was she going to go?

As she crept beneath the now-closed-in woven-stick floor, she heard the footsteps of the guards and jaetters storming into the room above.

She crawled down into the red-stained branches below, down into the dripping underworld of Dead Hollow, down past the whitened bones of the earth, into the darkness of a rocky, cavelike void until she found the cold, wet embrace of the stream that ran beneath the lair. The rocks all around her were streaked with black and red, cracked with the ancient movement of the mountain, and littered with the white broken sticks of hundreds of Faeran souls. They were the ones who had come before her. The ones who had stood. The ones who had spoken. They were the shattered twins, and the beaten down, and the silenced. *Knowing brings death.* But the cold swept around her, and lifted her, and carried her away.

The river was water, was blood, was all that had come before. As she floated with the current, she began to see horrific images in her mind, images of Gredic and the other jaetters pouring through the labyrinth and storming into her grandmother's room, images of her mother, father, and sister fleeing through the forest from dark figures with long spears, and images of the padaran writhing on the ground in bloody anguish with his leg in the trap, his face turning slimy gray—a thousand images that she could not bear.

She did not move her arms or legs, or turn her body. She drifted on her back, gazing up into the darkness of the cave. Far above her head, the footsteps of her swarming clan fell like shadows across the weaves of the sticks, like dark locusts flying across a reddened black sky. And the sky was blood. The sky was time. The sky was the past.

"Good-bye, Mamaw," she cried, feeling the ache of it deep down in her chest.

She floated with nothing but sadness, no will to move or live. She just let herself be carried by the blood of the earth, with no want or desire or need, other than to go back, to go back in time, to let them steal her satchel if that was what they wanted, to stay crumpled on the floor of the great hall with her voice silent and her eyes cast down, and more than anything, out in that forest, to un-throw that spear.

But she knew a river couldn't go back, and she had no will to fight it. She felt nothing but numb as the lair of Dead Hollow slipped into the distance behind her.

As she floated on the river, time had no meaning. No minutes or hours. There was only the movement of the water. All else in the world was still and did not exist. All else was ground. But she was moving, flowing with the sweep of the water that carried her.

And there was no time.

Her body slipped into an eddy of the river and bumped against the bank. She had passed through the underworld of the lair and into the living forest, but the thickness of the tree branches above her created a dark and shadowed world with no moon or stars.

She felt the touch of many small, wet hands with tiny fingers grasping at the skin of her bare arms and legs. Creatures with thick dark brown fur and large, flat, scaly tails surrounded her, their wide teeth chattering as they worked.

They dragged her body from the stream and partway up onto the earth.

She lay there on the bank of the river for a long time, too destroyed inside to move.

She woke to the growls of hunger stirring in her stomach. Her whole body hurt with a dull aching pain.

When she looked up through the canopy of the trees and saw the slanting rays of the setting sun filtering through the branches, she realized that she must have been lying there for many hours, through both the night and the day.

The water of the stream, which had been the color of blood beneath the lair, was clear now, sliding along a winding bed of smooth, round, pale gray stones through a thick forest of old trees, twisted and dark, with wet glistening branches hanging down from above and blackened roots twisting across the wet ground below.

As she slowly began to remember everything that had happened, she felt a pain in her heart unlike anything she had ever felt before, an aching, throbbing wound that sucked down into her soul so deep that it felt as if she was going to stop breathing if she didn't force her chest to keep rising and falling. She would never hear her grandmother's voice again, never feel her touch. She would never explore another forest dell with her, or look into her grandmother's eyes.

*"Gwen-elen den ulna, Mamaw,"* she said. *Wherever you're going, Mamaw, may you walk among trees.*

As she said these last words to her mamaw, she realized that not only would she never see her grandmother again, she would never again hear the Faeran language.

Willa laid her head back down in the black, soft, wet dirt that lived between the roots of the trees near the side of the river, and she shut her eyes.

There was a numbness in the darkness that gave her a sort of comfort that the sight of the world did not. The world was too painful, too empty, too full of thoughts to endure.

In the swarming clan of the padaran, love and family had become the smallest and rarest of leaves, struggling to survive, and now it felt as if the last of those leaves had withered and died. Her mother and father were gone, memories long passed. Alliw was gone, nothing but a handprint of paint on an echoing wall that she would never see again. And now her mamaw was gone, like the song of the morning birds had disappeared. It felt as if she were the only one still living in the world.

There was no one left to fill the quiet or hear her voice, no one left to warm her shoulder or touch her hand, no one left to forage with, or sleep with in their den, or tell her stories to, or learn from. It felt as if the spirit deep within her living body were nothing but a bleeding wound, and soon she would die.

When she awoke a few hours later, she heard the delicate sound of small, soft footsteps moving slowly toward her.

She opened her eyes to see a doe and a little spotted fawn stepping carefully through the fine grass that grew along the edge of the stream, their tiny hooves making no more noise than a breath as they touched the ground.

The fawn had beautiful tawny fur with white spots that helped her stay hidden in the forest and the fields—not that different from her own camouflage, except that the fawn's took a season to change.

The mother deer twitched her ears this way and that as she scanned the area for danger. But there was no danger. Only Willa.

While she was sleeping, Willa's skin had naturally turned as black and brown as the stream bank, with the color and texture of roots running along her arms and legs and chest. The mother deer could smell her and see her there, lying on the ground beside the stream, but Willa's presence did not alarm her.

Willa watched as the mother deer leaned down and drank from the stream, but the little fawn standing beside her stared at Willa, as if she wasn't sure what she was.

The mother deer nudged the fawn, reminding her to drink.

The fawn leaned down on splayed shaky legs, lowered her head, and drank a little bit from the stream, but then quickly raised her head again and stared at Willa.

There was something in the fawn's eyes, not just the curiosity that Willa expected, but something else as well. The fawn seemed to sense that she was upset, that she'd been crying . . . that she needed help.

Uncertain what the fawn was going to do, Willa didn't move.

Finally, with its nose twitching and its eyes blinking, the fawn took a few uncertain steps toward her, and then stopped.

*"Eee na nin,"* Willa said, which meant *It's all right* but had a gentler sound to it.

Fawns were sensitive little creatures. The slightest movement or the faintest whisper of the wrong word would send a fawn running. For the fawn to feel safe enough to come to her, Willa had to slow her breathing and her heartbeat. She had to find the stillness in her body and in her soul. She focused her mind on her heart, and brought it down slower and slower, until it was beating just once every few seconds.

The fawn's little white tail twitched nervously as she slowly made her way closer, her skinny little body suspended on her tremulous, overly long legs, and her dainty black hooves.

The fawn came very close, studied Willa for several seconds, then folded her legs, and curled up into a little spotted ball in the place between Willa's folded legs and her chest.

Willa felt the soft warmth of the fawn's silky fur against her skin, the minute movement of the fawn's gentle breaths, and the beat of her tiny heart. Willa slowly let the blood begin to flow through her heart again until her heartbeat matched the fawn's. While the mother deer fed on the nearby grass and watched over them, Willa and the fawn fell quietly asleep.

When Willa woke in the middle of the night, the mother deer was still feeding a short distance away, as if grateful to have a few moments on her own while she knew her fawn was safe. Willa, without disturbing the fawn, slowly reached out and grasped some of the fine, thin grass at the edge of the stream. It tasted wet and sweet in her mouth.

The presence of the mother deer feeding nearby, and the little sleeping fawn in the bend of her body, felt like a salve to her hidden wounds, as if one of the leaves from her mamaw's little tree had begun to touch her soul.

As she lay there in the darkness, she noticed a tiny point of glowing blue light hovering a few inches off the ground on the other side of the stream. Just as she turned toward it, it went dark and disappeared.

She thought she must have imagined it, but then another blue light appeared a few feet away from her, and then another farther out in the trees. A moment later, hundreds of tiny blue lights lit up the darkness around her, gliding slowly a few inches off the ground on both sides of the stream and all through the forest, setting the nighttime world aglow with steady, soft blue light.

Despite the sadness in her heart, Willa smiled. They were the blue ghost fireflies that her mamaw had shown her and Alliw years before. They were some of the rarest creatures in the world. These beautiful blue spirits appeared only in certain glens hidden deep in the forest on particular mountains, and only for a few moments on a few nights each year.

It was as if her mamaw had brought them out tonight just for her, to remind her of who she had been, and who she still remained.

And now, as Willa sat alone with the blue ghosts floating gently around her, their wandering lines of soft glowing light became a dance, with the humming of the forest insects and the babbling of the stream their music, and her heart filling with awe.

She slowly came to the realization that despite everything that had happened in her life, the *forest* wasn't dead. The *forest* was still alive. And she was alive within it, her heart still beating.

She knew that she had betrayed her clan. And she had betrayed the padaran. But more than that, she realized, *he* had betrayed *her*.

She didn't understand who or what the padaran was, or how he became the god of the clan, but he had betrayed the . . . What had he betrayed? The Faeran ways? But what were those ways in a world that moved like a river changing from season to season, storm to storm? She didn't know.

What she did know was that he had betrayed *her*, *her* ways, *her* heart. He had trapped and killed the animals of the forest. He had captured and imprisoned humans. He had sent his jaetters to kill her mamaw, to silence the last of the ancient whisperers.

Willa looked around her at the forest. She had followed the padaran loyally all her life. She had idolized him, struggled for him, stole for him, all for him, all for the clan. *There is no I, only we.*

But deep down, what kind of Faeran was he? What kind of Faeran could do these things that he had done? She didn't know. What she wondered now was what kind of Faeran she was going to become.

She slowly climbed up onto her feet. She looked down the path of the stream as it meandered between the trunks of the great trees and disappeared in the distance. She gazed at the blue-glowing mist curling through the branches that reached toward the sky. And then she looked up toward the slope of the mountain.

*The forests of the Great Smoky Mountain,* she thought. *The breath of life. My life. My grandmother's life. Food and water. Light and darkness. The trees, the animals, the flow of the river, the cut of the rocks, and all the world around me.*

The padaran had said that she would be cast out into the world on her own, and that she could not survive. But she *could* survive.

She knew how to forage for food. She knew the ways of the forest animals. She knew the spirit of the world.

*I'll live like the Faeran of old.*

And maybe there were other places she could go, places she'd never been before, places she couldn't even imagine. And maybe there were other people out here. Maybe there were other clans, places she could find warmth and shelter when winter came.

Standing there in the forest on her own, she didn't feel strong. And she didn't feel happy. But she finally felt as if she could go on.

She said farewell to the little fawn and the mother deer and she started walking. She wasn't sure it was even possible, but she decided that she was going to try to climb to the top of the Great Mountain and look out at the world in which she lived.

She didn't know exactly why she was doing it. She just wanted to climb, to feel the motion of it in her body.

It was an easy walk up the forested slope at first, eating the red berries of the mountain ash along the way. Then it became much rockier and steeper, and the difficulty of it drove her to keep going. The muscles in her arms and legs burned. The cold mountain air pushed through her lungs. As she pulled herself up the side of the mountain, the sharpness of the jagged rock tore at the bare skin of her hands. She didn't know why, but she liked the sharp, tangible, physical pain of it. The blowing wind pulled tears from her eyes.

Where the ground became too steep, she grabbed the roots and branches of the rhododendron like they were the rungs of a homesteader's ladder. When she spotted blackberries growing in the mountainside thickets, she stuffed some in her mouth. She drank from the little rivulets of water that dripped down the crevices of the rock past profusions of lush ferns.

With its steep rocky slopes, the mountain had always told people that it didn't want to be climbed, but she couldn't help but think that today it was providing for her along the way.

She followed the rocky streambeds that snaked up between the spurs of the mountain, up through the boulders and the old, weathered trees torn and twisted by the wind. She climbed hand over hand, up through the silent, craggy stone of ancient times.

Her heart worked painfully in her chest. Her lungs dragged for air. But she kept going. She wanted nothing now but for the pain in her body, and the loneliness in her soul, to block out what lay behind her.

She came into an area of thick fog where the Great Mountain often hid its head when it was sleeping, its dreaming mists floating across its smoky peak. But then she realized that it wasn't just the normal fog she was used to down in Dead Hollow and the valleys below. She was so high up that she was actually *inside* a cloud as it moved across the sky. She felt the cool touch of the cloud's tiny droplets on her cheeks as she climbed, and she tasted the sweetness of it on her tongue.

Way up in the sky now, the air had chilled, but her body was sweating despite the cold. Her muscles ached. Her fingers bled. Blisters pained her feet. But she kept climbing, pushing, driving her mamaw's death from her body. Reaching and grabbing and pulling and climbing, up and up and up she went. She wanted to get to the top of the mountain and see the entirety of the world.

And then suddenly there was nothing more to grab. She was surrounded by a dense stand of giant fir trees, with trunks thicker than her outstretched arms, but there was no higher ground.

She frowned in confusion. At first she thought she must have veered off course and reached a false peak, and that the real mountain was still above her—for the mountain had *always* been above her—but then she realized where she was. She had done it. She had reached the peak of the Great Mountain for the first time in her life.

Unable to see through the foliage around her, she went over to the thickest and tallest of the giant fir trees. She felt unusually nervous about approaching it. Without her mamaw gone from the world, did her own powers still work? Could she still speak to the trees? Would they still listen? Could she still learn and grow without her teacher? Or had all the magic of the world disappeared?

"I'm hoping you can help me get a little higher, my friend," she said softly in the old language, and she started climbing.

Her small, clawed fingers and her gripping toes clung easily to the rough bark of the colossal tree as she climbed, almost as if the two of them—her and this age-old tree—had grown up to be part of one another's lives. When she struggled or almost lost her grip, the tree lifted a branch or intertwined a vine around her hand to help her. She climbed and climbed, reaching for one branch after another, up and up through the mist-dripping boughs of the tree, until she came to the highest branches, her body finally swaying gently in the breeze.

She looked out from her eagle perch with excitement, but all she could see was the gray mist of the clouds rolling all around her. She was surrounded by them, inside them. But the clouds weren't just sitting still, blocking her sight, they were *changing*, rolling and turning, opening and closing the space around her, as if the Great Mountain was saying, *Just wait a moment, and I will show you . . .*

As the clouds began to clear, she spotted a patch of sky and the gleam of sunlight. She caught a glimpse of a forested ridge not too far away, and then a peak a little farther out. And then, as the clouds opened up, she began to see a vast world of rolling green mountains and shadowed valleys. Golden rays poured through the openings in the clouds and cast their light across the land.

She turned one way and then another, gazing out at the world—mountain ranges in every direction for as far as she could see. The forested slopes of the closest mountains lay around her with the evergreen canopy of the trees. The mountain ridges farther on were darker green in color, and the ones beyond those a deep blue, and beyond those a lighter blue, mountains so far away that they seemed to turn into the sky, layer upon layer of mountains, each one's shade of green and blue blending into the next, hundreds of colors for which humans had no names. It was the most beautiful thing she had ever seen.

She squinted her eyes and looked out toward the edge of the world, but beyond the distant mountains, all she could see were more mountains.

Then she remembered something that had happened the

year before. She had been creeping through the forest near Cades Cove, a quiet valley where a community of homesteaders lived, when she overheard two day-folk men talking as oxen pulled their carriage down the road.

"Well, ya know," one of the men had said, "back in the olden days, them folk reckoned the earth was flat."

"I can't see how they thought that," said his friend. "Even back then, I reckon they knew the earth was round. Look at the shadow cast on the moon."

But standing on top of the Great Mountain at this moment, Willa knew that the day-folk men were wrong. The earth was neither flat nor round. It was *mountains.* It was jagged rocks and steep ravines, treeless windy ridges and shaded wooded glens, streams winding through hidden forest realms, and high, rounded peaks that looked out across the world—and there, too, only mountains. *How could it be any other way?* she thought. *How could the trees and the mountains ever end? It would cease to be the world.*

She remembered floating through the underworld of Dead Hollow, thinking about the padaran, about the way of the Faeran and what that meant. The Faeran ways and the human ways. The *us* and the *them.* The *we* and the *I.* Maybe there wasn't just one way, but many. The earth wasn't flat or round. It was mountains.

As she gazed across the sky, she spotted something out of the corner of her eye and turned toward it. It was just a speck at first, very distant, but as it came closer she soon realized that it was a hawk soaring on the currents of air that flowed like rivers above the ridges of the mountains.

With the gentle tilt of its wings, the hawk steered its way through the sky. It was coming very close, and then her heart leapt a little when it glided right past her. For the first time in her life, she wasn't looking *up* at a hawk, but *down* at it. And as the hawk flew by, it tilted its head and looked up at her, as if surprised to see her there up on top of the world.

As the hawk soared on and looked back out across his aerial domain, she wondered again about what the men had said about the shape of the earth. *The hawk knows,* she thought. *He knows the air. He knows the earth. He can see it all up here.* She gazed out across the mountainous world, trying to imagine what was out there, trying to imagine where she could go.

As the mist began to slowly roll back in, it was as if the mountain was gently saying, *You've had enough now, little one. It's time for you to go . . .*

She knew the mountain was used to living in the mist and only seldom showed its true self, and she was grateful that it had decided to show itself to her.

As the incoming clouds formed along the ridges, she watched the mist roll down the sides of the Great Mountain into the valleys below. She thought about all the living creatures down there, the wolves in their dens and the bears by the lake, the mother deer and her fawn, the Faeran in their twisted lair, and the Cherokee tending their farms, and the homesteaders in their log cabins, and the newcomers with their iron machines, all coming together, the mist of the mountain, the breath of their world, providing life to them all.

An unusual scent touched her nostrils. Frowning, she sniffed the air, and then turned and scanned.

She wished she could ask the hawk what he could see, because she knew his eyes were far better than her own, but he was long on his way.

Then she spotted what looked like a thin line of gray mist floating up from a particular spot in the distance. But it wasn't mist. It was a trail of smoke rising from one of the valleys far below her.

She knew that particular valley well, with its coves of giant hemlocks, towering pines, and black walnut trees—old friends who had shaded her from the summer sun while they listened to her singing her Faeran songs of old.

She knew it must be a great outpouring of smoke for her to be able to see it from this distance. It was too much smoke to be the stone-steep breath of a day-folk lair. And too narrow to be the fire that consumes the world.

A tight and sickening feeling crept slowly into her chest as she stared toward the mysterious smoke.

A bright flash lit the spot. An area of trees disintegrated. And the trees around it collapsed to the ground, one after the other, like they were being eaten by a giant beast. A great eruption of smoke and debris rose up into the air.

And then the sound of it hit her in the chest, like a crack of thunder after a bolt of lightning. The booming sound flew across the sky and echoed off the mountains behind her.

A thick plume of black smoke rose up from where the trees had been destroyed. Even from this great distance, she could hear their screaming, their twisting, burning cries as their ancient spirits came crashing to the ground.

*"Anakanasha,"* she cried out in anguish, her heart aching for the wounded and murdered trees, and all the birds and animals that lived among them. The pain welled up in her chest so quickly and with such powerful force that it sucked her breath away. The tears burned in her eyes as she gazed toward the devastation.

*What vicious force had caused such terrible destruction?*

Willa ran across the rocky terrain, leaping from one jagged edge to the next, diving headlong through thickets of underbrush, and sprinting through the groves of the tall, growing trees, pushed on by the desperate hope that she might be able to help some of the animals that had been hurt by the destruction she'd seen from the mountaintop. But she had miles to go. She knew that her camouflage wouldn't protect her when she was traversing long distances like this. An onlooker would see a flash of movement and a blur of color as her skin changed from one rocky gray or leafy green texture to the next. It would leave her vulnerable to attack, but she had to find out what had happened.

Exhausted from running, she slowed to catch her breath when she reached Moss Hollow, a deep ravine dark with the green shadows of its protecting trees where thin runnels of water trickled through the mossy rocks and gathered into a stream. It was the place where the valley's river was forever being born.

After taking a quick drink, she continued on.

She followed the winding path of the young river until she arrived at the Three Forks, where several streams came together to become a true and powerful river with a life and soul of its own.

From here, she ran along the rocky bank as the great river began finding its own way and making its own decisions, moving boulders and carving through the earth, getting stronger and deeper as all the streams around it joined its cause, mile after mile, winding through the forest until it was strong and unstoppable, wearing down the mountains through which it flowed. She had seen with her eyes and learned in her soul that where a river is born, the earth shapes its path. But where the river grows up, it begins, in turn, to shape the earth.

When she finally reached the area where she had seen the destruction, she split off from the river and headed west into the forest. The sound of many footsteps scuffling through the leaves touched her ears. Then came the hushed whispers of muffled voices. A group of humans was coming her way. She ducked down into the bushes to hide.

A dozen Cherokee families were moving quickly and quietly through the forest. They were breathing heavily, their simple cotton clothing soiled and disheveled, and their faces tense with white-eyed fear as they glanced repeatedly behind them. Many of the Cherokee carried sacks and other supplies slung over their shoulders, as if they had hurriedly gathered their belongings from their homes and fled. One woman carried her baby wrapped in a blanket on her back. The men were bleeding from recent wounds and their faces were smudged with black marks.

She had often seen Cherokee walking on the gravel roads that connected the area's towns, and she'd seen them trading peacefully with the homesteaders, but she'd never seen them running through the underbrush like this before. They seemed to be fleeing some sort of danger, but they were also scanning ahead and looking all around as if they were searching for something they had lost.

Then she noticed that other than the one baby on the mother's back, there didn't appear to be any other children among them. Was that what they were looking for? Had they lost children?

And then, at the rear of the group, following behind all the others, she spotted one boy just coming into view. He was a lean, bare-chested boy a few years older than her. He had long black hair and the dark-striped markings of his tribe on his face and arms. He definitely wasn't from the same clan as these other Cherokee, but he was carrying one of their girls in his arms, and her hair was matted with blood.

He turned and looked into the distance behind him, his face racked with worry. Then he gazed out into the forest, as if hoping to see something there. *He's not just looking for their enemy,* she thought. *He's been separated from someone he loves.*

She wondered if this Cherokee boy knew the younger boy that she'd met in the prison beneath the lair, but she didn't think so. There was something very different about this boy. He seemed so strong and fierce of heart, and as he walked across the leaves of the forest, his footsteps made only the slightest, most muffled sound. She could smell the other Cherokee men and women just like she could smell the homesteaders, for they were human beings like any others. She knew it was impossible, but when this odd boy walked past her hiding spot in the bushes, his scent reminded her of something very specific: *mountain lion.*

At that moment, the boy abruptly stopped, turned, and looked right in her direction. His dark brown eyes scanned the forest intently.

Holding her breath, Willa wove herself deeper into the colors and texture of the woods and remained perfectly still.

The boy peered into the area she was hiding, like he knew she was there. But she could hold her breath for a long time if she had to. When it came to staying still, no one could outlast her. She had learned patience from the trees.

The shock of a booming explosion tore through the forest, rattling the leaves and shaking the ground. Flocks of startled birds flew up. Small animals darted for cover. The ricocheting sound echoed across the walls of the nearby ravines.

Willa ducked down with the Cherokee, cowering to the ground, white-cold fear surging through her body. She had never felt or heard such a deafening sound, one that slammed through her and everything around her. She was left lying on the ground, her lungs panting, and her ears ringing with a high-pitched whine.

"Everybody get up!" the Cherokee boy called to the others. "Keep moving!"

Willa climbed back up onto her feet. Just over the nearest ridge, a large plume of black smoke furled up into the sky. As the small band of Cherokee hurried away in the opposite direction, she went toward the smoke.

As Willa ran through the forest, an eerie gray smoke drifted through the trees. The smell of scorched wood hung in the air, tinged with a sharpness that reminded her of the blast of a killing-stick.

And then, as she pushed forward through the haze, something even worse invaded her nostrils: the sickening odor of recently cut trees. The overwhelming stench of hacked limbs, severed trunks, and spilled sap filled the air.

She came to a ledge where the ground had been broken to pieces by a powerful violence, with loose rocks and dirt crumbling down a cliff at her feet. As she looked out from the edge, a shocking sight opened up before her eyes.

The world was gone.

A vast area of the forest had been cut down and dragged away. All the trees for as far as she could see had been murdered, leaving nothing but a slashed clearing with thousands of stumps in a field of damaged earth, broken branches, and piles of sawdust.

Willa cried out at the sight of it. The trees had all been killed! *What kind of people would do this? Why would they destroy the forest?*

There were hundreds of men at work, savaging the trees at the edge of the forest. She watched in horror as two of them pulled a six-foot-long, jagged-edged saw back and forth through a living sugar maple tree, the sharp steel teeth ripping through the flesh of the trunk as sap oozed from the wound.

The murderers weren't the homesteaders or the Cherokee that she'd seen from a distance all her life. They were the humans that her mamaw and the padaran had called the newcomers. Now she saw why they had come to her forests.

"Timber!" the men shouted to their fellow killers as the majestic tree came crashing down to the ground. Then a dozen other men fell upon the tree with axes and hacked away at its limbs.

Trees she had known all her life—tulip poplar, black walnut, white oak, red maple—fell one after the other to the men's saws and axes. A few of these elder souls had lived their lives in these mountain coves for more than three hundred years, others for fifty or a hundred, but all of them were being cut down in a matter of hours.

Willa felt a rumbling in the earth beneath her feet and she heard a loud rushing sound. She turned to see a giant, black machine rolling on long steel rails that the men had laid across the earth. Even as distant as it was, the sound of the machine filled her chest and shook her body. Hot, spitting white steam poured out of the machine's stack, breathing heavy, chugging breaths as it pumped along the tracks. Sweating men riding atop the beast shoveled black coal into its burning belly.

When the machine reached the cutting area, crews of men used sweating, frightened, chain-enslaved horses to drag thick cables up the mountainsides and hook them onto the fallen trees. Then a second massive, belching steam engine mounted on the back of the moving beast dragged the bodies of the trees toward it, like a long-legged spider slowly pulling in its prey. A dangling, steam-driven boom swung out over the ground, grabbed the logs with huge claws, and lifted them onto the rolling beast's back.

The crews cut down the living, dragged in the dead, and stacked the carcasses one atop the other. She tried to imagine what they were doing with them all. She knew that they cut up the bodies of the trees to make their lairs and their tools and their weapons, their carriages and their toys and the cribs for their babies, but how many of the day-folk could there be in the world for them to destroy an entire area of forest?

A crew of men with shovels and wheelbarrows, spikes and hammers, approached the area where Willa was standing. They began digging and hammering away at the disturbed earth exposed by the explosions. They appeared to be laying steel tracks into a new area of the forest, establishing the course for the cutters to come with their machines. Where a rocky ridge or steep terrain thwarted their progress, they stacked small piles of red sticks and lit a long white vine on fire. They had blasted cavities into the sides of living mountains, broken apart large rock heads, and filled in the ravines of the river—flattening the mountainous land so that the black, steam-belching machine could come. Some of the fires from the explosions still burned nearby, great plumes of black smoke rising up into the air. *That's what I saw from the mountain,* she thought.

Unable to take any more of the devastation into her mind, she pulled back into the forest and stumbled away. It felt like someone had ripped a hole in her heart.

Saddened and disoriented, Willa found herself walking through an area of the forest that had been badly damaged by the recent explosion. The trunks of the trees were broken in half, their insides shattered, and their severed branches left to die on the forest floor. The bodies of dead birds lay strewn across the ground—blue jays and flycatchers, chickadees and woodpeckers—their feathers shredded and their necks broken. The carcass of a small red fox lay with its legs bent and its body twisted. She had come to the area of the destruction to help in any way she could, but it was too late. The fox's spirit was gone. The animals in this area were all dead. It left her feeling so hopeless, so powerless to do anything.

The disturbed earth beneath her feet suddenly gave way. She lost her footing as the soil collapsed around her. She found herself sliding down into the ravine of the dammed-up river, jammed with crisscrossing trunks and scorched trees from the explosion. She grabbed frantically at the dirt around her, but she couldn't stop her fall. She was headed straight toward the churning rapids pouring through the logjam. Despite all that the humans had done, the river would not be stopped. Every muscle in her body bunched with panic. She was terrified that she'd get sucked into the powerful currents and pinned against a log. She lunged out, grabbed hold of a branch, and held on, clinging to the side of the ravine, just a few feet above the swirling water.

That was when she saw it.

It was one of the largest animals she had ever seen. But it looked so small with its body crushed beneath the trunk of a tree. It was completely exhausted, and badly wounded, pinned half in and half out of the gushing water, its claws sunk deep into the bark of a tree, holding on with the last of its strength. It was seconds from drowning. The animal had jet-black fur and a long black tail, and its bright yellow eyes were staring straight at her.

The loose dirt crumbled beneath her feet as Willa plunged down the wall of the ravine toward the dark, churning current of the logjammed river. In a flailing, desperate leap, she flung herself out at an exposed root and clung to it, and then willed the living root to intertwine around her wrists and hold her in place. She hung there now, just above the dangerous currents. And trapped just a few feet away from her, there was a female mountain lion, a panther, as black as night, unlike any she had ever seen before.

She knew a predator like that could kill with a single swipe of her claws, but it didn't seem like the cat was going to attack, or was even able to. The panther's back was bent beneath the trunk of a fallen tree, and her bloody wounds looked excruciating. The cat's mouth was drawn up into a snarl, her whiskers trembling in pain. The panther growled repeatedly as she sunk her claws into the trunk she was pinned against and tried to pull herself free.

Willa had overheard the homesteaders and the Cherokee telling stories around their campfires about the Ghost of the Forest, and her grandmother had described these mythical beasts to her as well, but she never thought she'd actually see one with her own eyes.

She wanted to help the animal, but she was hanging on to the ravine wall by a spindly tree root, and she was terrified to go anywhere near the cat's sharp claws and deadly teeth. Panthers were one of the wildest, most vicious animals of the forest. She couldn't imagine how she could get any closer to her.

As the powerful flow of the river gushed through the narrow chute of the ravine, it pushed the tangle of massive trees that had jammed up all around them, rocking it back and forth. She could hear the logjam creaking and groaning like it was going to give way at any moment.

She had to get herself out of this ravine or she was going to get washed away when the river broke through. And she didn't have the strength to drag a panther out from under a fallen tree or lift a trunk from a panther's back.

When she heard the loud, jeering call of the blue jays in the trees at the top of the ravine, she knew it wasn't just birdsong. It was a warning. A warning to her in particular. Some sort of new danger was approaching. When she focused her ears on the area above her, she heard voices and footsteps at the top of the ravine. They were coming her way.

Expecting it to be a group of loggers with their axes, Willa pressed herself close to the wall and tried to blend, but dangling from the root, she couldn't stay still enough to hide herself very well.

Then she saw them. It wasn't the loggers, but Faeran.

Gredic, Ciderg, Kearnin, and a band of other jaetters were coming, wielding not just the sticks they had before, but sharpened spears now, ready to kill the animals of the forest and bring their pelts back to the padaran. The group of them were scavenging along the path of the destroyed ravine. They would soon discover the trapped panther just as she had.

Her grandmother had told her that one of the reasons that black panthers were considered magical was because they were so rare and elusive—very few people had ever seen one. Willa knew that the panther's black fur pelt would be highly valuable, far more valuable than a wolf pelt or coins or silver jewelry or anything else the jaetters might hope to get their hands on. When they saw the trapped and struggling panther, they would laugh with pleasure and chatter their teeth, then rush forward and stab her with their spears until she was dead.

Willa couldn't stand the thought of it.

When she looked again at the panther, she could see the desperation blazing in her yellow eyes. And she could see the panther heard the coming jaetters and understood the danger.

Willa's heart filled with a desperate sort of foolish courage. She willed the roots holding her in place to unfurl from her hands. Then she scrambled across the crumbling wall of the ravine to get closer to the panther. The panther's heavy, laboring breaths moved great rushes of air in and out of her lungs.

Her grinding claws gripped the bark of the tree trunk she was crushed against.

Willa thought she could make it over to the panther, but then the dirt beneath her feet and hands gave way. She slid down the slope of the ravine and splashed into the river. She reached out and grabbed the branches of the tree to keep from getting swept away, but the branches snapped in her hand as the rushing water pulled her under.

She had been trying to help, but now she was caught in the same vortex of swirling current as the panther. They were going to drown together.

Then something large and alive brushed past her leg under the water. She yelped in fear and scrambled up onto the bank of the river as fast as she could.

On the ridge above her, Gredic and Ciderg were shouting. They'd spotted the panther. And they had spotted her.

As the jaetters on the ridge looked for a way down the wall of the ravine, Willa knew she had to help the panther. But how? It seemed as if something other than just the fallen tree was preventing the cat from pulling herself free. But what was it?

The last thing Willa wanted to do was go back into the black swirling water and encounter whatever was lurking down there. But she had no choice. She sucked in a deep breath of air and plunged in headfirst.

She knew immediately that she shouldn't have done it. She could barely see through the cold murkiness of the water, and the undertow rushing between the logs was far more powerful than she expected. She tried to swim against it. She pumped her arms and kicked her legs and swam with all her strength. But it was useless. The current grabbed hold of her and slammed her against a submerged log, pinning her below the surface of the water. She couldn't swim free. She couldn't breathe.

She was going to drown in seconds.

Something brushed against her leg again. She reflexively squirmed away from it, but she couldn't even take a breath. She had to get to the surface!

Then she felt dozens of tiny hands against her calves and her thighs. Other hands were pressing against her side, trying to turn her body in line with the rush of the current. A lean body swam between her legs and another pushed against her ribs. She was being engulfed by furred attackers!

Her mouth came up out of the water and she sucked in a powerful gasping breath. She pulled the air all the way in, letting it flow down into her grateful lungs, and grabbed one of the larger branches of the nearest tree so the current couldn't pull her away.

A small, furred, dark face popped up out of the water in front of her. It had long whiskers, a little black nose, and dark, sparkling eyes. The river otter chattered at her, and then went back under the water.

Suddenly the water was filled with otters swimming all around her, rubbing against her, holding her, pushing her with their hands, shoving her with their shoulders against her body. She could see that some of the otters had been burned by the flames when the explosion destroyed their holt, but they seemed determined to help her.

The same otter as before popped up in front of her again,

scolding her with his chattering, as if he was irritated that she wasn't following his instructions. And then finally, she understood.

"But if I let go of this branch, I'm going to drown!" she told the otter in the old language.

But it was no use talking to him. *Let go, you foolish girl! Let go!* he seemed to be chattering.

There was a loud crack of timber and a jolting movement as the logjam began to shift. More water started pouring through the logs. It was the river's will to keep moving, and the river was going to win. It was going to push and swirl and wash all these logs away, and her and the panther and the otters with them.

Willa looked over at the trapped panther. She was barely hanging on. Her mouth was open, with its long, curved fangs, half in and half out of the water, and she was sinking deeper as the waters rose.

Taking one final breath, and fully expecting the current to sweep her away to her death, Willa finally did what the otters wanted her to do: she let go of the branch.

The otters immediately pushed in on her, twisting her body, showing her how to swim, how to dive, how to slip in between. *You're small like us,* they seemed to be saying. *You can't fight the current. You can't swim against it. You swim WITH it! You slip through it. You spin, you dive, you fly! Use the water's power to propel you! You twist, you turn, gliding through as fast and slippery as a fish.*

With the otters pushing against her like she was one of their little pups, she was suddenly doing it; she was slipping through the water.

The otter who had chattered at her on the surface led her deep into the dark, turbulent water beneath the tangle of submerged logs that were holding the panther's hind legs. The water was swirling red, filled with the panther's blood. And then she finally saw it: a steel trap had clamped onto the panther's back foot, and it could not escape.

# 35

Willa came up to the surface and took a gasp of air. "I'm sorry," she said, shaking her head to the panther. "I don't think I can get that trap off your foot."

Glancing up toward the edge of the ravine, Willa saw the jaetters making their way down through the loose gravel. The jaetters were hollering as they came, brandishing their newly sharpened spears.

The panther was being dragged under the water by the pull of the trap's chain. As her head sunk deeper and deeper, the panther opened her yellow eyes and looked at Willa. There was something about those eyes, something *knowing*, something pleading with her. But what could she do? It was a steel trap held down by a massive tree!

In a moment of careless sympathy, Willa reached out with both her hands and touched the panther's face and head, as if to comfort her, to hold her there, to save her from being dragged under, but she knew it was no use.

"I'm sorry!" Willa cried out as the panther's head went all the way under the water.

There was nothing she could do.

The panther was gone.

She was dead.

Willa was sure of it.

Then she saw her eyes. They were a foot under the water. But those yellow eyes were still open and they were staring up at her. She wasn't giving up. She was holding her breath.

*You can do this!* the eyes were telling her.

With the otters chattering frantically and swimming all around her, Willa pulled in a lungful of air, then dove deep into the water. She swam down through the swirling darkness toward the steel trap. The otters swam with her, guiding her through the tangle of trunks and branches. She grabbed the jaws of the trap with her fingers and tried to pull it open, but the trap's spring was far too strong. She pushed and pried and pulled, but it was no use.

Remembering how Lorcan and the other guard had tried to free the padaran by pushing down on the levers on each side of the jaws, Willa grabbed the levers with her hands and pushed as hard as she could. But the levers didn't move at all.

Hoping to use the muscles of her legs, Willa swam up through the tight, twisting tangle of submerged branches, positioned herself with her feet on the trap's levers, braced her back against a branch, and shoved her feet downward as hard as she could. But nothing happened. The levers didn't budge. The jaws didn't open. She just wasn't strong enough, or she didn't understand how the trap worked. She just couldn't do it.

The panther yanked and pulled her trapped leg like she understood exactly what Willa was trying to do for her, and was trying to help her do it. But it made no difference. The panther couldn't get free. Everything was trapped in the logjam. The trees, the branches, the cat . . .

Then Willa realized that these weren't just old, dead sticks submerged beneath the water. The humans had toppled these trees into the river with their saws and their explosives. The trees were still alive. They were still struggling to survive. Their spirits were still strong!

Willa swam down to the trap once more, but this time she didn't touch the cold, metal pieces over which she had no sway. She put her hands on the surrounding branches and closed her eyes.

She had practiced the kind of woodcraft she needed now when she was with her mamaw. But she had been in a healthy forest at the time, with her mamaw at her side, encouraging her, showing her the way. But now Willa was submerged in a logjammed river. She couldn't breathe. She couldn't speak. She could barely hold herself in one place under the water. But she had to try.

She gripped the branches, reached deep down into her sylvan heart, and awoke the spirits of the drowning trees.

As she infused them with her will, the branches of the trees began to twist and turn. They moved like fast-growing vines, winding through the murky water, furling themselves into and around the metal jaws of the trap.

This time, the limbs of the trees weren't moving of their own accord or because she'd asked them to. She was commanding them, controlling them, guiding them to grip the metal and pull.

As she tightened her muscles and gritted her teeth, the branches slowly pulled the jaws of the trap apart.

The panther pulled and pulled again. And then, finally, yanked her paw free.

As the cat swam frantically toward the surface, her sharp claws raked across Willa's thigh, tearing a painfully deep scratch into her leg.

With her leg bleeding, Willa swam upward toward the light. She broke the surface of the water and took a much-needed breath. But Kearnin loomed above her and drove the point of his spear right at her face. The panther burst out of the water with a snarling roar, and slammed into the jaetter with her claws, knocking him away. Gredic, Ciderg, and a dozen other jaetters charged forward, attacking with their spears.

The panther looked at Willa to make sure she was safe. Those bright yellow eyes were staring right at her.

"Yes, go now, go!" Willa screamed at the panther. "Run!"

Wounded and exhausted, but still filled with startling power, the freed panther bound straight up the steep slope of the ravine, then leapt into the forest and disappeared.

Willa felt a flush of happiness as the panther dashed to safety.

As all the jaetters surrounded her at the edge of the river,

Gredic said, "We've got you now, Willa. There's no place you can go."

But as the jaetters came forward, she let herself fall back into the river, right into the most powerful current. It swept her away instantly, hurtling her downstream with tremendous speed.

The spear-boys might be able to catch a Faeran girl, but they'd never catch an otter.

A long way downstream from the logjam and the jaetters, Willa crawled out of the river and collapsed to the ground, thankful to be out of the cold, rushing water.

*The rocks are strong,* she thought, *but the river wins. It turns. It tumbles. It chooses the path.*

As she lay on the bank, the sun gave her its warmth, the earth gave her its stillness, and the living trees held sway over the world once more.

She felt a sense of quiet and safety beginning to return, at least here, at least for a little while.

But her mind burned with memories of the devastation she'd escaped behind her, the earth torn apart and her mighty old friends crashing to the ground. She still felt the shake of the falling bodies in her bones, still heard the cracking limbs in her ears. The river had washed the sap from her hands, but the stench of the killing field lingered in her nose.

It sickened her how the jagged-tooth steel blades had cut so savagely through the living trunks of the trees. She remembered how the loggers with the axes had cleaved the helpless branches. And the shouting men with the snapping whips had yanked at the leather-bound heads of the wild-eyed horses to drag the carcasses of the trees across the ground.

The memories were aflame in her heart. But the worst memory of all were the birds, the hundreds of birds, their feathers torn and tattered, their wings twisted and broken, their bodies lying dead on the ground. A nest. A fox. A mantis. A fawn. A tree wasn't a tree. It was a world. And the men with the iron beasts were killing them by the thousands.

She didn't understand the newcomers. What was in their souls to make them want to destroy the beauty and sustenance of the world in such a way? What kind of evil drove them? Whatever it was, it was clear that they had come for one purpose: to cut down the forest and take the bodies of the trees back to where they came from. And they didn't care who or what they destroyed to do it.

But as dark and frightening as the memories were, the forest around her now provided a warm, soft, green refuge, peaceful and serene. A gentle breeze flowed through the hemlocks, the birches, and the dogwood trees that grew along the river. And she could hear the buzzy murmur and tiny, clawlike feet of a nuthatch climbing up the bark of a nearby trunk. A small flock of chickadees whistled and cavorted in the branches above. It was as if the forest knew what she most needed at this moment, that the quiet whispers of the olden ways would soothe her woodland soul.

When her mind turned to the panther, Willa smiled. Her heart swelled with pride. She'd actually saved the life of a black panther! Her mamaw would have been so pleased, and she would have wanted to hear all about it. In some ways, everything that had happened since she'd left Dead Hollow didn't feel real yet, like she hadn't truly experienced it, not until she'd told her mamaw all about it.

Still thinking about her grandmother, and her sister, Alliw, long ago, Willa gathered goldenseal and witch hazel leaves from nearby, then bound the wounds on her leg where the panther had scratched her. She knew the cat hadn't meant to hurt her. She'd just been trying to get to the surface. Even panthers had to breathe.

As Willa worked on her leg, she remembered the cat's striking yellow eyes staring at her from beneath the surface of the water. *You can do this!* the panther had been telling her. And she *did* do it.

She just wished there had been more time. She could have helped the cat with her wounds, or sat with her for a little while, speaking with her in the old language the way she did with the wolves and the bears. But everything had happened so fast, and then she was gone. She kept wondering where the cat came from. Did she have a family of some kind, or was the panther on her own like she was?

She couldn't explain it, but she longed to see the cat again.

She realized she was being foolish. That panther was a vicious predator. Given half a chance, she would have probably torn her to pieces and eaten her for lunch.

But sitting there by the side of the river alone, Willa missed her all the same. There was a kind of camaraderie in the danger they had shared, the way they had worked together, the way they had helped each other. Willa knew that the jaetter Kearnin would have killed her with that spear if the panther hadn't struck him down. The cat had moved so fast, faster than anything she'd ever seen. And it was for *her.* Not only had she saved a black panther, the black panther had saved her in return.

She spent the next several hours combing the forest, looking for the panther's tracks and trying to pick up her scent. Willa foraged along the way, eating the wild strawberries she found hiding beneath their white blossoms and the green sochan leaves growing along the little streams in the forest.

Eventually, she returned to the bank of the river where she had begun. It was no use. The Ghost of the Forest had truly disappeared. Willa plopped down on the ground in disappointment.

She knew that the truth was, she wasn't just looking for the panther. The panther wasn't what she longed for. She longed for her mamaw, and for her sister, for *anyone.* She wanted someone to talk to about what she'd seen, about what she'd done, about all the things that had happened.

She hadn't spoken with a living person in days. Her mamaw had been the last.

Where was she going to find a new den, a new place to hang her cocoon and sleep her nights? Her grandmother had given her the knowledge and skills to *survive* in the forest, but where was she going to find a place for her heart to live? How was she going to live in the world so alone?

She looked around at the forest, and then out across the water of the river, not sure where to go or what to do. Seeing the destruction of the forest had left her feeling so helpless, so small.

The Cherokee families she'd seen earlier that day were long gone now. The wolves, the bears, they had their own kind, their own lives to live. She was truly alone.

She stared into the river, letting the mesmerizing flow of the water wash over her mind. She wanted the motion of it to numb her, to sweep away the ache, to somehow blend her woeful spirit into the world.

But even as she watched the flow of the river, she knew where it would lead her. In all that had happened over the last few days, in all the violence and conflict she had seen, one act of kindness stuck in her mind. She kept thinking about it, the unexpectedness of it. She couldn't get free of it. She didn't want it to be the answer. She didn't want to take that path. It made no sense to her. But the whole time she was sitting there staring into the water, a part of her already knew what she was going to do. All the streams in her heart were leading her back to that one place. That one moment. And it wasn't far. All she had to do was follow the river.

Willa crept up to the edge of the forest, wove herself into the leaves of the undergrowth, and gazed toward the wooden lair of the day-folk man who had shot her.

The man was walking across the grass, his black-and-white dog following closely at his side. He wore a brown vest and a shirt with wrinkled sleeves rolled up to his elbows, and a wide-brimmed hat that shaded his eyes from the sun.

She didn't know all of the Eng-lish words the homesteaders used, but she was pretty sure that they called the lairs they lived in a "cabin" or a "house" depending on how they had cut up the bodies they had used to make it. They were crude words, and she didn't like them in her mind. And she knew that the "barn" was where they kept their animals. Many of the homesteaders lived in small log cabins, but this man had built a house, a barn, and a third building she didn't have a name for. And this was the building he was walking toward.

He had covered the roof of the building with overlapping slices of dead trees and he'd pieced together the walls from stones he'd stolen from the river. But the oddest feature of the building was that it had a large wooden wheel on the side, with a thick central shaft, eight spokes, and what looked like rectangular wooden buckets hanging on the curve of the wheel. She couldn't imagine what it was all for.

The man walked over to a narrow channel that he'd dug in the ground to take water from the river, and then pulled on a lever that opened some sort of divider. The stolen water came gushing through a chute and splashed down onto the buckets. There was a deep groaning sound, and then—to her amazement—the wheel began to turn, the buckets filling at the top and then emptying at the bottom, with the water pouring into a small pond, and then continuing on through another channel back toward the river.

She'd never seen anything like it. The man was stealing the water of the river, and then giving it back.

The shaft in the center of the wheel turned and turned, and something inside the building rumbled with the grinding, gritty sound of stone rubbing on stone.

She couldn't understand how he took the movement of the water and changed it into the movement of the wheel, but that was the spell he had cast.

But then a loud clanking noise erupted from the building

and the wheel shook violently, the wood twisting and creaking as if the wheel was going to tear apart. The man lurched forward and closed the divider as quickly as he could, bringing the wheel to a shuddering halt.

He gazed at his contraption in stunned confusion, then his face clouded with anger and he clenched his jaw, as if he suspected an enemy had purposefully sabotaged his machine.

He grabbed a tool with a long metal handle, then climbed up the giant wheel and crawled through the spokes into a dense thicket of metal branches. He cranked and he twisted. He hammered and he shoved, shouting out harsh words she didn't understand.

When he finally crawled out again, his knuckles were bloody. He went over to the lever and pulled it for the second time. The water came tumbling down as it had before and the wheel started to turn once more.

This time, he didn't just look satisfied that his machine was working, he looked defiant, as if he had defeated the most powerful of enemies.

Over the next hour, he carried large burlap bags into the building on his shoulder. She had seen the farmers in Cades Cove filling bags like these with wheat from their fields.

She stayed where she was in the forest, but she watched him through the open windows and door of the building. The man poured the bags into a metal mouth where the grains trickled down between two flat stones and were ground into a whitish-yellow powder.

While the water wheel did its work, the man walked over to the stack of severed limbs and trunks at the side of his house, picked up a killing ax, and started cleaving the logs in half. The wood was from the previous season, so she didn't hear its cries, but it was still difficult to watch. She hated how he used a wood-handled ax to cut more wood.

As he split one log after another, he grunted, slamming the ax into the wood harder and harder with each stroke, the wood making a sharp cracking sound as he split it. Sweat beaded on his brow, and he ground his teeth as he hurled the cloven slabs of wood aside.

It seemed as if he had fixed the problem with the wheel, so why was he so angry? Frustration seemed to be boiling up inside him. It was like he didn't want to just split those pieces of tree but crack open the earth they'd grown from.

His breathing got louder and louder. His whiskered face contorted with pain. And he just kept splitting, one log after another, until his hands bled onto the handle of the ax.

It reminded her of when she climbed the mountain, the way she hadn't cared that the rocks were cutting into her hands. She had *wanted* the rocks to cut into her hands.

Finally exhausted, he hurled the ax to the ground, collapsed beside the pile of wood that he had made, and dropped his head into his cupped hands.

He rubbed his face and eyes, as if he wanted to smear some memory from his mind.

In that moment, she remembered sitting by the stream that

had carried her away from the lair, trying to rub the images of her mamaw's dead body away. She remembered the longing in her heart and the sadness in her soul.

The man's shoulders drooped as he went quiet. And she watched as his anger melted into a slow and dying anguish.

He made no noise, but she could see his body shaking as he sobbed.

His dog, seeming to sense his master needed his help, lay down beside him. The man slowly stopped sobbing and rubbed the scruff of the dog's neck with his hand as he stared with glazed eyes out into the forest.

She didn't understand what was happening to him, why he was acting this way. But she could see that the man did not have his killing-stick with him, and his ax was out of reach now, a few feet away.

Her heart pounded and perspiration rose on her arms. She was finding it more and more difficult to breathe.

But she slowly stepped out of the forest.

And she showed herself to him.

The man looked at her in surprise, but did not immediately try to kill her. He did not run for his killing-stick when he saw her standing there at the edge of the woods. He did not reach for the ax or pull out the knife he carried at his side. He did not rouse his dog.

He did not move in any way.

But she knew he saw her. She could see his striking, bright blue eyes staring at her intently as if he could not quite believe what he was seeing.

She stood a dozen steps away from him, but she felt the movement of his chest as he breathed slow steady breaths.

"You're alive . . ." he said, his voice soft and low, but filled with a trace of amazement. "And you've come back to me . . ."

She did not speak, but she studied him, and she let him

study her. And for the moment—for the both of them—that was enough.

Her heart beat in her chest as he looked at her. The quills on the back of her neck tingled.

*This is my enemy,* she thought. *And he's seeing me.*

The man stood perfectly still, as if he knew that the slightest movement would scare her off.

When a breeze swept through the boughs of the trees, she stepped back, blended into the forest, and disappeared.

The next day, she watched him from the forest. He moved in and out of the house, sometimes working in his barn, feeding his goats and his chickens, or using tools she did not understand. Other times he worked in the building that used the water of the river to turn the giant wheel. He worked quietly and on his own. But sometimes he paused in his work and looked out into the forest, scanning the trees with a careful eye.

As the sun set and slowly withdrew its light from the trees of the surrounding forest, the man went back into the house. She watched as the window near the eating room lit up with the soft glow of a candle. The stars above the trees provided all the light she needed to see, but she liked watching the glowing radiance of the candle as the man moved from one room to another, the light moving with him, leaving darkness behind, until finally he went up the stairs, into the room where she had once seen him lying asleep in his bed, and the candle went out.

It was a warm summer evening, with yellow-green fireflies lighting on and off in the open area in front of the man's house while he slept. She walked over to a stand of beautiful, old sourwood trees growing near the side of house, with their craggy gray bark and their long, wavy limbs.

"Hello, my friends," she said to them in the old language, touching their trunks with her open hand as she walked among them. "It's good to meet you all."

Deciding not to make a cocoon that night, she picked the tallest of the trees and began to climb its trunk. "I hope you don't mind a friend for the night," she said as she reached its upper branches. Sourwoods weren't large trees, and they had bitter-tasting leaves, but she loved their nectar when their flowers blossomed and she appreciated their peaceful spirits. She always missed them when they slept in the winter and rejoiced when they came awake each spring.

She found a good spot in the branches near a tight ball of leaves with a bundle of baby squirrels snoring inside. As the tendrils of the tree gently encircled her body to make sure she didn't fall, she curled up and went to sleep. It was the first night in a long time that she didn't dream of stealing.

The next morning when she woke, the dog was sitting at the base of the tree, his ears perked and his eyes looking up into the branches.

Had the dog somehow detected her? Or had the nest of squirrels caught his attention?

He wasn't barking or growling, and he didn't seem anxious to attack. But he looked keenly interested, like he was certain there was something up in the tree, maybe the two-legged forest creature he'd seen the day before.

"Come on, Scout," the man called as he walked out of the house, down the steps, and toward the barn. But upon noticing the dog's position by the tree, he stopped.

The man turned.

"Scout?"

But the dog didn't move. His nose pointed straight up into the tree.

*This was a truly bad place to spend the night,* Willa decided. *Now I've been treed by the pesky dog!*

As the man walked toward the base of the tree, Willa's heart thumped. Goose bumps rose on her arms.

The man stood below her and peered up into the limbs of the tree. His eyes moved from one spot to the next, looking for her, but her legs and arms had taken on the appearance of the branches, and her face was nothing but leaves.

"What do you see, boy?" he asked as he crouched down beside his dog. "Is she up there?"

She'd shown herself to them two days before, but she wouldn't allow them to see her now, not like this, trapped up in a tree peering down at them like an opossum.

When the man and his dog finally gave up and left the area of the tree, Willa climbed down.

She watched the man go about his daily work. When he walked through his orchard, she became as dark and crooked as an apple tree's trunk. When he tended to his vegetable garden, she became as green and yellow as stalks of corn. And at the end of the day, while the dog napped in the shade and the man went down to the river to wash his hands and face, she crouched on a rock nearby, as blue as water and gray as stone.

The man finished washing up, then climbed back up onto the bank and headed toward the path.

Willa jumped from the rock she'd been perched on, and followed him into the forest.

It was there, on the path that led to the house, that she chose to reveal herself once more.

She pulled in a long, uncertain breath, relaxed the blend of her skin, and stepped onto the path in front of him.

She appeared before him in her natural green colors, her face spotted and streaked, her arms marked with marbled patterns, her dark hair falling around her shoulders, and her eyes emerald green.

When he looked up and saw her there, he stopped, surprised, his eyes wide for a moment.

But he stood very still.

"I was hoping you'd come around again," he said.

Suddenly, Willa became aware of her own breathing, the position of her feet, and the perspiration on her neck. She studied the man, looking for any signs of threat or attack, taking in all the details: his watching eyes, the light brown whiskers on his face, his hands freshly clean but scratched and worn from his work, his wrinkled tan trousers wet to the knees from standing in the river—all so different from any sort of living thing she'd ever talked to before.

"I'm sorry about what happened," he said. "It was so dark and you were moving so fast. I couldn't see anything. I shouldn't have pulled that trigger."

He paused, waiting for her to reply. She *wanted* to speak to him. She *wanted* to take a few steps closer to him. But she didn't know what to say to him or what to do. On the outside, she imagined she appeared to be standing very still, but on the inside, she felt like a trembling fawn, ready to dash away at any moment.

"But you don't seem to be too badly hurt anymore . . ." he said, almost to himself, as if he was mystified that her wounds had healed so quickly. "Listen," he added gently. "I know you and I didn't get off to a good start. But I want you to know that I will not harm you. You are welcome here."

She had never heard the Faeran of Dead Hollow use the Eng-lish word *welcome*, but she had always loved the word *eluin*, which she remembered her mother and father saying to her many years before. *"Esper dun eluin una,"* they had told her. *The trees will always welcome you.* It was one of the few memories she had of her parents.

And then the man said something else that surprised her.

"My name is Nathaniel."

Her ears took the unusual sound into her mind.

But still she did not reply.

"Do you understand the words I'm speaking?" he asked her softly.

Willa looked at him and took in a long, slow breath.

"I do," she said.

They were the first words she had spoken to him.

As soon as the man Nathaniel heard her voice, his face lit up with a sudden and genuine smile. She hadn't seen a smile in so long that it brought an unexpected wash of happiness through her, and she couldn't help but smile in return.

"I'm glad," he said. "I was beginning to wonder if you were some kind of spirit or something, or maybe my wits were finally leaving me for good."

"I'm as real as the trees around you," she said. "I'm just not used to talking to . . ." She let words dwindle and didn't finish her sentence.

"I understand," he said. "Sometimes no words is just the right amount."

She wasn't sure exactly what he meant, but she liked the kindness in his voice when he said it.

"Are you hungry?" he said as he began to walk toward the house and gestured for her to follow him. "Let's get something to eat."

But the instant he moved, she startled, and she was gone.

She had reacted quickly and disappeared, a reflex more than a decision. But once she had a moment to think about it, she realized the man hadn't been trying to hurt her. He had just started to walk up toward the house.

But after it happened, she felt too uncertain to rejoin him, and she withdrew back into the forest on her own.

The next morning, when the man Nathaniel and the dog, Scout, came out of the house, the man walked over to the base of the tree in which she was sleeping and set something on the ground.

"In case you change your mind," he said, and continued on into the forest.

When the dog lingered behind to sniff at the plate, the man said, "No, you've already had your breakfast. Now, come on."

Carrying his killing-stick in his right hand, the man followed the path that ran along the bank of the river, his dog trotting behind him. Soon they were gone.

As Willa climbed down the trunk of the tree and smelled the plate of food, she realized how hungry she truly was. It seemed like she was *always* hungry. Did the man know this about her? Was that why he had asked her this odd question about whether she was hungry? The Faeran of the Dead Hollow lair would never ask her this question. They did not care.

As she crouched on the ground and ate the food, she wondered where the man had gone with his dog and his killing-stick. He had seemed very determined to find whatever he was looking for.

But that evening, he returned exhausted and empty-handed, the dog walking along dejectedly just behind him.

As they came toward the house, she decided to stand in the open where they could see her. But she stayed near the edge of the trees just in case.

Her temples immediately started pounding, and she had to work hard to keep her breathing strong and steady, but despite the anxiousness welling up inside her chest, she kept her feet planted firmly in the grass.

The moment the dog saw her, he jolted to attention.

"Scout, *stay*!" the man said, stopping the dog in its tracks. "Down!" The dog went down on his haunches immediately, his whole body shaking with excitement. The dog obviously wanted to run at her, bite her, shake her, tear her to pieces, but the human's command held him in place. "She's a friend, Scout," the man said firmly. "You're gonna let her be. You got it? Let her be. She's a friend. You just *stay*."

The dog's eyes blazed with intense curiosity as he watched her, but he seemed to understand the man's instructions.

When she felt at least somewhat certain the dog wasn't going to attack her, Willa moved her eyes to the man, Nathaniel.

He was already looking at her, and he did not look displeased to see her.

"How was your breakfast this morning?" he asked.

"Thank you," she said, because she thought that was what day-folk said to one another.

"Yesterday, I introduced myself, my name is Nathaniel, and this here is Scout, but we didn't get *your* name . . ."

When she thought about telling him her name, her mind flooded with questions. What did a Faeran name mean to him, what did it sound like? In what way could he use it? Could he harm her with it?

There were many thoughts going through her mind all at once, and many of them frightened her. But unlike the day before, when her reflexes had acted before she could even think, now her thoughts came more slowly, more in her control.

"What do you wish me to call you?" he asked her.

"My name is Willa," she said finally.

Nathaniel nodded. "That's a fine and lovely name," he said. "It's good to meet you, Willa. Did your mother give you that name?"

"I do not know."

"Is your mother nearby?" the man asked, looking out into the forest. "Or your father?"

"My mother and father are dead."

"I'm sorry to hear that," he said, his voice filled with something she had never heard outside her own den, a tone, an emotion she didn't have a word for. "When did your parents pass away?" he asked.

"Six years ago," she said.

"Then who takes care of you out here?" he asked.

"Out where?"

"In the forest."

"The forest."

"I don't understand. Who feeds you and gives you shelter? Where do you live?"

"The forest," she said again.

"There must be someone—"

"I left my clan."

"Your clan . . ." The man looked around at the forest as if arrows were going to come flying out at him. "But you're not Cherokee, are you?"

"No," she said. "I'm not Cherokee."

"And you live around here in the forest? That's where you come from?"

Not sure she understood his question, she slowly pointed toward the top of the Great Mountain, which was visible from the open area in front of his house.

"You come from Clingmans Dome?" he asked in surprise, but it was clear that he didn't think he was understanding her.

"Don't you live in a town? Maybe down in the valley, in Cades Cove? Or maybe a new homestead I don't know about?"

"No. I live up there," she said again, but then she realized that wasn't actually true anymore. She didn't live in Dead Hollow any longer. She lived in the forest. "I live here," she said, knowing that she was probably confusing him as much as he was confusing her.

"But who were your parents? What is your last name?"

She didn't understand. She had already told him her name. She thought she knew the Eng-lish words of the day-folk, but she realized now that she must not.

"Well, in any case . . ." He turned very slowly this time and carefully gestured for her to follow him. "Come on into the house and get something to eat."

It had startled her before, but this time she held back her reflex to blend. When he walked, she walked with him, not quite at his side, but a few feet away from him. And the dog crept along with them, eyeing her with quick tilts of his head, but not biting her or even growling. He seemed to understand that the man Nathaniel did not want him to attack her.

As they went up the steps and through the front door, she paused, remembering the night she'd come here—the blasting noise of the killing-stick, the chomping teeth of the dog, the pain and blood of her wounds, her desperate escape out to the barn—it all started coming back to her.

"It's all right," he said. "You and I have made our peace and buried the hatchet."

"The hatchet?" she said, pretty sure that this was a kind of small, sapling-killing ax of the hand.

"It's just an old expression," he said. "Come on inside."

Willa stepped into the house and gazed around at the eating room and the main room beyond. Everything seemed so different from what it was when she had been crawling on the floor through the darkness.

"What do you have a hankering for?" he asked.

Willa knew immediately what she wanted, even before she could recall its name. She tried to remember what the Cherokee prisoner-boy had called them. The word felt wrong on her lips, garbled, like it couldn't actually be a real word, but it made her mouth water just to think about it.

"Cook . . ." she said. "Cookies. I have a . . ." She tried to remember the words he had used. "I have a hankering for cookies."

"Ah," he said. "I thought maybe somebody besides me and Scout had been into that jar." The man Nathaniel started to smile. He was trying to be kind to her—"welcoming," as he called it—but as soon as he said these words, he seemed to be suddenly overcome: his expression contorted and he turned away from her, rubbing his forehead with his hand.

"I'm afraid my supply of cookies has run dry," he said soberly, his voice shaking with emotion.

After a few moments, he regained his composure and turned back around. "But I've got some good, fresh cornbread from the latest batch from the mill, and I can cook up some venison if you want a proper meal."

"What is venison?" she asked.

He looked at her in surprise. "You know . . . meat."

When he saw the confusion in her face he said, "Deer meat."

"I sleep with deer, I don't eat them," she said.

"Ah . . ." he said hesitantly. "All right . . . No venison, then. What *do* you eat?"

"Shoots, berries, nuts, rock tripe lichen . . ."

He tilted his head, as if he wasn't sure if she was being serious with him.

"I've tried that sort of thing," he said, "but never been too partial to it. I'm afraid sticks taste like sticks, if you know what I mean. And I hate acorns in particular. My papa used to tell me you can eat 'em, but I think you'd have to be full-on starving to do it. Well, listen, let's try some of this cornbread over here and see how you like it."

"What animal did you kill to make the cornbread?" she asked, narrowing her eyes at him.

"It's made from corn flour from the mill," he said.

"The wheel in the water."

"That's right."

"So it's called a mill."

"Yes, that's right. People bring me their corn and their wheat and I grind it. I take one sack out of every eight in the way of payment. I figure, why plant and harvest crops, digging in the dirt for somebody else all day, when I can sit and watch a wheel go 'round on my own sweet time."

"You weren't watching the wheel go 'round on the day I first saw you," she said, trying to say the word *'round* like he did.

"No, that's true," he said. "Somebody did me a bad turn, shoved a hammer in the machinery, knocked everything all catawampus, trying to break the teeth off my main gear. Looking to put me out of business, no doubt. But I stopped it in time and got the gears lined up proper again."

Willa listened as carefully as she could, trying to understand all the confusing words he used, but she couldn't understand how the mill could have teeth.

"I'm competing with half a dozen other mills down in Cades Cove," he continued on. "So I need to keep working."

"Is that who damaged the mill?"

"No, no, those are good folk down there," he said. "We're competitors, sure, but they'd never do anything underhanded like that." He looked out the window toward the forest. "I know exactly who did it," he added bitterly. "And those are the ones you gotta be careful of."

This man Nathaniel talked in a peculiar fashion, and he talked a lot. It was as if for years he had been used to talking all day long, but lately he had been alone, and all the words pent up inside him came pouring out, like water splashing down through the buckets of his wheel.

As he continued, she didn't speak as much as he did, but watched him and listened to him. He fascinated her. He wasn't anything like what the padaran had told her the day-folk were. He wasn't violent or hateful. He didn't attack her or beat her or try to capture her or kill her. She'd seen other homesteaders only from a distance—small families building their log cabins, tending to their little farms, traveling on their carriages—but this man, this man who called himself Nathaniel seemed so different from the padaran, the jaetters, and the other Faeran of the clan. Were all the day-folk as evil as the padaran described other than this one man?

"Why do you cut the trees?" she blurted out suddenly, looking for his evilness.

"Ah . . ." He hesitated, unable to find the words to explain his actions.

"Why do you kill them?" she pressed him.

"I cut down trees to . . . make my house, to warm my home, to make tools . . . There are many uses for wood. I could not live here without it. Why are you asking this question? Are the trees friends of yours?"

She knew he had meant this as a joke, but she answered with the truth. "Yes, they are," she said. "And when you cut them they die."

He studied her for several long seconds, not saying a word.

"Yes," he admitted finally, quite softly. "The trees die. But I only cut what I need. We all have to survive."

"Do you need that wall?" she asked pointing toward the wooden wall. "Do you need the wooden wheel that turns in the water more than those trees needed their lives? Do you need the meat of the deer more than the deer needs her life, more than the fawn needs her mother?"

"I never looked at it that way," he admitted. And then he repeated, "I just take what I need."

"Like the wolf," she said.

"I don't know about that," he said, bristling. He didn't like to be compared to a wolf.

She could see he had no love for wolves. He was a kind man, but a fool, too.

She watched as he pulled out a sharpened blade of steel with an antler-grip, cut a slice of cornbread, and handed it to her.

"Have some of this and see how you like that mill," he said, smiling a little. "You want butter on that?"

"No," she said. She didn't know what butter was or what he killed to make it.

As soon as she put the bread between her lips, it began to melt in her mouth. It was unlike anything she had ever tasted before.

"You like that," he said, nodding and smiling. "You like it a lot. You see, I'm not all bad."

That first day, when she was watching him from the forest, he had seemed so sad, and then his melancholy shifted like the wind into a deep anger. And when he returned from his journey down the river earlier that afternoon, he had seemed so exhausted, not just in body but in spirit. But now he seemed to have forgotten a little bit of what had stormed through him a short time before, and she could feel the same thing happening to her. Their words and their smiles were affecting her, changing her in little ways, like the river shaping the stone.

In the days that followed, it was one strange incident after another.

She ate with the man Nathaniel while sitting at something he called his dinner table.

She sat with him and the dog by the warm glow of the fire in the evenings.

She watched him work in his mill in the afternoons, with the turn, turn, turning of the millstone grinding the wheat into flour while they talked.

Sometimes they walked together in the forest, teaching each other the way they saw the world.

She learned many new Eng-lish words, like that he called his killing-stick a "rifle" or a "gun." And she taught him the Faeran names of many of the plants and animals in the forest. When he showed her how to operate the mill, she taught him the songs of the birds flitting in the trees above their heads.

"There's something that has always confused me about the Eng-lish language," she admitted one afternoon, as they walked in the forest.

"What is it?" he asked.

She stopped and pointed to the needles of a pine tree. "What color do you call that?"

"Green," he said.

"In the Faeran language that color is called *erunda*," she said. "So, if the pine needles are what you call green, then what color is that?" She pointed to fresh grass growing in a small patch of sunlight.

"That's green, too," he said.

"But that's *finlalin*," she said in confusion. "They are totally different colors."

"Light green?" He shrugged. "It's still green."

"What about that color there?" she asked, pointing to the shiny, waxy leaves of a rhododendron bush.

"Green," he said.

"No!" she said in exasperation. "That's a different color. You can see the difference with your eyes, right?"

"Looks like green to me," he said. "Maybe a slightly different shade, but it's still green. How many words do you have in your language for the green colors you see in the forest?"

She shook her head. "I don't know. They're all different colors to me. But at least forty or fifty."

"I'll stick with regular old *green*, thank you," he said with a smile, bumping her gently with his arm.

As they continued through the forest, she couldn't help from taking a quiet, contented sigh. There was something about spending time with this unusual human that felt surprisingly like her soul was swimming in the warm water of the sacred lake of the bears.

But every morning, the man Nathaniel grabbed his killing-stick and trudged into the forest in the direction of the river with his dog Scout at his side. He did not tell her where he was going or what he was doing, and it was clear that he didn't want to talk about it.

Curious to know what he was doing, she slipped through the undergrowth and watched him from a distance.

He followed the bank of the river downstream, close along the jagged, moss-covered rocks, many of them towering over his head, others low and tumbled, with the water flowing between them.

The dog ran up and down along the bank, his nose to the ground looking for scent, working with the man Nathaniel, seeming to understand what he was looking for and as anxious to find it as he was.

The man and the dog came to a shallow section of the river where it was clear the man wanted to cross, but the water was running strong even here. To her amazement, the man slung his rifle by its leather strap over his back, picked his dog up in his arms, and began to wade across.

He plowed slowly through the current with forceful, deliberate steps as the water crashed against his thighs.

"Be careful," Willa whispered as she watched from the trees, the palms of her hands sweating.

She could imagine the powerful current pulling the man Nathaniel off his feet, and sweeping him and the frantically swimming dog down into the rocky rapids below.

When they finally reached the other side, the dog leapt from his arms and shook himself dry, and then the two of them continued on their way, receding into the distance farther downstream on the opposite bank of the river.

She thought the man and his dog must be going out to hunt for their food, and that he wasn't talking about it because he knew it would bother her. But when they returned later that afternoon, the man wasn't just empty-handed but solemn and exhausted, like he'd gone to the ends of the earth. His boots and trousers were soaked, his hands roughened by the abrasion of stone, and his clothes were torn.

Willa's brows furrowed in confusion. Where was he going every day? What was he doing out there?

She watched from her spot in the top of the sourwood tree as they came up from the river. The dog ran into the house, his tail wagging, excited to be home—maybe looking for her, she thought.

But the man Nathaniel didn't go in.

He walked in silence to the meadow near the house, where the rays of the setting sun were shining down. He stood there alone, unmoving and unchanging for a long time, except for the glisten of light trickling down his cheeks.

As she watched him, she felt as if the world was being held still, held in that moment, as if she couldn't breathe, couldn't move, her heart slowing to a low, steady thumping beat, as if in that moment she could reach out across the distance between them, and without any knowledge or understanding or words, know what the man Nathaniel was feeling.

Later that evening, with the feeling of that moment still in her heart, she went down to the river and sat by herself, listening to the water flowing between the stones, and remembering the sound of her grandmother's Faeran voice.

She remembered the look in her grandmother's eyes and the warmth of her touch, the way her mamaw had wrapped her in her arms, as if she were encasing her in a cocoon that would protect her forever.

And Willa remembered playing games of hide-and-seek with her sister, Alliw, in the dappled shade of the wooded dells—the two of them blending from one place to another as they took turns hiding from one another. She remembered the smile that lit up Alliw's little spotted face whenever Willa found her. They played through the sunlit days and the moonlit nights, running and blending and searching and laughing, over and over again.

Sitting there by the river on her own, she could see it all in her mind. And she could hear the soft sound of Alliw's voice as they explored the forest together with their mamaw and their parents. She remembered Alliw talking to a nest of frightened sparrows that had fallen from a tree, the way she cupped the little birds in her hands and reassured them that she would put them back where they belonged.

Willa remembered it all, but as the sound of the Faeran words drifted from her memory, it was like the whispers of the water flowing down the tumbling river.

And as the moon rose from the darkened peak of the Great Mountain looming in the distance, the man Nathaniel came down to the river, and sat beside her in the quiet, and seemed to understand not just her sense of silence, but her sense of loss.

He seemed to know, as if from his own experience, that there were parts of her life that he could not understand, words from her past that she longed to hear, but he could not speak.

# 43

The next day, while the man Nathaniel was away down the river, Willa remained in the forest near the house.

Every day, wherever she was and whatever she was doing, she had been practicing her woodland skills. Her mamaw had taught her the long history of her sky-reaching friends and the other plants, and all the ancient words and whispers she needed to converse with them. But now that she had begun to learn more and more on her own, she realized there was so much more she wanted to understand and do.

She practiced lying on the ground in a patch of ferns and vines, and then asking the plants to grow across her body until she disappeared, not just by blending the color and texture of her skin, but by physically covering the entirety of her body with the growth of the plants. She was able to achieve the growth she wanted. But it turned out to be surprisingly difficult to actually *get out of* the ferns and vines once they'd grown over her. The plants seemed to like holding on to her, with their tiny, sticky stems and their curling tendrils adhering to her skin.

As she was climbing out of the vines, she noticed a small slug slithering over a nearby rock. That was one of the few creatures of the forest she didn't like, but this time it repulsed her even more than usual. The slug's mucus-coated skin reminded her of the padaran when he caught his foot in the jaws of the trap. She still couldn't figure out exactly what she had seen when she glanced back to look at him. But the image had stuck in her memory. The padaran had always had deep bronze skin that seemed to be filled with light, but for that single moment when he was in terrible pain and distress, his skin had turned as gray and slimy as a slug.

Back when she was a jaetter stealing for the clan, she thought the padaran was a great leader, feared and respected by all, the wise father to her struggling people. But now that she had left the lair, she wondered why he had hated the old ways so deeply, why he had been trying so desperately to wipe out the last remnants of the woodwitches and their forest powers. What harm had they been doing?

She hated the dark memories of her old life. She didn't want to think about the Dead Hollow lair or the padaran. But questions kept sneaking into her mind like little worms: Where did he come from? Who was he?

She had heard stories that the padaran wasn't a normal Faeran like the other members of the clan, that he had come down from the top of the Great Mountain to lead the Faeran people. And it had been easy to believe. But what confused her now was that she had actually climbed the Great Mountain, felt its presence in her heart and heard its voice in her soul. She remembered vast clouds of mist, and a soaring hawk, and trees, and mountains for as far as the eye could see. But she didn't see any sign that the padaran, or anyone like him, had ever been there.

Near the end of the day, when she heard the man Nathaniel coming her way, she relaxed her blend so that he could see her. As he walked up to her, a vine was growing along her arm and around her wrist like a day-folk bracelet, and another was twining up into her hair.

The man watched the movement of the vines in silence, astonished and transfixed by what he was seeing.

"How do you do it?" he asked softly.

Willa tried to think of a way to explain it in Eng-lish words, but it was difficult. "With my mind, and sometimes my voice, I ask the vines to move."

"Have you always been able to do this?"

"My mamaw has been teaching me all my life, and I've been practicing more and more."

"What do you . . . What do you call what you do?"

"In the Faeran language, it used to be called *esperia*. In Eng-lish, we call it woodcraft."

"Woodcraft . . ." he repeated slowly, as if he was trying to absorb both the sound of it and the meaning of what he was seeing.

"Years ago, many of my people had the knowledge and the

power of woodcraft. It still runs very strong in the members of a few families. My mother and father, and my sister, all had the power. And my grandmother was the one who taught me. But I think I might be the last of the whisperers now . . ."

"The whisperers," the man Nathaniel said in gentle surprise. "I like the sound of that. And you and your people call yourselves *Faeran* . . . Is that right?"

Willa smiled and nodded. "And you and your people call yourself *human*, is that right?"

The man Nathaniel smiled. "Yes, at least once I've had my breakfast in the morning."

She liked the way he smiled when he said these words, and she liked the way it made her feel.

"Listen, I came over to ask you. I need to go check on something, and I thought you might want to come along with me. I think I could use your help."

Willa rose to her feet, pleased to be included.

A while later, as she walked along with the man Nathaniel and the dog Scout through the forest, she asked, "Where are we going?"

"We left the edge of my property behind us," he said, making his way through the undergrowth of the trees, "but I saw something back here in the woods that's been festering in my mind."

"What do you mean, your property?" she asked.

"My land," he said. "The property I own."

She still didn't understand.

As they walked along, Scout stayed close at her side. He had become used to her, and her to him. She liked the way he was always looking ahead, always scanning with his eyes and nose and ears. She thought there must be a little bit of wolf in him.

When she reached down to pet his head, he looked up at her, and she was surprised to see the worry in his eyes. He was smelling something ahead of them that he didn't like one bit.

She turned to Nathaniel and saw he was anxious as well.

They soon came to a footpath, and Nathaniel stopped.

"Can you sense anything?" he asked her. "Do you see anything unusual?"

Understanding that he wanted her to put her woodland skills to work, she crouched to the ground and looked at the earth, the lichen, and leaves. She noticed the way some of the ferns were bent and a few of the leaves were pressed down.

"Humans have been walking here," she said. "All of them wearing heavy boots, one of them dragging some kind of tool or object behind him."

"How many men?" he asked.

"At least four," she said, looking around at the footprints.

Fear clouded Nathaniel's face. "Can you tell how long ago?"

Checking the amount of wear and dryness on the edge of the footprints, and thinking about the last time it had rained, she said, "Yesterday."

"That's not good," he said, shaking his head. "Let's follow the tracks a little ways and see what we can learn."

As they walked on, they both noticed long red strips of cloth that had been tied onto some of the larger oak trees.

"What are they?" she asked.

"They're marking the most important trees to cut," he said, his voice filled with fear and anger all at once.

"I don't understand," she said. The thought of cutting down these beautiful trees made her eyes water, and she could feel the heat rising up into her face.

"These men are scouts for the logging company, surveying the forest to determine which groves to cut first, and finding the best route for their railroad to come up into the mountains. They've got a new kind of engine that puts power to all its wheels so it can handle hauling full loads of logs down the mountain slopes, but even the new engines have limits, so they have to map out their path."

"So, they're coming up here now," she said, her voice cracking in dismay.

"Right now, what they most want is my land," he said. "I own a section along the river, the only one flat enough for them to get their railroad line and their equipment up onto the rest of the mountain where they want to cut. So whatever you do, Willa, you need to avoid this area of the forest from now on. It's going to be too dangerous. Don't ever let those loggers see you."

As he said these words, she could hear the trembling fear in his voice. It felt like she could almost see the future he was seeing, and it frightened her to her bone.

At that moment, Scout brushed past her leg and took to sniffing something on the ground. Then he began to follow the scent off the path.

"Scout's onto something," Nathaniel said, moving toward him.

They followed the dog into the forest until Willa saw something on the ground up ahead.

"Wait," she whispered to the man Nathaniel, touching his side to bring him to a stop.

When she crouched down, he crouched with her.

"What do you see?" he whispered, peering in the direction she was looking.

It was well disguised in the leaves, but she could see it. It was definitely there.

"Scout, *come*," she said, her voice quiet but firm, using the word she'd heard Nathaniel use, and she was relieved that the dog quickly returned to her side.

"What do you see up there?" Nathaniel asked her again, sensing her anxiousness.

She pointed toward the ground ten or twenty paces in front of them. "Look carefully just ahead of us, by the roots of that oak there, and along the forest floor over to that chestnut tree. Do you see it? It's a net, hidden beneath the leaves."

"It's some sort of trap," he whispered. "Someone must be trying to capture an animal of some sort."

"Do you think it belongs to the loggers?" she asked.

"I've never seen them use anything like that before. They're more interested in laying railroad tracks and cutting trees than hunting and trapping, but maybe they've been having trouble with a local bear. But for the life of me, I don't understand why they would want to catch a bear in a net. Seems like it's just asking for a face full of claws."

"Do any humans other than the loggers use this path?" she asked.

"Yes, definitely," he said. "Some of the other homesteaders use it, and so do I."

Willa stared at the net, not sure what to do.

But Nathaniel suddenly rose up and moved past her. He picked up a large branch and heaved it into the center of the trap. The net sprang up with a loud, violent *swoosh*, bringing up an explosion of leaves with it. Then he pulled out the long knife he carried on his belt and cut the net down.

"I don't know who did this or why, but something like this doesn't belongs in these woods," he said angrily as he sliced the net to pieces and rendered it useless.

Then he touched her on the shoulder and gestured in the direction of the house. "Come on, let's get outta here before somebody sees us."

All the way back, she kept looking over her shoulder, convinced that the loggers or night-spirits or some sinister beasts she'd never seen before were going to chase them down and attack them, but they made it safely home.

In the days that followed, they continued on with the gentle patterns of their lives, working together in the water mill, taking care of their animals, and each morning, the man Nathaniel venturing out on his daily journeys down the river and back again, trudging with a grim and relentless determination.

In the afternoons, the man Nathaniel showed her how he had planted corn, squash, and beans in his garden to grow some of his food for the next season. And she showed him where to find the tastiest roots and berries that grew wild in the forest, and how to pick the sweetest brook lettuce from the shallows of the nearby streams.

When a group of otters moved into the section of river just downstream from the house, she took the man Nathaniel down to meet them.

"The otters seem to be looking over at us every time they come up for air," he marveled, as they watched them together. "But they don't seem nervous about us being here."

"No, they're not nervous," she said. "They want to know why I'm standing around with my feet on the ground instead of swimming with them."

One afternoon, after he'd returned for the day, Willa watched the man Nathaniel from a distance. After completing some of his usual chores, he climbed into an odd-looking cloth suit with long dangling arms and legs that tied at the wrists and ankles, a hood that went over his head, and a metal mesh that covered his face. Then he tramped down a path that led from the house.

Curious, she followed him through the stand of sourwood trees and then through a small field filled with white and purple clover, where bees and butterflies floated in the rays of the setting sun.

He walked over to a cluster of five black gum tree logs that had been cut into sections, stood on their ends, and turned into beehives. Honeybees were flying to and from the hives. It perplexed her that these bees would make their home in these human-cut contrivances rather than a natural hole in a living tree, but that appeared to be what they had done.

The man opened up the hive at the top and began to collect the wooden frames of honey as the bees buzzed and circled all around him. She could hear by their tone that they were a little bit agitated by his presence.

As Willa approached him, she shifted her color and made enough noise to make herself known.

The man Nathaniel looked up at her, peering through his mask.

"Stay back, Willa!" he shouted at her. "You don't have a suit on! Keep a safe distance!"

His face went white with fear as hundreds of bees swarmed toward her and landed all over her body.

"Willa!" he shouted in dismay, thinking the bees were attacking her.

*"Eee na nin,"* she said softly to him and to the bees as she watched them crawling over the bare skin of her arms. "They're just saying hello. They're telling me where to find the best flowers."

"What?" he said, frowning in confusion and doubt.

When he set down the rack he'd been working on and came over to her, she showed him how the returning worker bees danced in particular patterns to tell the other worker bees where the flowers were blooming that morning.

"That's incredible . . ." the man said. "I had no idea."

The bees in the colony worked closely together, communicating with each other, all laboring in harmony toward the common goal of keeping the hive healthy and strong.

*"Tia na lochen dar sendal,"* she said.

"What's that mean?" he asked.

"'We all have our ways to survive,'" she said.

"We sure do," he said, still watching the bees. And then, after a moment, he turned and looked at her.

"And what about you?" he asked. "What is your way to survive?"

She looked back at him, not sure how to answer his question. She knew he wasn't asking about the kind of leaves she ate or how she avoided predators. He had already seen these parts of her life with his own eyes. Although the words were the same, he was asking a whole different kind of question. And for the first time, it felt like she was beginning to see the hidden beauty of the language they were speaking.

"What is your way to survive?" he asked again.

"I survive here," she said.

That night, after they were done eating their dinner, Willa played with Scout in the main room while the man Nathaniel finished up the work in the kitchen.

She knew he was a cutter of trees and hunter of animals, but sometimes, over the last few days, it had almost seemed as if he understood the world the way she did. But other times, she grew dismayed by the life he'd been living, and her growing part in it.

When she looked over, she saw him chewing on a wooden sassafras twig as he swept the wooden-planked floor with a wooden-handled broom and then cleared the four-legged wooden kitchen table, sat down in a wooden chair, picked up a thin stick of wood in his hand, and began to scratch marks on a strange, impossibly flat sliver of whitish tree bark. He was surrounded by wood.

When they first met he had told her that he could not survive without it, and she was beginning to see what he meant.

Was the man Nathaniel evil for using the trees and animals to survive?

She didn't know the answer to that question anymore. Did that mean she knew more or less about the world?

"You said a few days ago that you own the land," she said.

"Yes," he said gently as he stopped and looked at her. "That's right."

"I don't understand what that means. How? In what way? The ground? The air? The trees? The animals? What does it mean?"

"It means that this is my property, an area where I can live my life the way I want to live, without asking anyone else's permission. I'm free. I can do what I want to do."

She stared at him, trying to understand.

"My great-great-grandfather earned this land back in 1783 for serving in the Revolutionary War," he said. "And there's been at least one Steadman living here ever since, sometimes many more. This land is the only thing I have, and that's one of the reasons I'm not going to let the loggers buy it from me, or take it away. As far as I'm concerned, it isn't for sale."

"But how can you or the loggers or anyone claim a place to be yours and only yours? I don't understand."

"I'll ask you the same sort of question in reverse," he said. "How can you wander through the woods without ever having a place to call your own, a place to call home?"

"I live in the world as it is, without disturbing it."

He nodded and took a moment to think about her words. "Disturbing it . . ." he repeated. "Is that what you call it? Is that what I'm doing when I'm fixing my mill, planting my sweet potatoes, or tending to my apple trees? I'm disturbing it?"

"Yes," she said.

"What about the bees?"

"What about the bees?"

"Where do you think your friends the honeybees come from?"

"They've always been here, like the trees and the river."

"No," he said. "They haven't. The people you call the homesteaders, the day-folk, brought them from England to America on their ships two hundred years ago. And then somebody brought them up into these mountains. Yes, the bees live here now. They've become part of the natural world. But humans brought them here. And humans brought the clover in the field as well. The clover, along with the sourwood trees, makes the honey taste better. It's true that we humans can do terrible damage, but we can do good as well. I'll give you an example: there are plenty of sourwood trees in these mountains, but there weren't any right here around our house and meadow, so my grandfather planted a hundred sourwood saplings every year for as long as he was living."

"I don't understand," she said, her brows furrowing. The bees that she knew so well—whose language of movement her grandmother had taught her—came from outside the world?

They came from the Eng-land of the homesteaders? How could this be true?

And did he say that his grandfather had planted the sourwood trees near the meadow? She had walked through those trees. She had *spoken* with those trees. She had *slept* in those trees. Day-folk didn't *plant* trees, they cut them down!

"I know how you feel about the trees of the forest," he said. "I can't live that way, but I understand it. And I know how you feel about the animals. Are you angry with me because I eat meat? Is that what's bothering you?"

She thought about his question for a long time. And then she slowly came to a realization, something she'd already known but hadn't truly understood before. "You are like a wolf."

"I am not a wolf!" he insisted, raising his voice as his face turned flush with sudden red.

It startled her a little bit, but then it made her smile.

He didn't like being compared to a wolf. He never had.

"I don't hate wolves," she said. "I love them. And I don't hate foxes or bobcats or otters. I don't hate any of the animals that hunt for their food any more than I hate the vultures or the mushrooms for living off the decay of dead things."

Nathaniel stared at her, studying her for several seconds with steady eyes. And then he smiled, and narrowed his eyes a little bit at her, as if he was unsure whether he had just been accepted or scorned.

A few nights later, after they had finished eating their dinner, Willa worked with the man Nathaniel to clean the table and wash up the plates. Then she went into the main room and sat on the sofa in front of the fire with Scout lying on her lap while she stroked the dog's ears. She liked the touch of his soft white fur on her fingertips, and she knew by the way he nuzzled into her that he liked to be petted there.

The man Nathaniel sat at the kitchen table, and as he had done a few nights before, he picked up his little stick of wood and began to make marks on what looked like a very thin piece of dead tree skin.

"What are you doing?" she asked.

"Making a list," he replied. "I have to go down to Gatlinburg tomorrow to take care of some business. It's a long way, so I'll spend the night and be back the following day."

"Will you be taking the path where we saw the footprints of the loggers?"

"Not that one, but one similar that goes down the mountain toward town," he said.

"You will need to be careful," she said, and he nodded in quiet agreement.

Willa didn't know what Gatlinburg was, other than a swarm of humans at the edge of the world, and she didn't completely understand what he had told her or how it related to the symbols he was marking on the tree skin, but she nodded her head and pretended she did. She didn't know why she said she understood when she didn't, other than that she wanted him to think that she did.

She wanted to belong, to know things, to be part of things. She wanted all of this: the dog's soft ears, the crackling embers in the fireplace, the washing up after dinner, and the man sitting at the kitchen table.

"Listen," he said softly as he turned toward her. "All these nights, you've been sleeping in the tree in the yard. I was thinking you might want to come into the house, maybe sleep inside here with us, if that's something you would want to do."

Willa looked at him. She knew what he was asking.

"I'll be back in a little while," she said and walked out of the house.

She went down to the river, gathered cane stalks and willow twigs, and started weaving them together into a fine, soft mesh until she had made a cocoon.

When she returned to the house and the man Nathaniel

saw what she had made, he got up from the kitchen table.

"Come on," he said softly. "I have just the spot for it."

He took the cocoon upstairs, and she watched as he hung it from the ceiling in his room near the open window where she'd be close to the leaves and branches of the trees, and be able to look out across the canopy of the forest toward the rise and fall of the distant mountains.

Later that night, as they were lying there in the darkness, he in his bed with his dog Scout on one side and his killing-stick on the other, and she hanging from the ceiling in her cocoon, the moonlight shone through the window the same way it had the first night she had come here.

Just when she was about to fall into a deep and welcomed sleep, he spoke in the darkness.

"Willa of the Wood," he said softly, the sound of mystery in his voice, as if there were things in the universe that he just didn't understand. "That's who you are," he said. "You're my Willa of the Wood."

"Willa of the Wood," she whispered to herself, smiling. She liked the sound of that, and she liked the sound of Nathaniel saying it.

Her life as a thieving jaetter seemed so far behind her now, like a cold, murky season with few rays of light.

Through all their days and nights together, they had talked of many things, but she knew there was far more that they hadn't spoken of.

She had told him of her life in the forest, of climbing the mountain high and seeing the blue ghost fireflies, of the sounds of the birds in the morning and the thrill of rescuing a wounded panther. But she hadn't told him of her life as a jaetter in the Dead Hollow clan, or of the death of her beloved mamaw, or of all the things she had done in the past. The past was pain, seemingly for the both of them, and it was a dark winter she had no want to return to.

And about him, too, there were thoughts she knew she shouldn't think. There were questions she knew she shouldn't ask. Why did he journey up and down the river every day? Why were the other bedrooms of the house so empty? What was the agony that lay behind his eyes?

Willa woke early the next morning when it was still dark and went downstairs. Outside, the sounds of the night had died down hours before, but the sound of the morning birds had not yet begun. An eerie silence held sway.

Standing in the kitchen, she watched Nathaniel in silence as he packed supplies into his leather knapsack for his long journey through the forest down to Gatlinburg.

"I'll see you when I get back," he told her gently.

She nodded quietly.

"I know you know how to take care of yourself in these woods," he said, "but if those loggers come around here causing trouble when I'm gone, then you do that thing you do, make yourself scarce."

"I will," she agreed. Making herself scarce, as he called it, was just about the only thing she was good at.

She watched Nathaniel grab his rifle and head out the door with Scout at his side, the dog content to go wherever he was going.

She followed them out and then stood in the yard. Seeing them fade into the thickness of the forest, she felt a peculiar pang in her heart that she'd never felt before, and she prayed they'd be safe.

She'd never been to Gatlinburg, but she'd seen it from a distance. Why would he go to there?

As she went back into the house and walked through it alone, she was struck by how different it seemed, so quiet and lifeless now. It felt like a hollow wooden cave, long abandoned by those who had once lived there.

She didn't want to stay in the house without Nathaniel and Scout there, so she went back outside. One by one, the birds began to sing and chirp and whistle in the darkness, each one making itself known to the others around it, until the morning light began to fill the sky above the trees.

She felt an unusual restlessness. She wasn't sure what to do or where to go. She fed the goats and chickens, and then made her way to the river. She gazed at the water flowing among the large boulders, then walked along the river's path. She traveled downstream, staying close to the river's edge.

She had intended to walk just a little ways, but once she started, she couldn't stop. She just kept walking, pushing herself hard. She went hour after hour, the cold water of the river soaking her feet and legs when she crossed through its shallow pools, and the rough surface of the jagged rocks abrading the bare skin of her hands as she climbed over them.

She didn't know what she was looking for. But Nathaniel had done it every day, and it felt right to be doing it in his stead, taking the same course he had taken.

As she journeyed down the river, she kept a sharp eye out for whatever Nathaniel might have been looking for. She was determined to figure it out.

She saw a family of raccoons, a mother and three little ones, foraging for crawfish in the shallows with their tiny hands. Another time, she spotted a fox staring at her from the undergrowth. She often heard the rapping of the woodpeckers, which always brought a smile to her face.

But then she heard a different kind of sound in the distance.

She stopped and listened, tilting her head.

It was coming from across the river, a dull, repetitive, thudding sound echoing ominously through the forest.

Her stomach wrenched into a twisting knot. It was the sound of axes cutting into the living bodies of trees.

She sucked in a quick breath and pulled back from the river into the underbrush of the forest.

The loggers were getting closer every day. Nathaniel had warned her to stay clear of them, and she'd seen their destruction with her own eyes. She had no want to see it again.

She turned and fled through the forest for home, glancing back over her shoulder as she ran. Sometimes she paused near a tree, blended into the bark, and waited just long enough to listen, then continued on.

As she made her way, she wondered if Nathaniel had been journeying down the river every day to guard and protect his land from the loggers, but she didn't think so. He always went downstream and always stayed close to the water, but she knew much of his property was upstream as well.

By the time she got back home, she was wet and exhausted, with no more understanding than when she ventured out. Her journey down the river had been a failure.

When she came to the grove of sourwood trees that grew near the house, she finally slowed to a walk and caught her breath, relieved to be back. As she made her way across the open grass toward the porch, she glanced over to the meadow where she sometimes saw Nathaniel standing by himself. And there she stopped.

She gazed through the opening in the trees toward the field, wondering.

Why did he go there?

Why that particular meadow?

If he was reluctant for her to see him crying, then why didn't he go into the barn or the mill where she could not see him?

What refuge did the meadow provide his weeping soul?

Curious, she turned and walked toward the opening in the trees.

To her surprise, the hair on her arms began to rise up.

Her temples began to pound.

Something was telling her to stop, to not go into the meadow.

She paused, debating whether she should listen to the warnings, but she didn't want to stop.

She wanted to *know.*

She walked into the center of the meadow, a small green field dotted with purple fringed orchids. A lively flock of chirping goldfinches and shimmering-blue buntings feasted on the coneflowers that drooped in the long rays of the setting sun.

Then she noticed something on the ground at the far end of the meadow.

As she walked toward it, her heart beat slow and steady.

At first she could not make it out, for it lay in the shade of an old, gnarled black cherry tree with long limbs that hung low over the grass. But then she began to see.

Someone had laid stones on the ground in the shape of a large rectangle. Inside the rectangle, there was a single mound of dirt. The mound had been swept clean of sticks and other debris, and it appeared as if someone had carefully smoothed the dirt with their bare hands. Periwinkle and ivy had been planted all around, and bunches of flowers from the meadow and the nearby forest had been laid alongside. At the end of the mound stood a cross made of wood. And beside that cross there were three other crosses, side by side in the grass, one after the other.

She swallowed.

Suddenly she felt very small, like a leaf floating in the wind, without will or destiny, other than to just fall to the ground.

*These are human graves,* she thought.

Each of the four crosses had a small wooden plaque carved with day-folk markings. She stared at the markings for a long time. But she could not read them. Suddenly, there was a part of her that felt as separated from Nathaniel's world as she had ever been. But there was another part of her, deeper down, that felt their connection, and knew that at this moment in the flow of time there wasn't another person in the world who was closer to him than her. They had become twins of the soul.

As she walked slowly back to the house, lost in her thoughts, she knew she shouldn't ask Nathaniel about the graves.

She shouldn't ask about the names that were on them.

She shouldn't ask about what happened before she arrived.

It would destroy everything.

The next afternoon, when Nathaniel and Scout finally returned from Gatlinburg, Scout dashed across the grass and ran up to her, his tail wagging excitedly.

"Hello, Scout!" she said cheerfully as she knelt, put her arms around him, and hugged him. "Welcome home!"

Her heart swelling, she glanced up to Nathaniel, but his face was more worn and haggard than she had ever seen it. She expected bright news of his journey, but when their eyes met, he just shook his head in discouragement, and walked on toward the house.

After putting his rifle and supplies away, he trudged into the mill and went to work, clanking and banging, as if he were smashing thoughts from his brain.

When he came out of the mill, he went to the woodpile and split logs with his ax in a fit of violence, slamming his blade down harder and harder with each chop until there were no more logs to split.

That evening, as they sat across from each other at the kitchen table and ate their dinner, she watched him warily, wondering if his dark mood had passed.

He ate his venison piled high with a relish of mashed-up squash, apples, and honey, and shoveled heaps of sweet corn succotash into his mouth, but he made no comments and asked no questions.

"The other day," she said tentatively, "you were making marks with a stick on the skin of a tree . . ."

"I was using a pencil to write letters on a piece of paper," he explained, and she could tell by his tone of voice that he didn't mind talking.

"What do the letters represent?" she asked. "Does each one have a meaning?"

"No, not exactly," he said as he cut another piece of meat and put it in his mouth. "Each letter is a sound."

"How can that be, when the skin of the tree is dead and the letters are silent?"

"I'll show you," he said as he left the table and went upstairs. She heard his boots as he walked down the length of the hallway. He returned a few minutes later with a set of wooden blocks.

"This is called an *A*," he said, holding up one of the letters. "It represents the sound 'ah,' like the word *apple*. Each letter represents a sound that we write on the paper so that people can understand what we're saying to them."

"Even though they are not there . . ." she said, amazed by the magic of it.

Nathaniel nodded, pleased with her reaction, and picked up another letter. "This one here is an *H*. It makes a 'hh' sound, like at the beginning of the word *home*."

"What is that one?" she asked, pointing to a letter that looked like one she'd seen on the plaques by the graves. It appeared to be a jumble of three sticks.

"That's a *K*, like at the beginning of the word *kitten*. You see, the alphabet contains all the different sounds."

Willa paused, trying to understand. "So . . . any word can be made from these letters?"

"Yes."

"What about Faeran words?"

"Yes, I reckon so."

"What about the name Willa, how do you spell that?"

"W-I-L-L-A," he said, then wrote the letters on the paper so she could see what they looked like.

"And what about 'Alliw'?"

He looked at her uncertainly. "Did you say, 'Alley Ew'?"

"Yes," she said. "Alliw."

"Is that a name?"

"Yes."

"Well, the beginning of the name might be spelled A-L-L-E-Y or A-L-L-I," he said. "But I'm not sure about the ending. Maybe an E-W or just a W. So it might be A-L-L-I-W."

She watched as he carefully wrote the letters out with his pencil for her to see.

She looked at the two names side by side.

W I L L A and A L L I W.

*Twins,* she thought. *My sister and I were twins, even in our sounds, in our letters, like the left hand and the right hand painted on the wall in the cave.*

"So how do you spell 'Nea'?" she asked next.

"I would imagine that would probably be N-E-A," he said, and wrote the letters down for her. "You see, you've seen the *A* before, but the *E* and the *N* sounds are new. The *N* is 'nn, nn.' Do you hear it?"

"I hear it," she nodded, mystified and satisfied at the same time.

"Is this Nea a friend of yours?" he asked. "Maybe a bumblebee or a squirrel?"

"No," she said with a smile, knowing that he was joking with her. "Nea was my mother. And Alliw was my sister."

"Oh, I'm sorry, I see," he said. "They're beautiful names, Willa."

He looked at her for several seconds, as if he wasn't sure if he should ask her more questions. "And they passed away six years ago, is that right?" he asked tentatively.

"My parents and my sister died when I was six," she said, but did not say the rest, that it had been *his* people, human beings, who had killed them.

"I'm so sorry, Willa," he said, saying it with such sympathy it was almost like he knew the truth of it.

Sometimes she wondered how they had been killed, why they had been killed. Had it been the metal-clanging newcomers with their saws and their axes? Had it been a homesteader like him with a killing-stick? Whenever she tried to think about her parents and her sister, she kept seeing images of them running through the forest, and then the darkness of the underworld of Dead Hollow.

Frightened, she tried to change the subject. "What about the sound a bear makes when it's happy because it's found a log full of honey or the voice of a tree when it whispers in the wind? Can the Eng-lish letters make those sounds as well?"

"Ah . . ." he said uncertainly. "I think you got me on those. But most other sounds, you know, that folk like us might make."

Willa nodded, smiling.

"What's so funny?" he asked.

" 'Folk like us,' " she repeated. "I like that."

He smiled in return, understanding. "So why all the questions about letters all of a sudden? Do you want me to teach you how to read?"

"As long as I can hear your voice, why would I need to read?" she asked.

"It would let you hear other people's voices, their stories," he said.

"Like who?"

"People who are no longer living or who live outside the mountains."

Willa tried to understand what Nathaniel was saying to her. Could these letters of the Eng-lish truly bring voices from outside the world? Could they truly bring back the voices of people who had died?

"I'm not explaining it very well," he said. "Let me try again. People write things down, and then later other people can read them. I might write down the story of what has happened in my life. Or I might write down a story that I imagine in my head. Or I might write a letter to someone who lives in a different place, or a message to tell you how I feel about something."

Willa listened carefully to everything he said.

By the flickering light of a candle made from the wax of the bees, they talked long into the night, of letters, and sounds, and stories told.

Later, she sat in front of the fireplace with Scout lying across her lap as he usually did and gazed into the glowing embers of the sleeping fire. As Nathaniel roasted chestnuts in a black iron skillet over the simmering coals, he reminisced that he had learned how to farm vegetables and plant trees from his father, how to cook meals and roast chestnuts from his mother, and how to read and write from his grandmamma. Many years ago, when he was growing up, they had all lived in the house together.

The following morning, when Nathaniel grabbed his rifle and headed out on his daily journey down the river, she wanted to tell him that she had gone down the river after him while he was gone. But she didn't.

She wanted to say, *What are we looking for out there? I've been down that river. There is nothing to find there.*

But she didn't. She didn't question him or push him. She didn't want to upset him or anger him. There were no more logs to split.

But she knew there was one thing she needed to tell him before he left.

"I heard the loggers in the distance yesterday," she said.

"You heard them?" he asked.

"Far off, but getting closer," she said.

"I understand," he said, nodding gravely.

"So be careful," she said, looking at him as steadily as she could.

"I will," he said, and then turned and began his journey. The threat of the loggers had clearly disturbed him, but he still had to go.

She watched Nathaniel disappear into the forest.

When she was sure he was gone, she went outside and walked over to the meadow.

The morning mist was rising from the dew-covered grass, and bright yellow swallowtail butterflies were fluttering over the field of purple fringed orchids.

She stepped into the rectangle of stones, careful not to disturb them, then sat down in front of the first cross. She studied the letters that had been carved into the plaque.

The first letter she recognized.

"Apple," she said.

The second letter looked like two vertical pine trees with a horizontal branch in between them. She was pretty sure that was the "hh" sound Nathaniel had told her about.

The third looked like a two-twig sapling sprouting from the ground.

The fourth looked like the moon.

The fifth was a kitten.

And the sixth was another apple.

She tried to sound out each letter one at a time, and then she tried to blend them together. It came out sounding like a garbled mess.

But as she sat beside the grave in the rectangle of stones and studied the letters on the cross, she knew that she could not give up.

The name was the path she must follow.

That evening, when the man Nathaniel returned from his trek down the river, he looked bitterly defeated, his eyes cast down and his teeth clenched, like he'd been walking all day up and down the river, searching and searching but never finding. As he came out of the forest his left hand gripped his rifle, and his right hand opened and closed repeatedly into a pumping fist.

*He's angry,* she thought. *He's going to clank around the mill or go cut down a tree with his ax or commit some other act of violence. I'm sure of it.*

But then, as he walked across the grass toward the house, he lifted his eyes and saw her standing there on the front porch.

The frustration and the fury lifted from the lines of his face.

The change in his mood was like the passing of a storm from the rocky heights of the Great Mountain. He looked at her with his bright blue eyes—suddenly filled with something that was not anger, and not rage, and not sadness—and he said, "I'm glad to be home."

The next morning, when Nathaniel was gone, Willa sat cross-legged on the ground beside the mound of dirt and the four wooden crosses.

She had learned from her reading lessons with Nathaniel that the sapling with the two leaves sticking out made the sound at the beginning of the word *yearling*. And the moon sounded like the middle of the word *hope*. So she thought she finally had the letters she needed to decipher the first plaque. She stared at it for a long time:

AHYOKA

She sounded out the letters one by one. "Ah-ha-ya-o-k-ah," she said, but it didn't sound right. She had never heard of any kind of word or name that sounded like that. She tried it again and again, but it was still nonsense.

Frowning in frustration at the confusing mess of letters, she studied the next plaque hoping that it would be easier:

INALI

She thought she had learned the sound of the little stick at the beginning and end of this string of letters, and the gorge with the mountain slope in between, and the apple, and the sound of the bent branch in the fourth position. But she thought she must be getting the letters and sounds mixed up, because this didn't look like any kind of name or word she'd ever heard either.

Then she came to the longest of the names on the four plaques. It appeared to be made up of the same sounds as the other two words, but they were in a different order.

HIALEAH

"Ha-i-a-la-ee-a-ha," she stuttered slowly through the sounds.

"Ha-i-a-lee-a," she said again, this time blending some of the sounds. It was beginning to sound familiar to her ear.

"Hi-a-lee-a," she said slowly, but gaining more confidence. Then she said it again, more quickly this time. "Hi-a-lee-a."

She said it again: "Hi-a-lee-a."

And then she understood.

This wasn't an Eng-lish word or name.

And it wasn't Faeran, either.

It was *Cherokee.*

She looked at the plaque on the first grave.

AHYOKA

"Ah-yo-ka," she said in the Cherokee way. She couldn't help but smile a little at the sound of it. It sounded right. These could definitely be Cherokee names.

But then she drew more serious again, realizing what it meant. Why? Why were there Cherokee names here? Most of the Cherokee lived on the other side of the Great Mountain. Why would there be Cherokee names in Nathaniel's meadow?

She turned to the last of the four plaques and studied it.

The stick.

The snake.

The kitten.

The apple.

She began to sound out the letters one by one.

And then she stopped, halfway through the name.

She did not need to go further.

She already knew what it said.

Her mind filled with a dark and cloudy fear. A feeling as cold as death poured into her chest.

She had made a terrible mistake.

# 50

Willa studied the letters on the fourth plaque one by one:

ISKAGUA

It was a long name, and she didn't know the sounds for all of the letters. But she knew the first four.

"Iska . . ."

When she said the name out loud, it broke her heart.

It was the name of the Cherokee boy that she'd met in the Dead Hollow prison. And it was too unusual of a name for it to be a coincidence. It was him.

*The cookies,* she thought. *That's all I did for him. I fed him cookies!*

She had been frightened to see a human boy imprisoned in a hole. She had run away from him. She hadn't wanted to see him. She hadn't wanted to think about him. She hadn't understood why he was there, why they had captured him, and she still didn't. But she'd been able to put it out of her mind. He was a *human*, nothing she was allowed to concern herself with, nothing she was allowed to help. That was what she had told herself.

But now, she knew so much more than she had before. She had experienced so much since then.

Her palms began to sweat and her stomach churned. Her mind clouded with shame and confusion. He was a living person. How could she have done what she did? She had left the boy lying in a prison cell in the lair of the night-spirits. How could she abandon him in that place? How could she let him suffer like that? How could she let him die? She'd been taught all her life that humans were her enemy, killers of the forest, murderers of her people. But how could she let *anyone* suffer like that?

As children, she and Alliw had saved the sparrows that had fallen from the tree. And she had healed Luthien from the wound of a hunter's gun. And she helped the panther. What kind of fear and hatred had lived so deep in her heart that she could abandon a human boy to rot in a dark, wet prison?

She couldn't move her body. And her mind went numb. All she could do was stare at the boy's name on the plaque above the grave. *Iska*, she thought. *His name was Iska.* She knew he had probably died in the prison cell where she had left him. He had probably died because of what she did.

But her brows furrowed and she rubbed her eyes, her mind filled with intense confusion.

How did Iska and those other children end up in the prison of the Dead Hollow lair?

She thought about the woodpecker she had disentangled

from the fragments of a net, and the band of Cherokee searching for their children near the devastation of the loggers, and the net-traps she'd seen in the forest on the other side of the river.

She knew the padaran was sending his jaetters out to hunt and trap the animals of the forest for bounty. Had he sent his guards down into the valleys to hunt for human children as well? But why?

And if that was what happened, if Iska was captured by the night-spirits and then died in that prison, how did his body get back here to this grave? Did his body come floating down the river? Why were these Cherokee people buried in Nathaniel's meadow?

Her mind swirled back into the past. When she saw Iska in the prison cell, could she have saved him? Could she have gotten him out? She'd barely been able to get herself out of the Dead Hollow lair. But she hadn't even *tried* to save him, she thought in shame.

She rubbed her face in agony. But she couldn't let her mind get pulled into the painful, twisting darkness of everything she'd done and hadn't done, all the terrible mistakes she'd made. She had to think about what she was going to do *now*. What did all this mean?

One thing was certain. She couldn't pretend any longer that she didn't know anything, that there was no connection between the past and the present, between the life she had led before and the life she was leading now. She couldn't hide behind the rocks of unknowing. She had to talk to Nathaniel.

She wiped her eyes, got up onto her feet, and ran toward the house.

When Willa arrived, Nathaniel wasn't there. His rifle was leaning by the door, so she knew he must be nearby. She looked for him in the mill house and the barn, but he was nowhere to be found. Noticing that his beekeeping equipment was gone, she headed out to the clover field.

On her way there, a bee buzzed past her face.

"Hey! What's the hurry?" she shouted to the speeding bee.

Then three more bees started buzzing around her, angry and agitated. One landed on her arm and immediately stung her.

"Ow!" she complained, pushing it away. "What'd you do that for? That's going to hurt you a lot more than it hurt me!"

As she approached the hives, the loud buzzing noise of the bees seemed to be filled with an intense, all-consuming malevolence. The vibration of the enraged insects ran up and down her spine as they swarmed all around.

Nathaniel, in his bee suit, worked over the hives, clearly trying to figure out what was happening. He had taken several of the structures apart and was looking inside them.

When Willa gazed in, she gasped.

Once there had been order—with every worker bee performing her job to collect pollen, feed the brood, care for the queen, and protect the hive—but now it had descended into pandemonium. Hundreds of bees were attacking one another, their mandibles chomping in violence and their legs entangling in fierce battles.

"Can you make them stop, Willa?" Nathaniel asked her, his voice filled with desperation.

Willa tried to speak to them in the old language, tried to soothe them with her voice, but the bees wouldn't listen. They were swarming in a mindless riot of killing.

"There's the queen!" Nathaniel said, pointing toward the bee that had a much longer abdomen than the others.

"Get out of there, queen!" Willa called to her.

Normally the worker bees gave deference to the queen, moved out of her way whenever she was crawling, and turned to face her when she stopped. They pampered her, fed her, and cared for her in every way. But now Willa and Nathaniel watched in grotesque fascination as the worker bees surrounded and murdered their queen.

All five of the hives fell into chaos. Hundreds of bees swarmed in wild, erratic circles all around. A worker bee stung Willa, and then two more attacked as well. Others flew off into the forest alone where they would soon die without the rest of their hive. All order had broken down, and for the bees that meant death. They could only survive by working together.

Nathaniel stood helplessly over the hives, his arms hanging uselessly at his side, his head hanging down, and his expression a tight grimace.

"What caused them to turn on their queen?" Willa asked him, her mind filled with confusion, not just about the bees, but about the names on the graves in the distant meadow.

"I don't know. Maybe some sort of putrefaction in the honey or a corruption of the hive," he said as he watched the last of the bees crawling across the killing field of the honeycomb, murdered bodies strewn all around them. "It's a total loss. They're almost all dead, and those few who survive won't last long."

As Willa and Nathaniel trudged glumly back to the house, Nathaniel didn't say a word. She was anxious to talk to him about the graves in the meadow, but he stared at the ground as he walked, dispirited like she'd never seen him. She didn't know why, or what to say to him, but she put her hand in his to let him know that she was there.

When he gripped her hand in return, she felt the urgency of it, the gratefulness that she was there with him, and a rush of emotion poured through her.

In that moment, as they walked back toward the house, she began to feel in her heart the answers to the puzzles that her mind could not work out. As she realized what was happening, it felt like her chest was expanding with air.

"You weren't the one who started those beehives . . ." she said slowly.

"No," he said glumly.

"You were taking care of them for someone else . . ."

He nodded slowly as they walked, but he did not speak.

"Did the bees belong to Ahyoka?" she asked gently, using the name for the first time.

The name, saying it out loud between them, with respect and care, was like a bridge over a dark and turbulent river.

He sighed, as if he knew the time had finally come. "Yes," he said. "The bees were Ahyoka's."

"And she was Cherokee . . ."

Nathaniel nodded again. "Ahyoka was a respected member of the Paint clan, the great-great-granddaughter of a famous chief."

Here he paused, as if he was uncertain whether he could continue through the emotion roiling through him. "And Ahyoka was the love of my life," he said finally, his voice cracking.

"The love of your life . . ." Willa repeated in a whisper of amazement. They were not words that she had ever heard in the Dead Hollow lair, but she knew in her soul what they meant.

"Ahyoka and I were married for fifteen years," Nathaniel said.

As Willa gazed at him, all the connections came together in her mind like the water of the three rivers becoming one. Suddenly she could see all the pieces of the broken world.

"What's wrong?" Nathaniel asked, seeing the troubled expression on her face.

"How did Ahyoka die?" she asked, her voice trembling.

Nathaniel shook his head in discouragement. The wrinkled

lines around his mouth and the pain in his eyes seemed to be filled with anger, sadness, and guilt all at once.

"I've been fighting the railroad and the loggers in every way I can," he said, "filing complaints with the county sheriff, disrupting town meetings, and trying to organize the other homesteaders to make a stand against them."

"And your land . . ." she said.

"That's right," he said. "The loggers have come to hate me, but to make matters worse, my land here on the river blocks their path upstream, so they're unable to take their railroad farther up the mountain. They've been sending their enforcers up here, threatening me and my family, scaring off my livestock, sabotaging my mill, doing everything they can to shut me up or drive me out."

"But why? Why have they come here into our mountains?" Willa asked in dismay.

"They're enterprisers, businessmen," Nathaniel said. "They've cut down all the forests up in the north, so now they're moving through the Southern mountains. They're meaning to come up here to Clingmans Dome and cut these trees, too."

"Which trees?"

"All of them," he said in disgust. "They're clear cutters. They don't believe in picking and choosing, letting some grow and harvesting others. They take them all."

Willa swallowed hard, remembering the destruction. "I've seen it," she said.

"Then you know what I'm talking about," he said. "That's where all this began."

He shook his head again, holding his lips tightly together and breathing through his nose, as if he was trying to find the strength to continue.

"I started a fight I couldn't win," he said, his voice grave and laced with regret. She could see that he was berating himself, racked with not just sadness but guilt.

There were so many questions swirling through her mind, and so many things she wanted to tell him, but through all that, all she could feel in her heart was a deep and abiding sorrow for what Nathaniel had been through. She could see that it had been bad. It had been unbearable to him.

She knew she didn't want to hear the story, but she held on to his arm, and said, "Tell me what happened to your wife . . ."

Nathaniel stopped walking and turned slowly toward her. She thought he was going to look at her, but his head stayed down.

"A whole gang of them came into the house in the middle of the night," he said, his voice low and struggling. "There must have been twenty or thirty of them . . ." As he was talking, he just stared at the ground and shook his head, as if he was living through it all again in his mind. "Ahyoka and I tried to fight them. I got off several shots. I think I killed at least two of them, then tore into them with my fists. Scout got hold of one them, too. I've never seen him fight so hard . . . But it was so dark, and then four of them grabbed hold of me . . ."

When his words faltered and dwindled down to silence, Willa slowly touched his arm to let him know that she was still there for him, still listening.

He raised his eyes and looked at her. "I tried to fight back," he told her. "I tried to save Ahyoka. I tried to save my children! But one of the attackers stabbed me with some sort of pike or spear, and the other hit me in the head with a club and I went down hard . . ."

He pressed his lips together and stared back down at the ground, pulling air in through his nose. Finally, he said, "Then I was out . . ."

"Your children . . ." Willa said, her voice catching in her throat. That was what she had heard: He had said, *I tried to save my children.*

"I've gone through it in my mind a thousand times," he continued, "but I don't know what happened next. When I came to, it was morning, and my wife and children were gone."

A sickening feeling welled in Willa's stomach. She had to make sure that she truly understood what had happened. She had to hear the words in her ears, not just see the Eng-lish letters scratched on plaques of wood in the meadow.

"What were your children's names, Nathaniel?" she asked him. "Tell me their names."

"My daughter Hialeah was twelve years old, so strong and brave. I remember hearing her screaming in the other room, fighting to protect her little brothers."

Nathaniel paused, unable to continue for a moment. Willa felt her heart pumping pulses of blood through her body as she waited for the name she knew would come.

"My little baby boy, Inali, was just five years old. And my oldest boy was ten. We named him in honor of his great-great-grandfather. His name was Iskagua."

Willa knew he was going to say the name before he said it, but her stomach still tightened at the sound of it.

"Iska . . ." Willa whispered in despair.

She closed her eyes against the tears, just trying to breathe as intense heat filled her face with pain. She wanted to cry, to turn away and hide. It seemed so long ago, like a different world, like a different her. But she had left Nathaniel's son in the prison. She had left him there with the spear-stabbing guards and the teeth-chattering jaetters. Iska had been Nathaniel's son, and she had just left him there to die!

"Why did you say his name like that?" Nathaniel asked her. "That's what we called him. We called him Iska."

"I know . . ." she said, her heart breaking.

How could she tell him that she'd seen his son alive, that she had actually talked to him, but that she had abandoned him in a dark, vile prison to die alone? Her mind swam with confusion and guilt and fear. There were still so many things she didn't understand.

"Tell me what happened next," she said, looking up at Nathaniel. "What happened when you discovered your wife and children were gone?"

"I looked all over the house for them. I thought maybe they had escaped or hid someplace. I knew that Ahyoka would never give up fighting for the children. And Hialeah was a very resourceful girl. But Scout kept barking and pulling on me, telling me he was onto something."

"Onto what?" she asked.

"He could smell them," he said. "When he ran out the front

door, I followed close. We tracked their scent across the yard and down to the river. And then, when we reached the bank, I saw . . ."

Nathaniel choked on his words so hard that he had to stop midway through his sentence.

He pressed his face into his hands, pulled in a long, deep breath, and then exhaled.

"I've never felt pain like that in all my life . . ." he said so softly that she almost couldn't hear it. "I remember I collapsed onto my knees . . ."

"Tell me, Nathaniel . . ." Willa urged him.

"The stones of the riverbank were spattered with blood, and my children's clothing lay all over the ground. That's when I realized what the attackers had done . . ."

"What?" Willa asked in dismay. "What did they do?"

"They killed them all and threw their bodies into the river," he said.

"I . . ." she began to say, but her words faltered. She was too shocked to speak.

"They killed them all," he said again, as if it was necessary for him to feel the full pain of it.

"The night I broke into your house . . ." she said.

"I wasn't in my right mind," he said. "And I haven't been since."

"Down the river . . ." she said. "That's where you've been going every day."

"That first morning, I started searching for them. I found my wife downstream, her body pinned against a rock under the water.

I had to use a rope and pulley to get her out. I nearly drowned in the process. There was a point when the river was trying to pull me under that I wanted it to win. I wanted to let the river take me like it took her. I wanted to get out of this world."

"But you didn't," she said softly, trying to find some hope in that.

"I *couldn't*," he said. "I hadn't found my children's bodies, so I couldn't go. Not yet. I couldn't stand the idea of my children in that cold water. When I finally got Ahyoka out of the river, I carried her home, dug a grave in the meadow, and buried her. I kept her wedding ring because I knew she'd want me to have that, for us to be together."

"Tell me what happened to your children . . ." Willa said.

"I was exhausted after digging Ahyoka's grave, but I went back out and continued the search for my children's bodies. I've been looking for them every day since, scouring the banks of the river and the whirlpools and the deepest holes, but it feels like every day I don't find them they slip farther away from me."

Nathaniel slowly shook his head. "I'm at a point where nothing has any meaning anymore, where it's time for me to leave this world, but I can't. I can't think straight. I can't do anything. I'll find no peace in my life, or in my death, until I find their bodies and can bury them beside their mother."

"But there are four crosses . . ." she said.

"I couldn't let them go, couldn't accept a world without them. It just didn't feel real. So I had a memorial service for them, just Scout and me, trying to come to terms with what had happened. I put the crosses next to Ahyoka's and I prayed for their souls like I had found their bodies, like it was a real funeral. I thought that might help me to accept that they were gone, but it didn't . . ."

Willa held his hands in hers as she listened to the words pouring out of him.

"It just makes me angry," he said. "Those loggers are still out there, still slashing down trees. I heard their infernal machines on the other side of the river this morning. Their scouting crews are getting closer every day. I haven't been able to stop them legally, but if they come anywhere near my land, I'm gonna raise a living hell like they've never seen. I went down to Gatlinburg looking for justice for my wife and children, but when I accused the railroaders and the loggers, the sheriff turned stone cold. He didn't believe a word of what I told him. He looked at me like I was crazy. Most of those men down there are bought and paid for, too many people making good wages with the railroad and the lumber company to let anything get in the way of it. Their enforcers have started spreading rumors that they saw me beating my wife and hurting my children. Now the sheriff is investigating me for the crime of what happened to my family."

As she listened to his story, a thick and heavy feeling caught deep in Willa's throat. In this one moment, it felt as if she could see all the broken pieces of the world in a way that no one else could. And one of those broken pieces was her.

She knew that what Nathaniel thought happened hadn't happened. The loggers hadn't been the ones who attacked his family. And what the detectives thought happened hadn't happened, either. Like the two men arguing whether the earth was flat or round, they were both wrong. The world was mountains.

But how could she tell Nathaniel that her own people had attacked his family? How could she tell him that she had seen Iska in a night-spirit prison and left him to die? If she told him what really happened, he'd go through the cruel pain of Iska's death all over again. It would destroy what little was left of his clinging soul. And it would shatter the life that she and Nathaniel had shared together for these last few weeks.

She racked her mind trying to figure out if it was in any way possible that Iska could still be alive, that he could have somehow survived in the prison all this time. Why were the night-spirits capturing and killing human beings? What use did the padaran have for children?

She tried to think back to what she'd seen in the lair. Who was the bronze-faced/gray-faced padaran, the god of the clan? How was he able to hold such terrible power over those who had once been such a good and honorable people?

She was so deep in the convolution of her own thoughts that when the dog burst into a fit of wild barking she jumped in surprise.

"What is it, boy?" Nathaniel asked Scout as the dog carried on barking, staring out into the forest.

Willa's ear twitched. "Wait," she said, touching Nathaniel's arm to hold him still. "I hear it now, too."

It was faint, but she could definitely hear the sound in the distance.

*Thud. Thud. Thud . . .*

"What are you hearing?" Nathaniel said, the tension rising in his voice.

The incessant pattern of the sound seeped into Willa's chest like black leeches. *Thud. Thud. Thud . . .*

"I hear axes . . ." she whispered.

Nathaniel's face filled with anger. "It's those godforsaken loggers!"

He started walking fast toward the house, more upset than she'd ever seen him.

"What are you going to do?" Willa asked in a panic as she hurried to catch up with him. He was in no condition to confront the loggers.

Nathaniel stormed into the house, threw down his beekeeping equipment, and grabbed his gun.

"Come on, Willa," he said as he charged out of the house and headed into the forest. "We're going after them."

Nathaniel stormed out of the trees, gripping his loaded rifle in his hands, and bore down on the loggers. Scout charged with him, growling viciously. But Willa stayed in the undergrowth. She wasn't a fighter or a killer. She couldn't threaten or shout or intimidate. She'd be lucky if they could even *see* her.

A crew of twenty stubble-faced, hard-bitten lumbermen had come with horses and a wagon full of saws, mauls, chains, and axes. They had already felled one beautiful black cherry tree. Half a dozen axmen were chopping off its limbs as the teamsters harnessed the horses. Two men with a six-foot-long, jagged-tooth saw had already cut halfway through the trunk of a second tree, an old oak that looked as if it had stood for more than 150 years.

"Stop!" Nathaniel shouted. "This is my land! You have no right to cut these trees!"

One of the men, gripping his ax, walked up to Nathaniel, and shouted, "It's a free country, ain't it!" into his face.

"We can do anything we feel like," another man said as he chopped the limbs of the tree. "Isn't that what freedom means?"

"You don't have a permit to cut here," Nathaniel said.

An older man, grizzled and one-eyed, spat out a dark brown stream of chewing tobacco onto the ground. "We don't need no stinking permit."

"I'm Nathaniel Steadman," he said, facing off with the boss of the crew. "I own this land."

"It's forest," the boss said. "No one owns the forest. It's public land. Free for taking."

Willa's muscles tensed as several of the other lumbermen walked up to stand in front of Nathaniel beside the boss. They weren't going to back down.

"Ain't Nathaniel Steadman the name of the man who done beat his wife and killed her?" one of the lumbermen said.

"Is that true?" the boss asked, squinting at Nathaniel's face. "That you? You kill your wife?"

"No, I didn't kill my wife!" Nathaniel said. "You can't just come in here and start cutting!"

"Who says I can't?" the boss said. "You? How you gonna stop me?"

"I've got a God-given right to protect my land," Nathaniel said, brandishing his rifle.

The man standing next to the boss slammed the butt of his ax into Nathaniel's face.

Willa's whole body jolted with the shock of it. She lurched forward to help Nathaniel, as he toppled to the ground.

Scout charged in and bit the attacker, but the man kicked the dog in the head and swung his ax at him. Scout leapt back and dodged the blade, then sprang forward and clamped onto the man's wrist, snarling and biting.

Nathaniel tried to scramble back up onto his feet, but three of the men rushed in. They kicked him in the sides and punched him with their tightened fists. They struck him with the handles of their tools.

Willa cried out and tried to block their blows, but there was nothing she could do. They beat him, one punch after another. She felt every blow against Nathaniel's head like it was against her own. Every kick to his side struck her ribs.

With tears smeared across her face and anger welling up inside her, she threw herself to the ground on all fours and gripped the thick roots of the nearby trees.

"If you want to live, then you must help us!" she shouted in the old language. There was no kindness in her voice, no compassion. She was demanding this, screaming at the trees. "I know you can help him! Do it now or you're all going to die from the cuts of their axes!"

Driven by sheer desperation, Willa focused her mind down into the ground beneath her. She drew upon everything her mamaw had taught her of the forest and the trees and the flow of the world. She intertwined all that she had learned on her own of the tendrils of growth and the bend of limbs. And she reached deep into her woodland spirit, weaving the most powerful woodcraft she could imagine in her mind. The earth, the water, the root. The trunk, the branch, the leaf. It was all hers. She called out a string of old Faeran words that had never had a meaning in the Eng-lish and never would. They were the ancient phrases of her people, the summons of her ancestors to rouse the ire of the trees, to bring movement to roots that hadn't moved in a hundred years.

The tree roots that ran along the ground all around her and beneath the feet of the lumbermen began to vibrate in agitation. The roots creaked and bent, pushing against the ground around them. Then the roots broke up through the earth like long, quivering, clutching fingers. Willa sucked in a startled breath, astonished by what she had done. She pushed into her fear and carried on. The roots of the trees were moving to her command, like slithering snakes from the ground, twisting and grasping, trying to touch everything around them. They were the *mireroots*, the primeval spirits of the trees, coming to life.

As the earth itself erupted around them, the eyes of the lumbermen went wide with terror. Their faces filled with expressions of shock. The writhing roots coiled around their legs, clamping onto knees and calves. The branches of the forest trees thrashed back and forth above their heads as if angered by a violent storm.

One of the men tripped backward and fell. The mireroots intertwined his arms, his legs, his throat, sucking the life and nutrients out of him like he was the earth itself. His skin withered and cracked, his fingers shriveled into broken twigs, and his eyes turned into black seeds of what they had been.

The other men shouted and screamed, and tried to flee. In

a fit of wild panic, one lumberman swung at a mireroot with an ax, but the blade ricocheted away and struck deep into the shin bone of his companion. The man shrieked in agonizing pain and collapsed into the clutching death of the mireroots as the other men backed away in horror.

Several of the men leapt onto horses and galloped away. Others just ran. But the one-eyed boss pulled the rifle from his horse's saddle and aimed at Nathaniel, thinking he was the cause of all that was happening. Scout charged forward and leapt at the man just as he pulled the trigger.

Willa watched in relief as the terrified loggers fled in panic, tearing away by foot and by horse.

When they were finally gone, she let go of the tree roots and collapsed to the ground in exhaustion.

She lay in the dirt, shaking and gasping for breath, just holding on to the steadiness of the earth.

The branches of the trees stopped thrashing.

The roots retreated slowly back into the ground.

The screaming storm of violence that had filled the world just moments before faded into an eerie silence.

The badly wounded Nathaniel lay on the ground a few feet away, cradling his dog's limp body in his arms.

"No, not you, Scout," Nathaniel cried as he hugged his dog to his chest.

There was blood and bruises all over Nathaniel's face and

head, and she knew he must be in terrible pain, but he wrapped his arms around his dog and held him.

"Not you, boy, not you!" he wept as he stroked Scout's head.

And then Nathaniel looked over at her and met her eyes. "We've got to help him, Willa. We've got to help him . . ."

But Willa knew it was too late.

The logger's gun had done its damage.

Scout's spirit was gone.

The last living member of Nathaniel's family was dead, taken from him by the forces of the world.

"I'm sorry," she said, as she wrapped her arms around Nathaniel. "I can't save him." And Nathaniel wrapped his arms around her in return, holding her like she had never been held—holding her as if she were the very last being on earth he could hold on to.

After a long time lying on the ground with Nathaniel and Scout, Willa rose, and she pulled Nathaniel slowly up onto his feet. She put her shoulder under his arm and they limped back to the house in silence.

As he slumped down, bloody and wounded, into his bed, she tried to say gentle words to him that might soothe him, that might help him through the pain of his loss, but she knew that her words meant nothing. Nathaniel had suffered too much. He'd lost his wife, his children, and now his dog.

She wanted to tell him that she'd seen Iska alive, to give him hope, to give him something he could cling to. But she knew she couldn't. Not at this moment. Not like this. After all the time that had passed, Iska was probably dead by now. She couldn't hurt Nathaniel with this new uncertainty, this new pain, the agony of knowing that he might have been able save his son if he'd only known where he was.

As she thought about what to do, she went out and gathered seal berries and herbs from the forest. When she returned, she applied poultices to his bloody cuts and bruises, trying to help him in any way she could.

He lay in the bed without moving, his eyes glazed with hopelessness.

She wondered again whether she should tell him about what she had seen in the prison. She knew it wasn't right to hide what she knew from him. But if she told him about seeing Iska in the night-spirit lair, he'd drag his bleeding, damaged body up onto his feet, grab his rifle, and head up the mountain to find his son. It would be impossible to stop him. He'd go with or without her. But there was no way he could make it up through the ravines and ridges to Dead Hollow. And she couldn't bear the thought of him collapsing in exhaustion and lying dead and alone among the rocks. She couldn't bear the thought of the jaetters getting hold of him the way they had her grandmother.

But as she wet a rag and cleaned the dirt and blood from the wound on Nathaniel's head, she was already beginning to see what she must do.

She didn't want to do it. She didn't want to leave. She didn't want to go back up there to that dark place. She knew she was probably going to die. And if, by some thread of strength, Iska was still alive, and by the grace of the Great Mountain she managed to get him back to his father, then she knew what would happen next. And it would break her heart.

From what she'd seen and experienced all her life in the withered lair of Dead Hollow, love was a rare and tenuous thing, families small and fragile and dying. Love was a thing that shattered. It was a thing that could not last.

She had finally found in Nathaniel a place for her heart to live. And it felt like a shaded, magical forest dell unlike any other. But if she succeeded in returning Iska to him, and maybe even his other children if they were still alive, then she knew everything would change. Nathaniel would have his real family back, his *human* family, the family he'd been searching for and yearning for. The family he truly loved. His need for her and her strange night-spirit ways would fade away like mist from the top of the mountain, all around her in one moment, then drifting away in the next, as if the Great Mountain was saying, *You've had enough now, little one. It's time for you to go . . .* And she knew it was a pain she could not bear.

But despite what was going to happen, she knew in her heart that she had to go.

Nathaniel lay in his bed, broken and wounded, body and soul, mourning not just his dog Scout but his beloved wife and children. Willa knew that one way or another, whether she lived or died up on the mountain, whether she succeeded or failed, this would be the last time she would ever see him, the last time she would ever touch his shoulder with her hand, or hear his voice.

As the man Nathaniel's eyes finally drifted shut and he fell into a troubled sleep, she wanted to say *Thank you* to him, thank you for all that he had done for her, for the kindness he'd shown her that first night in the barn and every day they'd been together since. And she wanted to say how sorry she was about everything that had happened, what had come before, and what had come after.

But as she turned and went downstairs, she couldn't find a way to say any of these words, or express any of these feelings, in the new language or the old. And although he had taught her some of the Eng-lish letters, she did not yet know how to write the sounds of feelings on the skin of trees.

So she walked outside alone, made her way across the grass, and disappeared into the forest.

It was just the way she had come.

Willa followed the edge of the river like she had many times before, but traveling upstream now, against the flow of fate, against the flow of time, back toward the world she came from.

She made her way high up into the mountains, through the darkening forest as the mist rose up into the moonlit trees and the owls took wing.

Hours later, she finally came to the rocky gorge that led into Dead Hollow.

The Watcher—the weathered carcass of the upside-down tree wedged between the narrow walls of the ravine—loomed over the path, a black guardian against the enemies of the clan.

*And tonight, that's me,* she thought.

She had told herself that she'd never come back to this dark and wretched place. But here she was again. She wanted to turn away, to skulk back down the mountain and slip quietly into her soft cocoon hanging in Nathaniel's room. She wanted to go back to Scout and pet his ears, and run and play with him in the soaring groves of trees. But she knew she couldn't. Her life with Nathaniel and Scout had been destroyed by four symbols on a piece of wood and a logger's gun.

She had no choice now. She knew what she had to do. But she felt the weight of it in the pit of her stomach as she watched bands of jaetters and guards moving in and out of the entrance of the Dead Hollow lair like hornets around a nest.

It struck her how the members of her clan always ventured out of the lair in groups. *There is no I, only we.* But when she had been a thieving jaetter she liked to go out on her own, to use her own skills and make her own decisions. She hadn't even realized at the time how much that had set her apart from the others, how infuriating and incomprehensible it had been to Gredic, and how suspicious it had seemed to the padaran.

*Now there is an I,* she thought. *I, the woodwitch, the weaver, the jaetter, the thief. Move without a sound, steal without a trace. That's what I'm going to do, steal without a trace, just like old times.*

But as she gazed at the Watcher, she knew if she walked in through the front entrance of the lair they'd swarm her and kill her on sight.

And she suspected that the prison guards had probably found the crack in the stone she had used the last time. They were probably guarding it or had blocked it off. It was no use to her now.

This time, she needed a different way in. Something small.

Something quiet. And something that would reserve her strength for the battles to come. One of the things she had learned as a jaetter was that nights of thieving were long and filled with many perils.

She pulled back into the forest and headed for a nearby stream to find some help.

A short time later, she crept through the dripping understory of the blackened trees that grew along the back walls of the lair. The shuffling, tail-dragging movement of her new allies followed just behind her.

When she finally came to the spot that she thought was nearest to the prison, she whispered "Here" in the old language, touching her fingers to the base of the wall.

The two beavers moved forward and started chewing, chomp after chomp with their sharp, strong teeth, cutting their way through the thick layers of interwoven sticks.

Three of the beaver colony's young kits, and two of the adults, had been trapped and killed by the jaetters for the bounty on their fur since she had last visited the colony. It seemed impossible, but the Faeran of the Dead Hollow clan, who had once lived in harmony with all living things, had become their gravest enemy.

"Thank you, my friends," she whispered when they finished boring a small hole through the wall for her to fit through. "It's going to get bad from here on, so you better get back to your lodge. Stay safe."

As she crawled on her hands and knees through the dark, slimy hole, her stomach tightened. She loathed the smell of it, the closed-in feeling of it. But how could she have stayed with Nathaniel knowing what she knew? How could she abandon Iska to the night-spirit guards if he was still alive? He was Nathaniel's son!

She crawled through several feet of densely layered sticks, then finally made it through to the other side.

She slowly peeked her head out and looked around. The hole hadn't brought her directly into the prison but into one of the lower tunnels of the lair. She checked one way and then the other for any signs of the guards. For now, her path looked clear.

*Move without a sound. Steal without a trace,* she thought again as she crept carefully out of the hole and crouched down to the floor.

She stayed very still, listening for the faintest sounds in the distance, her quills oscillating, ready to detect the slightest movement coming in her direction. Every sense in her body was tuned to the take.

She dashed up the tunnel quickly and quietly, scanning ahead. She reached one turn and then another, making her way toward the prison.

It was hard to imagine that the boy Iska had survived very long in the cruel conditions she had seen him in. The prison guards had seemed determined to make sure he wouldn't last. The small hole they had crammed him into hadn't been much larger than his curled body, and the guards hadn't even been feeding him.

It seemed even less likely that his brother and sister had survived. She'd seen no signs of them at all.

But she had no choice now. For Nathaniel's sake, one way or another, whether they were alive or dead, she had to figure out what had happened to them, or Nathaniel would drive himself insane searching up and down the river for their bodies.

If she could somehow find Iska in the prison and escape with him, it would be the greatest take a jaetter had ever achieved, to steal a human being right out from under the noses of the night-spirit clan.

She came to a corridor where she could hear the sounds of footsteps and voices just ahead. She stayed close to the wall, and moved slowly forward.

As she peered around the corner, a guard ran toward her, spear in hand. She threw herself to the wall, wove herself in, and disappeared just as the guard ran past her.

Before she could even take a breath, two more guards came down the corridor dragging a screaming human girl behind them. The girl flailed her body in wild, jerking motions, lurching one way and then the other, trying to escape the guards, but the guards had clamped onto her wrists with their bony hands and would not let her go.

"What's wrong with this one?" the larger of the two guards asked, as they dragged the girl down the corridor.

"It keeps trying to escape," the other guard said. "Lorcan said that it wasn't cooperating, so we should throw it into the abyss."

Willa watched in horror as they pulled the screaming girl away.

They were taking her toward the labyrinth where they

would heave her into the black void of the bottomless pit and she would never be seen again.

Willa's fists tightened and her jaw clenched. A desperate need to help the girl welled up inside her. But she didn't know what to do. She couldn't leap out in front of the guards and suddenly overpower them. She felt so helpless.

*Get what you came for,* she told herself fiercely, trying to focus her mind. *Find your take and go.*

She moved deeper into the prison, sneaking unseen and unheard from shadow to shadow, blending here and darting there. She soon found herself surrounded by wailing, captured children crammed into prison cells up and down the corridor, guards shouting at them through the lattices in the cell doors. Some of the children were wounded and weak, others strong and defiant and fighting back. But what struck her was that the humans were still here—and at least some of them were still alive.

It seemed as if the guards were holding the various prisoners in different types of cells, feeding some extravagantly and starving others, talking to certain children in kind words, but then isolating the others in total darkness. She couldn't figure out why the guards were doing all this. But somehow, it felt strangely familiar to her. There was something about it that reminded her too keenly of her own nightmares.

*Just get what you came for,* she told herself again, and tried to continue on. *You're a thief. Find your take and go.*

Deeper down in the prison, where there were no guards, she followed a long, winding tunnel with dozens of cells no larger than holes for curled-up bodies. Little human fingers reached out through the lattices of woven sticks as she went by. She tried to push her way through the dark, nightmarish confusion, but the sounds and smells were unbearable.

Finally, she came to the cell she was looking for, where she had fed Iska the cookies.

She crouched down and peered into the darkness of the hole. The body of a young, dark-haired boy lay crumpled on the floor.

*"Wake up,"* Willa whispered into the cell.

But the boy did not reply.

*"Iska, wake up!"* she whispered again, louder this time.

But the boy in the cell did not move.

She looked up the corridor, knowing that a guard could come running in her direction at any moment, and then she turned back to the cell.

"Iska, it's me, it's Willa," she said. "You've got to get up. We've got to go!"

But still the crumpled shape in the cell did not move.

She felt her world starting to close in, the heat rising to her face, and it was getting more and more difficult to breathe.

Her hand trembled as she reached slowly into the darkness of the cell to touch the body.

"Iska . . ." she said again as she put her hand on the boy's shoulder. But he did not respond.

She shook him to rouse him, to make sure he was all right.

But still he did not move.

She reached over and put her hand on his bare arm.

His skin was cold.

Too cold.

She swallowed hard, and then she slowly withdrew her hand.

She peered through the lattice of sticks, trying to get a different view of the boy lying on the floor in the cell. She had to see his face to be sure.

*It looks like him . . . But the hair . . . Maybe the hair isn't right . . . It's dark brown, not jet-black like Iska's had been.*

When she finally found an angle where she could see some

of the boy's face, she realized that it wasn't him. She didn't know who this poor, dead boy had been, but he wasn't Iska.

But whoever he had been, he didn't belong here on the floor of this cell. There had to be someone out there looking for him, someone who loved him, someone like Nathaniel or her mamaw, someone who had been a part of his life, and he a part of theirs.

She looked down the corridor, her heart so overwhelmed with emotion that she couldn't stir herself to move.

The only thing that brought her back was that none of this made sense. *Why are they treating the various prisoners so differently? Why are they taking care of some but not others? What are they doing to them? What is the purpose of all this?*

As the questions raced through her mind, she remembered something from years before. She and Gredic were lying bloody and beaten on the forest floor on the first night of their initiation as jaetters.

She realized that the guards weren't treating some of the prisoners well and others badly. They were treating them all badly at first—breaking them down—then slowly feeding them and taking care of them, making them more and more dependent and obedient.

*They're initiating them,* Willa thought in horror. *They're adopting these children into the clan and turning them into jaetters.*

And she knew the reason why. She had seen it all her life, in the crumbling ceiling of the great hall, in the echoing corridors and empty dens, in the stories her mamaw had told her of the many years past. The Dead Hollow clan was dying. There had been fewer young ones born every year.

When the padaran took her into his rooms behind the throne, she had seen the fear in the depths of his mind and the lengths to which he would go to save the clan. He had adopted the tools and weapons of the humans. He had taken on their language. He had even started killing the animals of the forest, something no Faeran of old would ever do. But even with all the changes he had made, the clan continued to wither year after year.

She could see now that the padaran had ordered the night-spirit guards to capture these human children for a purpose. If children weren't being born, they'd be stolen, brought up in the ways of the clan, and grafted into the jaetter life by force. The padaran would train them just as he had trained her and Gredic and the others—with food and care, and threat and violence, all in careful measure, until they were faithful servants of the clan. *There is no I, only we.* She hadn't had a choice about whether she was part of the Dead Hollow lair. She hadn't had a choice about whether she wanted to be a jaetter. And neither would they.

But looking now at the body of the dead boy lying in the cell, she knew that some of these children weren't going to make it. They were going to die here. The guards would drag their bodies to the labyrinth and throw them into the black abyss.

Hopelessness welled up inside her. She looked down the corridor of cells. How could she ever find Iska in all of this? How did she know he wasn't already dead and gone?

Gathering up her strength, she moved down to the next cell and peered in.

"Iska?" she whispered, but without hope. A little girl groaned and looked up at her with pleading eyes. Willa felt a pang in her heart, but she knew she couldn't help the girl. There were just too many of them.

*Get what you came for, Willa,* she told herself again. *Get your take and go.*

She pushed herself on to the next cell.

"Iska . . ." she whispered.

But every hole she looked into offered a new nightmare.

Willa checked cell after cell for Iska, but she could not find him.

She went down one of the lower side corridors to a place where the cells were mostly empty. It seemed to be where they were isolating certain prisoners in an unused part of the prison.

"Iska, are you here?" she whispered into the darkness.

She didn't find him in those cells, either.

She went down another side corridor and kept looking, using her eyes, her nose, her ears, every sense in her jaetter body focused on finding him.

*Find your take, Willa,* she kept thinking.

"Iska . . ." she whispered into the next cell, trying to keep her voice from losing hope, but the cell was empty.

"Help me!" came a gasp from farther down the corridor.

Willa ran forward to the cell door and looked into the hole.

A pair of brown eyes peered out at her, filled with hope.

"Iska!" she said, her heart leaping with joy.

"It's me," he said, their fingers touching through the lattice of sticks.

"I'm so glad I found you," Willa said.

"I knew you'd come back!" Iska said excitedly.

She could hear the sounds of Nathaniel's voice in his. Iska was so much a part of her now. And he was alive! Iska was actually alive!

She didn't remember giving him any indication that she'd come back for him, but it broke her heart to think that he'd been waiting for her to return all this time.

She pressed her fingers against his through the lattice of the interwoven sticks, just holding on to them. There was so much to tell him.

"Do you live in this place?" he asked. "Who are you? Where do you come from? Do you have food?"

"I'm a friend of your father's," she said, ignoring the rest.

Iska's face flushed with relief and happiness. "Is he all right? Where is he? Is he here?"

"No, but he's been looking for you."

"I knew he would be," Iska said, nodding his head.

The boy seemed to have been living on nothing but hope in his time here, hoping for her to bring him food, hoping for his father to rescue him. But Willa could hear in Iska's tone of voice that he had known it was quite possible that his father was dead.

"What about my mother?" Iska asked, his voice ragged with fear. He seemed to already know what Willa was going to tell him.

"I'm sorry, Iska," she said, her voice trembling. "Your mother passed away the night you were captured."

She had seen the light in Nathaniel's eyes when he spoke of Iska's mother. She had seen the life Ahyoka had lived with him in their home. She had cared for Ahyoka's goats and her bees, and she had sat on Ahyoka's grave and read her name.

"Your father buried your mother in the meadow by the house," she said sadly.

Iska's lips pressed together as he slowly nodded his head and wiped the tears dripping from his eyes. "I saw her lying on the ground," he said. "By the river . . ."

"I'm so sorry, Iska."

"But who are these creatures?" he asked fiercely, looking at her through the lattice. "Where are we? What are they doing with us down here?"

"You're in the lair of the night-spirits," she said. "They've been capturing human children."

"But I don't understand. What do they want with us?"

"For you to join them," she said gravely. It didn't seem possible, but she knew that was what they were doing.

*"Join them?"* Iska said in horror.

She was relieved to hear from the revulsion in his voice that there was still some fighting spirit inside him.

"I've come to get you out," she said. "To take you back to your father."

"But I can't get out of this cell," Iska said. "I've been trying to dig through the sticks, but it's impossible."

"Step back away from the door," she said.

As Iska followed her instructions, Willa put her hands on the door that separated them. "You're not going to want to watch this. Turn your eyes away. Quickly now."

"What are you going to do?" Iska asked, but in that instant, the door boiled into a wall of writhing, undead sticks and collapsed onto the floor into a slimy pile of twisting black worms.

Iska wrenched away in startled terror. "Oh my god, what is that?"

"I told you not to watch!" Willa scolded him as she reached inside, grabbed his arm, and pulled him out of the cell.

"Come on," she said, gesturing for him to follow her up the corridor.

"We need to get my brother and sister," he said as he followed her.

"I'm sorry, Iska," she said, as they quickly turned a corner. "I haven't seen them."

"I know they're here someplace," he said. "My sister wouldn't give up."

"But where are they?" she asked.

"Please, Willa," Iska said. "We can't leave without them."

Willa's stomach tightened as she looked uncertainly into the darkened bowels of the rest of the prison. She knew how difficult it was going to be to find two more prisoners in the chaos of all these cells and get them out alive. But she knew that if it was Alliw who was imprisoned here, she could never leave her behind. It was the bond that could not be broken.

"All right, we'll start looking for them," she said. "Starting down here in these side tunnels."

As they ran through the lower tunnels of the prison, searching from cell to cell, Willa's legs pumped beneath her, propelling her forward. Her eyes scanned ahead, looking for danger at every turn. Iska ran beside her, trying to keep up, and whispering his sister's name into the cells.

The corridors of the prison had already been dangerous for her, but with Iska in tow, they were far more so now. His skin was alarmingly consistent in color from one moment to the next, and was sure to give them away.

"You've got to run faster!" she whispered back to him as they raced through the tunnels. "If they catch us, we're dead!"

She shouldn't have even said it.

At that moment, three guards came running down the corridor, spears in hand.

# 59

Willa hurled herself against Iska and pinned him to the wall with her body, then blended into the brown surface of the woven-stick wall just as the guards came.

"What are you doing?" Iska whispered.

"Stop wiggling!" she hissed beneath her breath as she pressed herself against him.

As the guards rushed down the corridor, Willa saw that the larger of the two was Lorcan, the commander.

"I've been feeding the prisoners in the upper cells just as you ordered," the smaller guard said. "But two of them won't eat, and there's one in the lower cells who has tried repeatedly to escape. It bit one of my guards."

"Keep culling out the weak ones," Lorcan told him. "And the next time the one in the lower cells tries to escape, drag it out of here and throw it into the abyss. They need to obey or they die."

Willa smelled the stench of the guards' bodies as they passed. When they had finally gone out of sight, she exhaled a long breath of relief and uncovered Iska.

"How did you—" he started to ask in amazement, but she grabbed his hand and pulled him down the corridor in the opposite direction from the guards. If they were going down into the lower levels, then she was going up.

"Just trust me, Iska," Willa said. "Follow me as fast as you can."

They ran up through one tunnel after another, turning corner after corner, up through the main corridor of the prison, then down the side tunnel and the many turns that followed, until they finally came to the hole she'd used to sneak her way into the lair.

"Crawl in there and hide," she told him.

"What? I can't," Iska protested. "We need to find my brother and sister."

"Just listen, Iska," she said. "I'll go back into the prison for your brother and sister. I swear I will. But I can't have you with me. You're too conspicuous."

"Because of that thing you do with your skin," he said.

"That's right," she said. "I can blend, but you can't, so I need to go alone."

"I'll wait here, but we've got to find them," he said.

"Listen to me," she said, grabbing his hands as hard as she could and looking into his eyes. "If I don't return, it means I failed and you need to make it home to your father on your own. If I don't come back, you've got to get out of here without me."

"I understand," he said, nodding. "Be careful."

She had put on a good front for Iska's sake, so that he'd follow her instructions, but as she ran back up the corridor toward the prison cells, she felt the bile rising up in her throat. Her whole body was filling with dread. A terrible premonition invaded her mind.

*You're not going to survive this, Willa,* she thought as she ran.

She had lived in the vast Dead Hollow lair all her life, but after the time she'd spent in the forest, she realized what a truly lifeless place it had become. It had once been the hidden domain of the forest folk, her people of old, living in harmony with the trees and animals around them—the woodwitches sculpting its glorious, green, living walls—but now it had become a dark and sapless hiding place. She had always known that her powers didn't work well in the unnatural lairs of the day-folk, but this place wasn't much better. After years of the padaran, there was nothing left here but rotting sticks and dead souls, lifeless Faeran followers who'd given up on the beauty of the world.

*You were born here and you're going to die here.* The words came into her mind as she turned the final corner toward her fate.

Without her animal allies and the full powers of the forest, how was she going to find Iska's brother and sister? How was she going to fight off the guards? There were no living trees, no wolves or bears or otters—nothing she could draw on for strength and no one to ask for help.

*You're not going to make it,* she thought as she ran toward the prison cells.

Willa turned the corner and immediately came upon two guards near the entrance of the prison. She jerked back, pinned herself to the wall, and blended.

"That human has been fighting hard," one guard was saying to the other as they came out of one of the larger cells.

"Then don't go easy on it," the other said. "The harsher you are, the faster it will break."

Her skin crawled as the guards walked right past her. She waited for them to go up and out of the prison toward the main area of the lair before she moved.

At that moment, an idea came into her mind.

The answer had been right here in front of her all this time, but it had taken the guards to remind her.

The shouts and screams that she'd been hearing, the pleading eyes peering out at her through the lattices of the cells . . .

She had thought there was no one who could help her. But that was wrong. There *was* someone who could help her. There were *many* who could help her. They all had mothers and fathers to get home to. They all had brothers and sisters like Iska. And she was surrounded by them.

There were no animals or trees she could draw on here, but there was something else. In each of these cells there wasn't an "it." There was a "he" or a "she." There was a *human being*, a living, breathing, thinking soul, with wants and desires just like her—someone fighting to survive.

She quickly crept over to the closest cell.

"Hey, I'm Willa, what's your name?" she whispered.

"I didn't do anything. Why am I here?" the voice asked angrily.

She couldn't see the prisoner in the cell, but it sounded like an older human boy.

"I'm sorry, I didn't put you in here," Willa said as she studied the outside of the door. "But I'm going to get you out."

"Who are you?" the boy asked, coming to the lattice and looking out.

"My name is Willa, and I need your help."

"I'm Cassius," the boy said, his voice strong and determined now, almost hopeful.

The doors of the cells were bound tightly shut from the outside with knots of vines. Every time she used her power to reanimate the twisted dead sticks of the lair, it sucked the energy out of her, so she knew she couldn't continue with that. It was a slow process, but she pulled and pried at the vines with her fingers, hoping to unfasten them.

"You're green," a small female voice said behind her.

Willa turned to see a little girl's pale face peering out at her through the lattice of sticks on the other side of the corridor. The little girl looked like she was no more than seven years old, and Willa could see the streaks of the tears that had fallen down her cheeks.

"Yes, sometimes I am," Willa said. "What's your name?"

"Beatrice," the little girl said in her tiny voice.

"I'll come for you next, Beatrice," Willa said as she finally figured out how to unfasten the vines and open the door to Cassius's cell.

"We don't have much time before the guards return," she said to Cassius as he came out of the cell. He was about fourteen years old, and had dark brown skin and short black hair. "Now listen," Willa said. "Do you think you're able to run?"

"Yeah, I can run," Cassius said, nodding.

"I want you to take Beatrice," Willa said as she opened the little girl's cell. "Can you do that?"

"Yeah, I can do that," he said. It sounded like he'd do just about anything she asked him at that moment.

"All right, good," Willa said, looking up and down the corridor for any signs of approaching guards. As Cassius took Beatrice into his arms, she told him exactly what he needed to do. "Go up this first corridor a little bit, but take an immediate left, follow it around the curve, then turn right, then left, then two more lefts, and then down . . ." She could see he was listening intently to everything she said. "If you encounter any guards, then pull back into the shadows and hide. If they corner you, then watch out for their spears. They're very sharp. When you reach the escape hole, there will be a boy there named Iska. Tell him Willa sent you. He'll show you the way out. Do you understand?"

"Yeah, I got it," Cassius said, holding Beatrice. "We're ready."

"Now go, Cassius, run! And tell Iska to expect more."

# 61

In the next cell she found an eight-year-old girl, gave her the instructions, and sent her limping on her way.

One door after another. Cell after cell. Prisoner after prisoner. She freed them as fast as she could untie their doors, asking them if they'd seen the two children she was looking for, and then telling them to run, to hide, and to help each other get to the hole. "If you see the guards, run as fast as you can!" she told them.

*That's twenty-three so far,* she thought, as she went to the next cell. The more she freed, the more she knew the guards would come. They'd hear the noise. They'd see the commotion. Every child she freed put her further from her own freedom.

A little boy with freckled skin, ragged red hair, and a muddy face touched Willa's arm as two of the other children ran up the corridor.

"I've seen her!" the boy said. "I saw the Cherokee girl. She was in the cell across from me when I was down in the bad part. She kept telling me not to give up."

"The bad part?" Willa said. "Where is that?"

The red-headed boy pointed farther down the corridor. "There's a tunnel off to the side that goes to the right, through an area where there's been a cave-in, and then curves way down deep. It's the third door."

"Thank you," Willa said. "Now run."

As the boy made his escape, Willa ran in the opposite direction, down into what he had called the bad part of the prison.

The rotting ceiling sagged so low that she had to duck beneath it to get through. Other areas she had to climb. Black mold coated the woven-stick walls. A dank, unbearable stench filled her nostrils. Finally, she came to the third door and peered into the darkness.

Willa saw the arms and legs first, all folded up in the corner of the cell. The hands, the thighs, the whole body was wrapped around something.

The brown skin of the arms and legs was dirty, scraped, and bruised. The long black hair was matted, hanging all around the arms and legs and the thing inside.

And then the eyes opened and looked at her, brown in color, and staring warily back at her.

*She's alive,* Willa thought in relief.

The girl's arms and legs pulled inward, wrapping more tightly around the small boy she was protecting in the bend of her body.

"Whatever you are, stay away from us," the girl said, her voice laced with intense fear as she jerked deeper into her cell. "Get away from us!"

Willa pulled back, startled.

Crammed down in this darkened cell, this girl had been through too much.

Willa slowly crouched to the floor, lowering herself so she looked less threatening, and spoke in her softest voice.

"My name is Willa," she said. "I'm a friend of Iska and your father, and I'm here to help you, Hialeah. If you'll let me, I'm going to get you and Inali out of this cell."

Hialeah stared back at her in shock. It appeared to be the first time anyone had said her name in weeks.

"How do you know my name?" she asked.

*I saw it written on your grave,* Willa thought, but she did not say it. "I know your father," she said. "He told me all about you and your brothers."

"You're going to get us out?" she asked in amazement, her voice filled with disbelief and uncertainty. "Is this a trick?"

Willa slowly opened the cell door.

"Don't come any closer!" Hialeah shouted at her, holding her crying brother tight to her body.

"I'm not coming in," Willa said, moving back away from the door. "The choice is yours . . ." she said, speaking so softly now that she knew the girl could barely hear her. "Iska's waiting for us, Hialeah. But we don't have much time. We have one chance to get out. And that chance is now. But we've got to run. We've got to fight. I'm not certain we'll succeed. If they catch us, they're going to kill us. But we have this one chance, to either cower down here in this cell, or to run for home. Which do you want to do, Hialeah?"

Hialeah stared at her, still holding her brother. "I want to run," she said.

When Willa extended her hand, Hialeah took it. She pulled the girl and her brother out of the cramped confines of the cell. As Hialeah rose to her feet, Willa saw she was surprisingly tall, with a long, lean body, and arms and legs to match. She had long, straight black hair that fell down to her waist, and her face was filled with stern determination. Her little brother, Inali, clung to her chest, looking around with bewildered eyes, but he'd stopped crying. It seemed as if Hialeah had been holding and protecting her little brother for weeks. It was the bond that could not be broken.

"We've got to hurry," Willa said, leading them up the corridor.

When Willa began to run, Hialeah ran with her. The girl had been resistant to trust her at first, but now that she understood what they needed to do, she was moving quickly. When Willa ran faster, Hialeah stayed right with her. The girl's legs were strong, and pumped hard. She and Willa ran side by side, both of them scanning ahead and looking behind them, ready for the worst.

"Just hold on, Inali, I've got you," Hialeah whispered to her brother as they ran. "We're getting out."

When they came to an obstruction in their path where part of the old tunnel had caved in and blocked their way, Willa climbed up on top of it and then reached down. Hialeah handed Inali up to her, climbed up herself, then took her brother back into her arms on the other side.

As they ran through the corridors past the other prison cells, Willa could see that they were all empty. She had freed every last prisoner she could find.

She, Hialeah, and Inali ran down winding tunnel after winding tunnel.

"It's not much farther," Willa told them.

As they turned the final corner, Willa saw the last of the escaping children at the end of the corridor. They were getting down onto their hands and knees and crawling frantically into the hole. Only one small face remained peering out.

"Iska!" Hialeah cried out with relief.

Willa's heart swelled with hope. They were going to make it! They were all going to make it!

But then a rushing sound rose up behind them, the pounding of many feet and the clatter of weapons.

"Run!" Willa screamed at Hialeah, then turned to stand her ground against the coming guards.

The first guard charged toward her and thrust his spear. Willa leapt back just in time. But another guard attacked from the other side. There was a swarm of at least a dozen of them.

"It's the jaetter!" Lorcan shouted, looming above the other night-spirit guards as he pushed through them to reach her. "It's Willa! Get her!"

Two of the guards charged in, stabbing frantically. Willa dodged and dodged again. She glanced back behind her to see

Hialeah running for the hole with her brother in her arms.

A guard lunged forward and grabbed at Willa, but Willa leapt out of his grasp. Lorcan jabbed in with his spear. Willa tried to leap to the side, but the sharp tip grazed her leg and sliced through her skin with a painful, ripping tear.

That's when Willa realized that Lorcan's spear wasn't just a wooden stick like it had been before. The tip had been equipped with one of the flint arrowheads that she herself had provided to the clan, so sharp that it could easily slice through muscle and bone.

One of the other guards thrust his spear and stabbed her in the arm. Bolts of pain radiated through her shoulder and hand, driving a scream from her lungs. She tried to dodge the next stab. She tried to fight them all. But it was no use. She couldn't hold them off any longer. She turned and fled for the hole.

She could feel herself getting farther away from them with every step she took. Her heart swelled with hope that she was going to make it. But as she ran away, Lorcan pulled back his arm and hurled his killing spear like a javelin. It shot through the air and struck her in the neck with a shocking blow and knocked her to the floor.

She looked down toward the end of the corridor, and the last thing she saw was Nathaniel's children disappearing into the escape hole.

Her body lay facedown, flat across the floor. Searing pain throbbed from the wound where the spear had cut through the flesh of her neck. She couldn't lift her head to see the guards charging down the tunnel toward her, but she knew they were coming. She could hear their shouting. She could feel the pounding of their footsteps in the vibrations of the floor. She had seconds to live. And after stabbing her in the heart with their spears, the guards were going to grab Iska, Hialeah, and Inali as they tried to crawl to their escape.

Somehow, some way, she had to stop the guards. Nothing else mattered to her.

She closed her eyes, pressed her hands to the woven-stick floor, and conjured up the darkest woodcraft she had ever used. She had grown up asking the tendrils of the plants around her for their gentle assistance, and she had learned how to move the living trees with the force of her will. But this was different. To bring these old sticks back—to waken the dead—she had to infuse them with her own blood, her own life. She had to let the vile black twigs absorb the nutrients of her soul. It had weakened her every time she did it, dragging the life from her body. But she had no choice. She pressed her bloody neck wound against the floor, infusing it with the last of her living power. She could feel it sucking the life from her blood so rapidly that she flooded with cold. As the guards rushed forward to grab her, the floor beneath them erupted into a slime of black and twisting undead sticks.

The first guard screamed in horror as he fell through the wormy floor. The writhing, grasping sticks sucked the life from his withering body as he plummeted into them. She gasped in astonishment when the wave of his energy coursed back through the floor around her. And then something jolted up into her body, filling her with a surge of strength she'd never felt before. For just a moment, the floor had become the roots, and she the tree. The remaining guards recoiled in shock and fear.

"She's a woodwitch!" one of them screamed, as they all backed away and fled.

Gasping for breath, she climbed up onto her feet, her arms and legs shaking, not just from exhaustion but from the pulsating force that had wicked up into her body. She pressed her trembling hand to the bleeding wound at her neck as she stumbled toward the hole in the wall.

All the other children had crawled through the hole and

escaped the lair. Only Iska, Hialeah, and Inali remained. They were waiting for her. When they saw her coming, they rushed forward to help her.

"Your wound is bad," Hialeah said, quickly tearing pieces of fabric from her dress and beginning to work on Willa's neck. "We've got to stop the bleeding."

"I gave us a few seconds, but Lorcan and the other guards will go around to the other side and find another way through," Willa gasped. "You need to crawl through that hole and don't come back."

"But, Willa—" Iska tried to interrupt her, but Willa kept talking.

"On the other side of this hole, you need to run as fast and as far as you can. Climb the ridge, and then head west through the forest until you reach the creek."

It hurt to talk. It hurt to move. Her neck throbbed. She could see that blood was all over Hialeah's hands as she worked on the bandage—but unlike Iska, who was just shaking his head in refusal, Hialeah was listening intently to every word she said.

"When they realize what's happened, the night-spirits are going to send out search parties looking for you," she told Hialeah. "They can see far better than you can in the darkness, so don't travel at night. Follow the creek downstream, and look for a very small cave in the rocks. Crawl inside and get down into the water to hide your scent. Stay quiet and hidden until morning. When the sun rises, many of the night-spirit guards will return to the lair. That will be your chance. Follow the creek the rest of the way downstream until it joins up with the river, and then follow the river all the way home. The journey will be difficult, Hialeah. Many hours and many miles. But you can do this. Get your brothers home to your father. That's what you need to do. Do you understand?"

"I understand," Hialeah said, looking at Willa with steady eyes as she tied off the last of the bandage. "I'll do it."

"No!" Iska said, grabbing both of them. "You've got to come with us, Willa!"

"She's not coming," Hialeah said, her voice grim and steady.

"I'm sorry, Iska, she's right," Willa said. "I'm not going with you, and you'll not see me again after this. I'm going to stay here. I'll close this hole behind you and lead the guards away so they won't know where you and the others have gone. Now that they've seen me, they're going to be looking for me. The one who kills or captures me will gain great pride in the clan. In the meantime, if you and the others can get far enough away, then you'll have a chance."

"You can't give yourself up," Iska said, shaking his head.

"You're not listening," Hialeah said. "She's made her decision. She doesn't want you with her."

"I only need one more thing," Willa said, looking at the two of them. "Your father taught me some of the letters of the Eng-lish words, but we weren't able to finish."

"Tell me what you need," Hialeah said.

"While I was at your house, I learned how to spell my mother's name, but not my father's. How do you spell 'Cillian'?"

As Hialeah quickly spelled out the letters for her, Iska tried to keep arguing. "Willa, no, don't give up on us. Forget about all this. Come with us." But even as Iska said the words, Willa's mind focused on the sounds of her father's name, and she heard the echoes of the distant past, of the forward and the back, the left and the right, and the River of Souls. She turned back to Iska knowing more than ever what she had to do. "No matter what else happens, Iska," she said, "the most important thing to me is that the three of you get back to your father. He loves you and he needs you. Do you understand? You must get home."

"But what are you going to do?" Iska cried. "You can't fight them all alone!"

"I'm not going to fight them," she said. "And I'm not alone."

The last she saw of Iska, Hialeah, and little Inali, they were crawling through the hole and escaping into the darkness.

The moment they were gone, she pried and twisted the sticks at the edge of the hole with her fingers, pushing and pulling them, weaving one stick into the other, her bloody fingers dancing across the old rotting bark until the sticks began to move on their own, sucking the life force from her skin and her bones, intertwining like black, slithering snakes until the hole was closed and the snakes went still.

As she lay crumpled against the wall, trying to keep herself steady, she imagined Iska and Hialeah escaping from the lair with their little brother, running through the forest with the other children. *Keep running,* she told them in her mind. *Keep running.*

A roar of sound came rushing down the tunnel from the upper part of the lair. Pounding feet and pumping legs, laboring breaths and shouting voices, clattering spears and chattering teeth, and a thousand other sounds, all crashing toward her.

Holding the blood-soaked bandage to her neck, and knowing what she must do, she slowly rose to her feet to meet them.

Her eyes glazed as she waited for them.

She could see it in her mind. She could see it all. The long withering of the Faeran race and the rise of the padaran, god of the Dead Hollow clan. The steel traps, the captured children, and the glistening face. The words of guiding wisdom, the towering strength, and the missing voices. The running parents, the screaming sister, and the red flowing stream beneath the lair. She could see it all.

But even through the winter of all of this, there had still been a trace of hope in her mamaw's voice when she taught her the lessons of old, and there had been a glare of anger in Gillen's eyes when she saw the injustices in the padaran's hall—and these were the saplings that might someday grow into the light once more.

When twenty guards came charging down the corridor, she couldn't help but suck in a startled breath. She wanted to run, to blend, to hide, but she stiffened her legs the best she could and made her stand.

In her mind and her spirit, she detached herself from the world, like a branch broken from a tree, from the sound, from the fear, from the pain that she knew was to come.

Lorcan charged forward and slammed the butt of his spear into her face with a battering blow that knocked her to the ground.

She lay flat out, facedown on the floor, spasms of excruciating pain radiating through her head and neck.

She lay there on the floor very still.

She closed her eyes.

She slowed her heart.

She stanched the bleeding of her wounds.

And she stopped breathing.

"Is she dead?" one of the guards asked, jabbing at her limp body with his spear.

Lorcan crouched to the floor and clamped onto her neck with his hand to hold her securely in place as he leaned down and listened for her heart.

He listened for ten seconds.

And then thirty seconds.

And then he rose back up to his feet.

"She's dead," he said.

"Tie the body's hands," Lorcan ordered bluntly.

Two of the guards immediately knelt down and bound her wrists with vine.

"Now drag it," Lorcan said.

As they dragged her down the corridor, Willa let her body fall limp and her head hang low with her hair covering her face.

As they pulled her along the floor, she took a quiet, unnoticed breath and slowly released a few beats of her heart, pumping just enough blood through her body to stay alive.

She knew where Lorcan and the other guards were taking her.

Time was all she needed now. Time for children to run. Time for children to hide. Time for children to escape out into the world and return to the arms of their mothers and fathers where they belonged.

She heard the hisses first, then the snarls and the jeers, and she felt the air change as the guards pulled her into the Hall of the Padaran, which was already crowded with hundreds of the Dead Hollow clan.

The other Faeran spat at her and shouted at her, enraged with her treason against the lair.

Her fellow jaetters were worst of all, snapping and biting at her as the guards dragged her through the clamoring crowd, her legs scraping along the floor.

"Traitor!" Kearnin and Ciderg shouted as they leapt forward and struck her limp form, sending bolts of pain through her body.

As she glanced through the narrow slit of her eyes, out through the tangled fall of her hair, she saw Gredic watching, too stunned to speak or move, as they dragged her dead body past him. She could see her old friend Gillen, too, her face filled with despair. And many of the Faeran in the crowd stood in aghast silence at the sight of a dead girl being brought before them.

Finally, Lorcan grabbed hold of her and threw her body brutally onto the floor at the padaran's feet.

The slamming pain reverberated through her bones, but she did not cry out, and she did not move.

"The woodwitch is dead!" he declared. "May the wisdom of the padaran always guide us."

The padaran sat on his throne staring down at her body with grim satisfaction, his shoulders hunched and his quills raised all around his neck and head, making him seem even more massive than he was. There was a bandage wrapped around his right foot, but the skin of his face and arms glistened with the bronze, sparkling colors of his divine power, and his eyes blazed with certainty.

As she lay there on the floor, Willa thought that she had

been here before. She had been dragged. She had been kicked. She had been hissed at and attacked. But she knew that this would be the last time she would ever be hauled before the padaran. This would be the last time she would ever see the ancient Hall of the Glittering Birds.

Through all the strikes and all the pain, Willa had pulled herself inward. She had not fought back. She had not cried out. She had taken the punches and the kicks, the bites and the spits. She had taken it all. She knew that death was near. But when it came, it was going to be in her own way.

All she needed was time.

She lay wounded, tied, and beaten on the floor in front of the padaran, but she did not feel defeated. She had given Nathaniel's children a hole to crawl through and the time they needed. She imagined Hialeah leading her two brothers through the forest. She could see them climbing through the rocks of the creek. They were going to make it home.

"Nothing has any meaning anymore," Nathaniel had said to her, but now it would. She had saved his children. She had saved Nathaniel.

She slowly released the muscle of her heart, and let it start beating again. She felt the blood beginning to pump fast and strong through her veins. She began to take air into her lungs, in deep, steady breaths.

As she lay on the floor, she slowly lifted her eyes and looked around her at the padaran and the jaetters and all the members of the clan.

It was finally time to do what she had come to do.

Lying crumpled on the floor of the great hall, with her hands still bound at the wrists, Willa slowly raised her head and began to gather herself together.

Gasps of shock and confusion erupted from the crowd as they saw her moving.

"She's alive!" Gillen yelled, rushing through the other jaetters to try to help her, but the massive Ciderg grabbed Gillen and shoved her back.

"Willa is moving!" someone in the crowd yelled.

"But she was dead!" shouted one of the guards who had seen Lorcan strike her down. "Her heart was stopped!"

Everyone watched in disbelief as Willa, with her hands still tied, leveraged herself onto her shoulder, got her legs beneath her, and slowly rose to her feet.

A wave of murmurs and fear ran through the crowd.

She stood a few feet in front of the throne and looked squarely at the padaran.

The padaran stared back at her, his lip curling with malevolence. Unlike many of the others in the great hall, he didn't appear frightened that she had risen from the dead. He seemed to be thinking through the best way to kill her in front of all the members of the clan, to make her an example of what happened to those who raised their voices against him. But he showed no signs of fear that she possessed some unnatural power that might actually be a danger to him. And it was at that moment that she knew for sure that her hunch about him was right.

*It's all a trick,* she thought, *a disguise, a blend. It always has been.*

The padaran rose from his throne and stood to his full height in front of her and the onlooking crowd, the majesty of his glimmering quills raised around his head, and his steel spear of power gripped in his hand.

"You dare to stand in front of me?" he snarled.

"I stand in front of whoever I choose," she replied.

"You're a traitor to the clan!" he roared, raising his spear at her.

Willa tried to stand tall, but Lorcan struck the back of her legs with the shaft of his spear and sent her crashing painfully to her knees. "Kneel before your padaran, you vermin!"

"She's a traitor!" someone yelled from the crowd.

"She attacked the padaran with the steel traps of the humans!" one of the jaetters hissed.

"And she released the prisoners!" a guard shouted. "They've all escaped!"

"Traitor!" people started screaming all around.

"String her up!" Ciderg bellowed, raising his muscled arm.

Willa scrambled back up onto her feet as a wall of enraged, mottled-gray faces and tightening fists came toward her. Gredic and his pack of gnashing, hissing jaetters surrounded her with the rest of the attackers. Gillen and a few others pushed toward her and struggled to help her, but they were powerless against the mass of bodies.

The mob of people surrounded her, grabbing her on all sides. She felt hundreds of clawed fingers gripping her arms, her legs, her hair, her neck. Her skin crawled and twitched as their hands and bodies pressed against her. She tried frantically to escape, to wrest herself away from them, but they were all around her, drowning her in their grasping hands.

She felt as if she was moments from death, but then a thought poured into her mind.

*The River of Souls.*

She could see it, and she could hear her mamaw's voice in her mind.

*You are forever among your people,* her mamaw had told her. *The past, the present, and the future to come.*

Doing everything she could to steady her fear, she stopped struggling or trying to get away from the mob of Faeran around her. She looked into the grimacing faces of those trying to hurt her. And she looked into Gillen's eyes as the girl fought to protect her. She looked at them all.

*Believe,* Willa told herself. *Believe in your people.*

Pulling in a deep breath, she stood in the middle of the

thronging crowd, stretched her bound wrists above her head, and screamed in the old language, "I want you all to stop right now!"

The startling sound of the Faeran words echoed across the hall, up into the decaying wings of the ancient sculpted birds that adorned the ceiling.

Gasps rippled through the crowd: the little woodwitch had dared to speak the old language in the Hall of the Padaran!

"Just stop!" she screamed again, this time in both the Faeran words and the Eng-lish, so that all of the people could understand her. "Just stand still and listen to me!"

The crowd watched in awe as the vines binding her wrists began to move of their own accord, twisting and twining with life until they unfurled from her hands, and fell away to the floor.

Lorcan charged forward to slam her with the shaft of his spear like he had before, but she caught the shaft of the weapon in her hand and instantly melted it into a writhing wooden snake and threw it to the ground.

The crowd shouted in dismay and shrunk back in fear.

"Listen to me," she said as she looked out across the many faces. "You know my name is Willa, and I've been a loyal member of this clan all my life. I just need you to listen to what I have to say . . ."

"Listen to her!" Gillen shouted.

"She's a traitor!" one of the jaetters hissed.

"Let the little one speak!" yelled one of the other Faeran in the crowd.

"I did not come here to die," Willa said. "And I did not come here to fight you or harm you . . ."

As she continued speaking, she felt many of the people in the crowd moving closer, trying to hear her. They were pressing in on her, but it had a different feeling now. They were listening, touching her with their hands, crowding around her.

"I came to the great hall this night to speak to all of you about *Naillic*."

It was as if she had thrust a stick into a hornet's nest. A buzz of whispers and agitation whirred through the crowd. Suddenly the movements in the room began to shift. She felt new forces driving toward her, others pulling away.

"I've heard the word before," someone said.

"What does it mean?" asked another.

"It's forbidden!" one of the jaetters whispered.

"Don't say it!" another hissed.

"Death will come!" one of the older Faeran shouted.

"Don't say the word!" someone warned.

"But it's not just a word," Willa said. "Naillic is a *name*, the name of a Faeran boy who was born in this clan."

"Seize her!" the padaran screamed from the dais of his throne.

Lorcan and the other guards shoved forward to follow his orders, but it was too late. The crowd had engulfed her in a river of Faeran bodies, a River of Souls.

Willa pointed toward the padaran standing by the throne. "Those who knew the truth have been killed. Those who raised their voices have been silenced. The memory of the past has been pushed from our minds. But I came here to tell you that his name is Naillic. He is not an all-powerful, glistening god. He's a normal, mortal Faeran just like the rest of us!"

"Don't let her speak another word!" the padaran screamed at his guards. "Kill her!"

The guards pushed into the mass of people, shoving with their arms and stabbing with their spears, forcing their way toward her, but shouts of terror and anger rose up from the crowd. Gredic and many of the jaetters attacked, biting and clawing their way toward her.

The mob of people around her rose up into a swarm, like bees around a developing queen of a new hive, pressing in on her, protecting her.

"He claims to be the great leader of the clan," she shouted above the rising clamor of the crowd. "He says that we must always stick together, that we must always care for one another, but has he cared for the ones we love?"

"She's a traitor!" Ciderg spat as he tried to fight his way through the crowd to get to her.

"She speaks the truth!" one of the elders called.

"Don't trust her," someone shouted.

"She's a woodwitch!" somebody else screamed.

"Trust in the padaran!"

"Let her speak!" Gillen shouted out. "Listen to her!"

"Kill her!"

Feeling the rise of the clan all around her, Willa turned toward the padaran and pointed at him. "We all know that all Faeran are born with a twin to whom we are bound and connected for the rest of our lives—the left hand and the right, the forward and the back. But where is your brother, Naillic? Where is Cillian? Where is the man who was my father?"

She had finally said the words she had come to say. And when she said them, all of the Faeran in the great hall stared up at the padaran in utter shock, slowly coming to realize the full meaning of her accusation. Hushed murmurs of confusion and uncertainty ran through the crowd.

"She's a traitor, kill her!" the padaran ordered his guards again, pointing his long, crooked finger at her, but hundreds of Faeran surrounded her, blocking the guards.

Climbing up onto the base of one of the great hall's old, rotted sculptures, Willa shouted at the padaran across the heads of the crowd.

"My father was another traitor, just like me, wasn't he, Uncle!" she yelled. "He kept clinging to the old ways, like so many of our loved ones who have gone missing." She knew that many in the clan had lost people dear to them—those who had spoken up, who had resisted, who had put the love for their family before their obedience to the padaran.

She wasn't sure anyone was listening to her, but then a voice called out to the padaran from the crowd. "Tell us what happened to Cillian!"

And then many of the Faeran started pushing toward the throne, anxious to understand. "Tell us!"

"What happened to Nea and little Alliw?" someone else cried out from the back.

Willa's heart swelled when she heard her mother's and sister's name. Someone must have remembered her family from years before, but they'd been too frightened to raise their voices until now. *Knowing brings death.*

"All my life, you told me that the humans killed my parents," she shouted at the padaran. "But I suspect that the truth is that my mother and father committed a crime in your eyes, the crime of raising their daughters in their own way, speaking the Faeran language with them, and teaching them the lore of our people. And worst of all, my father knew your name, knew who you truly were, Naillic. He was a constant reminder that you were not the padaran, you were not a god."

As she spoke, the Faeran looked upon the padaran, and they looked upon her, and they whispered and discussed among themselves, trying to put the truth together.

"You call me a traitor to the clan for what I've said and what I've done," Willa shouted at the padaran and the guards surrounding him. "And you say I'm a traitor because I freed the humans from the prisons below. But I have never stabbed a

Faeran with a spear, never punched one with a fist. I live in the old ways, where the members of a clan take care of each other and love each other."

Willa gazed across the faces of the crowd, all of them turned toward her now. "The padaran not only murders his own people, he traps and slaughters the animals of the forest who were once our friends and allies! He has abandoned the ways of the forest that keep us alive! He sends out his guards to kill innocent day-folk and capture their children! He poisons our ears with lies about the humans even as he hoards their machines in his private dens, trying to make sense of what they do!"

"If we don't adapt, we're all going to die!" the padaran bellowed, trying to intimidate them with the force of his will, but turmoil swirled through the crowd, like hundreds of bees buzzing in a corrupted hive.

She turned back to the padaran. "I ask you once again, Naillic. Tell us all. Where is your brother? Where is Cillian?"

"Stop saying that traitor's name!" the padaran spat, seething with venomous anger. His whole body seemed to glow with scintillating power as he pointed his spear toward her.

"You killed your own brother!" someone screamed. There was no greater loss to a Faeran than losing a twin brother or sister. And there was no more heinous crime among the Faeran people than killing your own twin. It was the bond that could not be broken, and Naillic had broken it. The entire crowd erupted with rage.

"He's a twin-killer!" someone yelled in the old language, and it brought a burst of joy to Willa's heart. She had thought she would never hear the language again, but now they were actually shouting it. The clan was rising up against the padaran!

"Where is my mother?" someone cried out.

"You killed my sister!" screamed another.

"What have you done, Naillic?" yelled a voice from the back.

"All the traitors of the clan must be killed!" the padaran shouted back at them, gripping his spear of power as if he was going to hurl it into the crowd. They shrank back in fear, but they did not flee.

"All of you," Willa shouted out to the Faeran people as she pointed at the padaran. "I want you to look now at Naillic with your own eyes. Can you see him? Can you truly see him? He's not a shimmering god. He's been tricking us all. He's *blending*! He's a woodwitch. He comes from a powerful family of woodwitches. He comes from *my* family! Even as he vilified the Faeran of old who built this glorious hall, even as he took this sacred place in his own name, he used his own Faeran powers to deceive us. He's disguising himself to look like everything we want our leader to be. It's all a lie!"

As everyone in the crowd gazed at the padaran in amazement, the glistening of his face and body seemed to fade.

"I see it!" someone gasped. Many of the Faeran maneuvered to get a closer look. Others pointed and whispered, their faces filled with suspicion and surprise.

The luster of the padaran's aura dimmed. The wrinkled, gray skin of his massive, old body started to become more visible.

"I see it, too! He's been tricking us!" someone called out.

"The Faeran people of the past used their woodland powers

to conceal themselves from our enemies," Willa shouted. "Naillic is the first woodwitch to use his powers to conceal himself from his own people, to trick the eyes of all the Faeran who see him."

With the help of Gillen and several of the other Faeran around her, Willa quickly climbed down from the base of the old sculpture and moved through the mass of people toward the passageway that led into the padaran's private chambers.

"Stop her!" the padaran commanded, waving his hands frantically at Lorcan and the other guards.

"We have to help her!" Gillen cried, rallying the Faeran around her. "We have to protect Willa!"

"Everyone come with me!" Willa shouted above the commotion. "Come see what the great padaran has hoarded in his dens!"

"No one gets through!" the padaran ordered his guards as he hurried to block the passageway.

"Follow me!" Willa shouted again, raising her arm above her head, and suddenly the mass of the crowd rushed the dais of the throne.

"I command you to stop!" the padaran roared.

But the people did not stop. They poured around him like water around a stone. His skin was entirely gray now, his body dripping with sweat, and his face mangled from years of deception. The padaran lunged forward with his spear and stabbed one of the oncoming Faeran in the chest, sending him dead to the ground, then he lunged again and stabbed another.

Lorcan grabbed a spear from one of the other guards and charged into battle. He thrust his spear into one rioter after another, sending them staggering back with bloody wounds. But then five of the rioters surrounded him and struck him down, wrenched the spear from his hands, and drove it into his heart. Lorcan, the commander of the padaran's guard, was finally dead.

The padaran grabbed a torch from the wall and blocked the entrance to his den.

"Stay back!" he screamed at the encroaching mob as he brandished the burning torch from side to side. "I will burn anyone who comes near!"

Leading a pack of jaetters, Gredic and Ciderg barreled into the rioters to take back the area around the throne and protect the padaran. Ciderg grabbed one of them by the head, and hurled him aside. A whole new wave of attacking guards and jaetters pushed into the crowd with their spears. But then the swarm of the angry mob fell upon Ciderg in force, striking him with many blows.

"No!" Gredic screamed, trying to save his brother, but it was too late. Ciderg's body toppled to the floor with a crash.

A new storm of confusion and violence erupted all around as jaetters and guards fought against the surging crowd.

"Stay out!" the padaran screamed as he grabbed two more torches and propped them up in the passageway to create a barrier of flame. The torches popped and smoked, and the flame burned high as he added more and more torches to the barricade.

In the midst of the chaos, a group of three hissing jaetters shoved their way through the mob. One clawed Gillen across the face. The other two knocked Willa to the ground. The teeth of the attacking jaetters chattered with anticipation as they came at her.

The flames of the padaran's torches burned upward, joining together and scorching the walls.

"If you try to get in here, you're all going to burn!" the padaran shouted at the rioters as he retreated into his private dens.

One of the torches fell and hit the woven-stick floor, catching it aflame.

As the fire spread across the floor and walls, the great Hall of the Padaran began to fill with smoke, and screams of terror rose up from the chaos of the crowd.

Willa found herself engulfed in a wave of running, screaming people and burning flames. A foot hit her in the head. Another foot stepped on her back. She tried to get up, but the running crowd trampled over her.

Crushed to the floor, she looked over to see Gillen fighting to get closer.

"Gillen!" Willa cried as she reached for her. For a moment, their fingers touched and they were almost able to grasp each other's hand, but then the mob swept Gillen away like the current of a great river and she was gone.

Filled with new determination, Willa growled and tried to get up, only to be knocked down again.

Finally, someone in the crowd stopped to help her. He held her arm and pulled her up onto her feet. She could finally breathe. She got her legs underneath her and was able to stand. Someone was saving her life. She turned with hope in her heart, but then saw Gredic's face and felt his hands clamp painfully onto her arms.

"You're coming with me, Willa," he snarled as he dragged her through the fleeing crowd.

Willa tried to yank away, but it made no difference. He held on to her tighter than he had ever held her before, as if he knew this was his last chance. He wasn't going to let her go.

The fear boiling up inside her, she fought and flailed against him, but he was far too strong. He dragged her out of the burning Hall of the Padaran and down one of the smoky side corridors.

Angry at her resistance, Gredic slammed her up against a wall and pinned her with the force of his body.

"Stop it, Willa!" Gredic shouted into her face.

She couldn't move. She couldn't breathe. He pushed against her so hard that it was like a rock had fallen against her.

"The lair is going to burn," he said, his tone ragged with fear. "Do you understand me? It's all going to burn! But you and I are going to stop fighting each other."

Willa could see what was happening. He'd lost his twin brother and his jaetter allies and now he was alone, which terrified him more than anything he had ever faced. His instinct now was to clan together, even with someone he hated. "We're going to escape. We're together now, Willa."

She could see the violence in Gredic's eyes, the need to control, to dominate, but more than anything, she could hear the desperation in his voice. She tried to jerk away from him, but he held her firm, pressed against the wall.

"We're together now, Willa," he said again, as if he could force the thought into her mind.

She knew there was no way out of this. He was never going to let her go. And even if she managed to escape him, he'd follow her. He was going to hunt her down.

She needed a different way, a different path.

She could only see one way out.

Sometimes you had to do things you didn't want to do, things that went against everything you had ever done before.

She stopped fighting him.

She became very still and she looked into his bloodshot eyes.

"All right," she said, nodding her head in agreement. "We'll leave together, through the labyrinth to my old den. I know a way out of there."

Gredic grunted, pleased that she was finally beginning to cooperate with him, but he clutched her arm, wary of a trick, and shoved her along in front of him like one of the human prisoners.

She tried to wrest her arm away from him, but he wouldn't let her go. He pushed her and dragged her down through the tunnels of the lair, leaving the smoke and flames and shouting behind them.

"The whole lair is burning up there," she said in dismay.

"We're going to make it on our own," Gredic said. "We're together now," he repeated with a clinging insistence that sent a cringe down her spine.

When they finally reached the labyrinth, she guided him

down through the stone tunnels that led toward her den.

When he realized she was leading them in the right direction, she felt his grip on her arm relax a little. She stumbled and collapsed to the floor. Gredic reflexively reached down to pull her to her feet. She leapt up and sprang away from him with all her speed. But he reached out just as quick, grabbed her by the hair, yanked her back, and pulled her off her feet. She screamed in pain as she fell backward and hit the floor, banging her head hard.

*"You're not going to escape, Willa!"* Gredic rasped as he pinned her to the ground with his hand gripping her neck. Her refusal of his offer, her rejection of him, had filled him with rage. "You're going to regret the choice you've made trying to get away from me again. I can see now the nasty little lying beast that you really are. But you're not as smart as you think you are. After I'm done with you here, I'm going to track down those three little humans of yours that you seem to care so much about. You forget how long we've been together, Willa. I know exactly where you hid them. And after I'm done with you here, I'm going to track them down and make sure they never get home."

Willa exploded with anger and squirmed from his grip, twisting her body and knocking his clutching hands away.

She leapt up and darted out of his reach, then sprinted down the corridor.

She followed the winding passageway, but she could hear his footsteps coming behind her. There was no way to outrun him for long, and he was too close for her to blend into the rock wall.

She turned down the tunnel on the left, then turned to the right. Gredic followed right behind her, growling with anger.

When she came to the end of the long, winding tunnel and took the passageway on the left, she did it knowingly. But when she felt the air turning cold, her chest seized with panic despite herself. It was a choice she could not come back from.

The blackness of the abyss was just steps away.

She came to the edge of the dark hole at the end of the tunnel, and there was nowhere else to go.

She was trapped.

The hole of the abyss fell hundreds of feet down into pitch-darkness. No one knew how deep it was, or if it even had a bottom.

Gredic lunged forward and clutched her with his bony hands.

He had grabbed her so many times over the years. She had fought him for so long. But this time, she didn't try to leap away. She didn't try to dodge him or fight him. As he charged forward, she pulled him into her, wrapped her arms around him, and held on.

*I'm going to track them down and make sure they never get home,* Gredic had said. And that was his mistake.

She leaned way back.

"We're together now, Gredic," she whispered into his ear.

In a flailing spasm of wild panic, Gredic tried to escape her embracing arms.

But it was too late.

The two of them fell together.

Willa fell through the black darkness of the abyss. Her mind screamed with fear that these were the last seconds of her life. She felt the sensation of falling in her stomach and her limbs. Her hair floated around her head. The cold air rushed past her, touching her cheeks, her arms, her legs, getting colder as she fell, deeper into the darkness.

Gredic had let go of her and she had let go of him. She knew he must be falling with her, but she could not see him.

When she hit bottom, the force of the blow struck her so hard that it sent splitting bolts of pain through her ribs. The crash bludgeoned her face as she splashed down into the churning rapids of an underground river. Her body plunged deep into the water, propelled by the force of her fall. There was no up or down, just wild spinning and tumbling over and over as the current took hold of her and swept her away.

Willa tried to pump her arms and her legs, tried to swim to what she thought was the surface and take a gasp of desperately needed air, but the river was far too powerful. It hurled her through its twisting underground tunnels, flowing through watery caves and narrow chutes. There was no surface to reach. No air. Just water flowing through stone.

But she was not alone. She had inside her everything every creature of the forest had ever taught her. She was everything every friend had given her. She was a soaring hawk and a roaring panther. She was a healing bear and a running wolf. But most importantly at this moment, she was a *river otter*.

She stopped fighting the water, stopped trying to swim against the current, stopped trying to exert her will. She tucked herself smooth, and let herself be taken with the flow, slipping through the water, *with* the water, part of the water, like her teachers had taught her. Twist and turn, slip and slide, the water was her domain.

There was no up or down, left or right, there was only one direction: the flow of the river. And she propelled herself through it as fast as she could, knowing that her only hope lay on the other side of the darkness, the other side of the caves and tunnels through which she moved. She didn't need eyes or ears or other senses. She only needed to go where the water wanted her to go, and get there as quickly as possible.

The flow of the river hurled her into a cave with a pocket of air. At last, her head broke the surface of the water. She pulled in a blessed breath, filling her lungs with the cold, damp air of the cave. Then she held her breath and went back under, continuing through the next tunnel until she reached the cave on the other side.

The underground river finally emerged out of the caves and poured fast and smooth through what felt like a world of giant boulders.

Floating easily on the current now, with her head well out of the water, she pulled in long, grateful breaths of air.

Above the water and the boulders and the trees that lined the river, a thousand stars cast their glistening light across the nighttime sky. She had never been more relieved to be alive.

Something floating in the water bumped her shoulder. Startled, she flinched away from it, and turned to defend herself.

But when she realized what it was, her heart filled with a different kind of dread.

Gredic's body was floating down the river with her. He had drowned fighting what could not be fought.

She knew she should have been happy to see him dead. But she wasn't.

The jaetters had been shattered. Kearnin had died days before. Ciderg and at least a dozen others had been killed in the battle. And now Gredic was gone as well.

She knew she should have been filled with triumph that she had defeated her enemies, but loneliness darkened her soul. Gredic and the other jaetters had been members of her clan. She had known them all her life.

A memory from years before came into her mind. Just after her sister and parents died, she and Gredic were pulled into the jaetters. The padaran and his guards took her and Gredic out into the forest alone for their initiation. By the time the guards were done with them, she and Gredic lay exhausted and bleeding on the forest floor. Jaetters weren't born; they were made. Willa remembered lying there in the dirt and the leaves, looking over at Gredic on the ground a few feet away from her. Wincing in pain, she got up onto her feet, and then she helped him up as well. He limped a few feet away, picked up two long, spear-like sticks from the forest floor, and put one of them into her hand. "We don't give up, Willa," he said to her.

As she floated down the river with Gredic's body beside her, Willa treaded water over to the river's edge, reached up to the low-hanging trees, and pulled a stick from the branches. Moving through the water back over to him, she opened Gredic's cold, white fingers, wrapped them around the stick, and then let the current take him downstream with his spear in hand. "We don't give up, Gredic," she whispered.

She was left drifting down the river alone now, beneath a jet-black sky and a spray of stars. It was quiet, almost peaceful, but there was a faint, orange light flickering on the smooth surface of the river.

Still treading water, Willa turned and looked back, up the slope of the Great Mountain. It felt like it was always there, always watching.

The Dead Hollow lair was on fire. It was a great blaze of snaking flame and black smoke rising upward into the midnight sky. From a distance, it almost looked like the Great Mountain itself was burning.

# 69

Leaving Gredic to float down the river without her, Willa crawled up onto the rocky bank.

The night air hung about her in a drifting haze of gray smoke and orange flickering light.

That was when she noticed something dripping onto the ground. It was her own blood.

Over the past few hours, she'd been speared in the neck, dragged on the floor, slammed against a wall, kicked in the side, and stepped on. Now that she'd come out of the cold water of the river and the all-consuming urgency of escape had faded behind her, her body began to hurt in places she didn't even realize could feel pain. Hialeah had bandaged the bloody wound on her neck, and the twisting roots of the floor had infused her body with a startling jolt of vital power, but she knew that she was losing too much blood. She couldn't make it very far in this wounded condition.

She gazed up toward the burning lair. She didn't want to go back up there, but there was a chance that one area of the lair in particular had survived the fire, and that it could help her.

She climbed hand over hand, up through the rocks and trees, toward the blaze. She watched as the flames consumed one area after another, the crackling of the burning sticks and the rush of the fiery wind drowning out all else, as the odor of burning wood filled the air.

*Do not say it out loud until you wish to destroy everything . . .* Her mamaw's warning about saying "Naillic" echoed in her mind. Her old den, the great hall, the homes of all the Faeran people were being destroyed by the fire. She couldn't help but feel the weight of it as she climbed.

By the time she reached Dead Hollow, most of the lair had burned down into ruined, smoking piles of charred wreckage, the dry sticks of its old walls and floors providing ample fuel for its own destruction. Where once there had been a vast hive of twisted-stick tunnels and rooms, now there was nothing left but the blackened remains of disintegrated walls and heaps of smoldering ashes.

All the Faeran of the clan had fled the lair to escape the fire, so the entire area was abandoned, and most of what remained was unrecognizable. But there was one small part of the lair at the bottom of the gorge where the fire could not go. And that was what she was hoping for.

She climbed through the ashes and debris until she reached the lowest, oldest part of the lair.

She had been in this area just a few hours before with Gredic, but now it looked completely different. All the woven-stick passageways and walls were burned away, and all that remained was the labyrinth of stone tunnels and ancient caves where she and her mamaw had lived.

Willa climbed down inside and then made her way through the tunnel that led to her den, down the passageway with the painted figures of the Faeran past. Despite the burning that had occurred above, the paintings on the stone walls had survived. She came to the River of Souls, thousands of hands touching the wall, her mother's and her father's, Alliw's and her own, the left and the right, the forward and the back, all together.

W I L L A and A L L I W, she thought, remembering the strange human symbols.

"Good morning, sister," she said, touching her living hand to her sister's handprint as she walked by. "I'm glad you made it through."

Finally, Willa came to the den where her mamaw had raised her.

Those areas of the floor that had been made out of woven sticks had burned and were gone. And the intense heat of the surrounding conflagration had melted and destroyed their cocoons and all their other belongings. Most of the small trees and other plants that her mamaw had nurtured in the small circles of light were wilted from the heat and dead.

All except one.

The little tree was still alive.

She sighed with happiness and smiled. It was sitting in a stone pot on a stone ledge, protected and safe in its little niche. It was an ancient tree, miniature in size, its small branches gnarled with age, but its tiny leaves were green with living spirit. Her heart warmed to see that the little tree was waiting for her.

"Hello, my friend," she said as she moved closer. "I know it's probably been difficult to breathe these last few hours, but don't worry. I'll get you someplace safe, with plenty of light and water and nutrients."

She took several of the leaves that had fallen from the tree and pressed them to the wound at her neck. The relief from pain was immediate. She felt the intense power of the tiny plant surging into her skin, through her muscles, and deep down into her blood. One by one, she treated the most painful of her wounds.

"Thank you, Mamaw," she whispered softly, not just for nurturing and protecting the little tree all these years. Not just for teaching her how to use it, and for the many other gifts of the mind that she'd given her. But for the love that had come with it.

"Protect it, hold on to it," her mamaw had pleaded with her before she died.

Willa hadn't understood at the time. But she knew now that her mamaw wasn't telling her to hold on to the little tree, or to the secret of Naillic's forbidden name, or even to the ancient lore of the forest. She was imploring her to hold on to what was in her heart: her love, her compassion, her sense of her soul; not just her instinct to blend, but sometimes her willingness to stand up and make herself known, to throw the spear, to spring the trap, to set things in motion that cannot be undone.

Her mamaw had been watching the decline of the Dead Hollow clan for many years, and Willa came to realize what her mamaw already knew: that the Dead Hollow clan hadn't started dying because of the arrival of the day-folk, but with the rise of the padaran who came after—the quelling of the Faeran words, the disconnection from the forest, the drowning of love and compassion and sympathy in a swarm of fear and malice and control.

Without love there could be no families, no children, no elders. There could be no future.

As she held the little tree, she came to a realization, something that she didn't think she could have understood before. For years, her mamaw had been unable to fight against the growing power of the padaran and his control of the Faeran people. To go against him meant death. Willa realized now that she herself had been her mamaw's last try. She was her last hope, to live and to love and to follow the path of the heart.

"I'll protect it, Mamaw, I swear I will. I'll protect what's in my heart," Willa whispered in the old language. "I'll never let it go."

Willa carried the little tree slowly up and out of the old stone tunnels and walked through the ashes until she reached what was once the center of the Dead Hollow lair.

She looked around her at the vast gray field of ashes.

Her premonition that she would never again see the Hall of

the Padaran—the Hall of the Glittering Birds—had been correct.

The once magnificent walls of the great hall had burned and crumbled down. The hall wasn't just empty or damaged. It was *gone.*

The great throne of the padaran had burned into a charred, blackened heap.

She stepped slowly forward, into the area that had been behind the throne.

She began to make out a dark shape on the ground. It was burned and blackened, but she could see the outline of what was once a leg, and the oblong mass of a scorched and smoldering head. The knees and elbows were folded up to the chest. The person had died cowering in fear.

A sickening feeling crept into Willa's chest. It was the dead body of the padaran, the charred bones of his gripping fingers still clinging to his spear of power.

He had run into his private rooms and blockaded his door to protect his precious human-made objects from the hands of the mob. He had gathered the looking glass and the other human-made things all around him, coveting them to the very end. He was so frightened of losing control of them that he would not leave, even as the smoke and fire came.

The spear of power and the other metal objects had survived the fire.

But he had not.

She stared at what was left of her uncle for several seconds, and then she turned away.

As she made her way out of the burned wreckage of the lair for the last time, she found a spot in the center of the destruction.

She knelt down, dug into the ashes and dirt with her hands, and planted the tree into the ground.

"I know, I know, you don't want me to leave you here," she said gently. "But you just wait and see. You'll like this new spot when the sun rises, and the rains come, and the ashes wash down into the rivers. There will be plenty for your roots to grow into."

After a few moments sitting with the little tree, she rose and started to walk away.

She took a few steps.

But then she stopped and turned and looked back at the tree, sitting so small and frail in the ashes all alone.

*Maybe you don't have to wait,* she thought. *Maybe I can give you a little bit of a head start, help you out, like you always did for me.*

She walked back over to the little tree and knelt down in the ashes in front of it.

Then she touched her fingers to the tree's tiny roots and trunk, and she closed her eyes.

At first, nothing happened, but then she began to softly sing the song that her mamaw had taught her when she was six years old, the night her parents and sister died.

The roots of the tree began to extend, reaching down into the ashes.

"That's it, little one," she whispered. "Keep coming . . ."

As the roots pulled the nutrients from the ashes of the past, the tree began to grow, its branches reaching upward and spreading outward, the leaves unfurling bright and green, and the trunk thickening as it reached toward the sky.

It was a song of death and a song of life, of growth and rebirth, with words as ancient as the mist-filled forests.

Soon the tree had grown as tall as she was, with its branches as wide as her outstretched arms. "That's it, little one, keep coming . . ." she said again, and the tree kept growing. It grew and grew, until the trunk was thick, the branches strong, and the leaves reaching far above her.

Willa smiled as the energy of the tree flowed through her body and her heart, and her own power flowed through the tree. And the moment she smiled, the branches above her head curled and turned and brightened into the shape of glittering flying birds, glowing with a bounty of blue ghost fireflies, their sparkling abundance reaching to the glistening starlit heavens above. She was sculpting like the Faeran of old.

When she was finally done, the magnificent, glowing tree stood more than a hundred feet tall in the center of the ashen devastation that had once been Dead Hollow, the moon shining down through its branches and lighting up the world around her.

Willa looked up at the tree and smiled with happiness. "Well, it's a good start, little one, a very good start indeed," she said, her heart overflowing. "I think you've got it from here."

And only then, with the little tree settled into its new home, did she rise from her knees and walk away.

As Willa made her way out of the smoking devastation of the lair and went out into the nighttime forest, the magnitude of everything that had happened began to soak into her mind.

The padaran—the god of the clan—was dead.

The ancient lair of her people had burned to the ground.

Gredic would never be able to attack her again.

Her fellow jaetters—her rivals and tormentors—were gone.

And the clan was shattered, cast out into the winds of uncertainty, without shelter, without a leader to bind them together toward a common cause.

She felt it all, swirling inside of her.

What had she done?

Was she the one who had caused all this? Had she destroyed the Faeran people?

Too dismayed to take it all in, she just kept walking.

A short time later, she came upon a Faeran boy, a little bit older than her, wandering alone among the trees, a stunned look on his face. He was one of the few young Faeran she'd ever seen who still had spots and streaks like she did, instead of mottled gray skin. He had been a jaetter like her and the others, but he had never tormented her, never stolen her take.

"Are you all right, Sacram?" she asked as she approached him, but he did not reply. And he did not look at her.

A jagged cut dripped red down Sacram's forehead. His shoulder was burned and bleeding. His hair was singed and his face was blackened with soot. The boy was mumbling to himself, but she couldn't understand him, and his eyes were glazed, as if he had taken in more than his mind could absorb.

"Sacram, it's me, it's Willa," she said, touching his arm, trying to let him know she was there. He did not resist her or pull away, but he did not respond to her, either.

"I will help you," she said, taking his arm and leading him. "Let's go this way, toward the others . . ."

As she and the lost boy walked along together, she wondered what kind of life they would lead now. In the chaos of a scattered clan, would this boy remain a jaetter like he had been before? Would jaetters even continue to exist? Would this boy even survive the winter? Or was he one of those bees flying around looking for a hive that had been destroyed?

She walked with Sacram for nearly an hour, down the mountain, away from the last burning remnants of the Dead Hollow lair, following the tracks and disturbed leaves that told her that at least some of the other Faeran of their clan had fled in this direction.

"Where is everyone?" the boy asked blankly. She wasn't even sure if he was speaking to her or himself or to someone who wasn't there.

"Where is everyone?" he mumbled sadly again, repeating himself over and over again.

She knew he needed help. He had seen too much and he was suffering from clan-shock. But if she could get him back to the others, then he might get through it.

As she walked along through the forest with the boy, she came to the decision that she wouldn't just help him. She'd help gather all the members of the clan back together. That was what she needed to do, not just for the sake of the others, but for her own clan-shock, which she knew was lodging deep in her leafy soul with every moment that passed.

Now that the padaran was gone, things were going to change. People were going to need help. They would need to relearn the ways of the forest. They would need to listen to their own hearts again and turn to each other, build families again. They would all need to work together, side by side, to make a better lair for themselves.

She began to feel an unfamiliar kind of hope in her heart, the kind of hope that could only come after desolation, after destruction, a sense that maybe, just maybe, that which had forever been unchangeable was about to change.

She picked up a scent in the air.

"We're almost there, Sacram," she told the boy. "Some of the others from our clan are just up ahead. We'll get you some food and water, and you'll be able to see everyone, and you'll start feeling well again. It's all going to be all right."

The boy's face did not change. It did not light up with hope. But his walking seemed to gain new strength and speed.

Finally, she spotted a small group of twenty or thirty Faeran in the forest ahead.

Willa held the arm of the boy as she came upon them, just to make sure he stayed steady on his feet, and to show the others that she was a friend, not a foe.

"I just wanted to make sure Sacram found his way," she said as she approached. "I've come to help in any way I can."

At first, no one seemed to see her or hear her. They were just stumbling along, their eyes staring ahead or down at the ground.

"I came to help," she said again, more loudly this time.

One of the women looked up, and then pointed at her and shouted, "There she is!"

"She's returned!" said one of the men.

Willa's heart leapt that they recognized her and were welcoming her among them. She was part of the clan again.

She led Sacram over to his mother.

"I want to help in any way I can," Willa said. "We'll gather everyone together. We'll help each other forage for food and keep warm."

"We don't need your help," the boy's mother said, grabbing Sacram by the arm and yanking him away from her.

"Burner!" one of the men hissed.

"Get out of here, burner!" said another, scowling and then spitting at her. "We don't want you here!"

"Destroyer!" the first woman shouted.

Willa stepped back, startled and confused, her heart sinking in despair. "I didn't start the fire," she said, but they didn't seem to care.

Many of them had believed in her for a little while, and they had finally been able to see through Naillic's blend. They had swarmed around her and protected her. But most of her allies had been struck down by the padaran's guards, and others had been swept up in the fear of the fleeing crowd.

*Fear follows fear.*

The Faeran had lived in Dead Hollow for hundreds of years. It had been their protection, their way of life, their hive. And she had been the one who had clenched her fist and raised her voice.

Without the lair, there would be no walls, no warmth, no protection, no clan, not the way it was before. They didn't care what she had said or what she could do. They hated her.

Then she saw one jaetter girl coming forward through the group. Willa felt a rush of relief. Gillen was alive! Her face was smudged with soot marks and her shoulder had been badly burned, but she looked as strong as ever, and she seemed as relieved that Willa had survived as Willa was that she had.

"Don't you see?" Gillen shouted out to the rest of the group. "Willa has done us a great service! She has defeated the padaran!"

"You want us to thank her for burning down our home?" one of the older Faeran sneered.

"She's given us a new chance!" Gillen said, her voice filled with hope and determination. "We're free! We'll start over. We'll build a new lair."

"Freedom is all fine and good until it snows," one of the other Faeran said.

"Or we get hungry," someone said. "I'm hungry now!"

"Willa is knowledgeable in the old ways," Gillen argued. "She can help us!"

"She's a traitor against the clan!" someone spat.

"Traitor!" called another.

As Willa looked around her at all the faces, it surprised her that many of the older Faeran in the group appeared to hate her even more than the others. She had hoped they would remember the Faeran of old that her grandmother had taught her about, but instead they seemed the most set in their ways, the most angry that their lives had been disrupted. But she could see in the hopeful faces of some of the younger Faeran that they understood that things could be different now, that a new kind of clan could be created. When she looked at her old friend, Gillen met her eyes with a brave and steady gaze. Willa could see it. Something had changed in Gillen. Something had kindled a new courage in her, and Willa knew there would be others like her.

"Now that the padaran's gone," Willa said, trying to move toward her Faeran kin, "we'll find a better way to live . . ."

"Get out of here!" one of the older Faeran hissed, and chattered his teeth at her.

"Burner!" some of the others started screaming again. "Burner!"

"I came to help . . ." Willa said, but she could see that most of the clan was against her.

It was clear that change would come soon. Gillen and the others would lead the clan anew. They would begin to find a better way. But Willa could see that very few wanted anything to do with her.

Sacram's mother ran forward and pointed at her, her face wrinkled with revulsion. "She's a clan-breaker!" the woman screamed.

Gillen and several others tried to stop them, but it was no use.

Many of the Faeran hissed and shouted at Willa. And then some of the men picked up long sticks from the ground and charged at her. Others hurled stones. Willa ducked down and covered her head with her hands and arms as she ran away, the stones striking her ears and neck and shoulders with painful blows.

She ran down into the narrow gulley of a stream, scrambled beneath a fallen log, and curled into a shaking ball.

Hiding in that dark little hole, she buried her face in her hands and wept.

Willa rubbed her eyes, then crawled out from beneath the log. She brushed the dirt and the centipedes and the little bits of bark from her hair and her arms, and looked around her.

She had once again been cast from her clan. What was she going to do now? Where was she going to go? Should she howl for Luthien? Should she go back to the sacred lake of the bears? Should she find the mother deer and fawn that she had met by the stream? She knew she had the knowledge and skill to live safely in the forest on her own for many years. But she also knew that a tree needed more than water and soil to survive.

As she clambered out of the gulley of the stream and came up onto a mound of high ground, she caught a glimpse of movement across the river.

Her heart leapt. The black panther and a dark brown mountain lion were traveling along the edge of the river.

The two big cats were moving quickly and with determination, traveling east, as if they were on a long journey over the mountain to some distant land.

They were such beautiful and majestic beasts, filled with a power and confidence that amazed her. She could see that they had sustained wounds from some sort of battle, but the wounds didn't seem to be slowing them down.

She was so glad to see the cats. She didn't know who or what they were, or why normally solitary animals were traveling the way they were, but she loved how they were together.

"Good-bye, my friend," she whispered in the old language to the black panther, wishing her well wherever her journey would take her.

After everything that had happened since the night she was shot, and as she watched the departing panther, she felt such a profound and aching loneliness, a sense that she was truly on her own now. But there was something about the panther that gave her hope as well, hope in friendship, hope in alliance, hope in a future that she knew she could not yet imagine. She knew that she wasn't like the black panther. She wasn't fierce of heart or sharp of claw like many of her animal friends. She wasn't a leader or a fighter. She had never raised a weapon or struck a blow against anyone or anything, and she vowed that she never would. She was just a Faeran girl, a night-spirit named Willa, trying to find her way.

"Willa of the Wood," she said to herself, knowing a little better now exactly what that meant.

She had said the words very quietly beneath her breath, but

the moment she spoke them, the black panther stopped on the trail, turned its head, and looked across the river toward her. The panther's yellow eyes stared straight at her.

Willa's normal instinct when she was spotted by a predator was to blend into her leafy surroundings and disappear. And it would have been easy to do here, easy to never be seen again.

But that was not what she wanted.

Her heart was beating heavily in her chest, but she held her blend back.

She wanted the panther to see her.

The panther gazed at her for a long time. Was the panther wondering where she'd come from and exactly what she was? Was the panther wondering if she would make a good ally in the fight against the dark and mysterious dangers of the world?

Willa held the panther's gaze with her bright green eyes.

"Willa of the Wood," she said again, and she smiled. She was a creature of the forest, with the lore and spirit of her grandmother within her. She spoke the old language and the new. She could sense the movement of the rivers and hear the whispers of the trees. And she thought that someday, just maybe, she and this panther might meet again.

As the hours passed, the smoky haze of midnight flames slowly gave way to the coming dawn, with Venus, the Morning Star, rising from the black silhouettes of the mountain ridges, up into the dark blue of the glowing sky.

As the sun began to rise from behind the Great Mountain, Willa's thoughts turned to the humans.

She just hoped that in all the chaos and violence of the night none of the guards or jaetters had found Cassius, Beatrice, or any of the other children as they fled through the forest and down the mountain. *Keep running,* she thought to her young day-folk friends, *keep running all the way home.*

And then she thought about the last of the three human children to escape through the hole.

*Follow the east side of the creek and look for a small cave in the rocks,* she had told Hialeah. *Stay quiet and hidden until morning.*

She didn't know what she was going to do in the world now that the lair had been destroyed, or where she was going to go, but she wanted to finish the one thing she had begun: to make sure that Nathaniel's children made it home.

She followed the creek toward the spot she had told them to hide.

As she approached the area, her mind clouded with dark thoughts she couldn't control. She'd seen so much fighting and death. What if the children never made it to the hiding spot? What if they had been attacked or recaptured?

When she saw Hialeah crouched near the crevice in the rocks, Willa's chest flooded with relief.

*She's there,* Willa thought. *She made it.*

Hialeah had light brown skin and beautiful chestnut eyes, which made a striking combination as she stared out from the rocks, scanning the forest for danger. Her long, straight black hair fell evenly on either side of her face, and her mouth was set in a serious expression. Her plain brown dress was dirty from weeks of imprisonment and the trek down into the gulley of the creek, and it was torn where she had used it to make a bandage for Willa's neck, but Hialeah looked strong and capable.

Willa moved forward through the broken tumble of giant rocks until she was no more than a few steps from Hialeah, then slowly revealed herself, trying not to startle her.

Hialeah's face immediately lit up. "You made it!" she said as she moved toward her. It startled Willa when Hialeah wrapped her arms around her and pulled her close. Willa couldn't help but smile. Hialeah was probably her same age, but taller and stronger than her, and there was something invigorating about her embrace. It was a strange and glorious feeling to be held by this bold human girl, to feel the arms of her friendship around her.

"Thank you for saving me and my brothers," Hialeah said.

"You're welcome," Willa said happily.

When they separated, Hialeah looked Willa over more closely, checking the bandage on her neck.

"The cut . . ." Hialeah said in astonishment, ". . . and your other wounds . . . They're almost healed."

"I got a little help from an old friend," Willa said.

"You came back!" Iska said enthusiastically as he crawled out of the cave, holding his little brother by the hand.

"Sshh! We're supposed to be hiding!" Hialeah scolded him.

"It's all right now," Iska insisted. "Willa's here! She'll protect us!"

"I don't know if I can protect anyone—" Willa started to say, but following his sister's lead, Iska leapt at Willa and embraced her, wrapping both his arms around her. "During the night, we decided we weren't going to leave this cave until you got here."

Willa frowned and looked at him. "I told you that we wouldn't see each other again, that you should go home without me," she said in confusion.

"We saw the flames during the night," Iska said. "We knew something bad happened."

"We were worried about you," Hialeah said.

"I knew she'd make it," Iska said proudly and defiantly.

"No you didn't," Hialeah contradicted him. "You were

fretting about her all night. We all were. Even Inali was asking about you."

Willa was glad to see her friends were all right, and she was happy to see their smiling faces, but she knew they had a long way to go before they were home.

And she also knew that it was those same smiling faces that were going to change everything when the three children came back into their father's life.

She felt as if her time with Nathaniel had been as rare and ethereal as the soft glow of the blue ghost fireflies on a long, dark night, but his reunion with his real children would be like the rise of the sun. The faint magic that had warmed Nathaniel's wounded heart for a little while would fade into nothingness in the brightness of the coming day.

And she knew that with his children sleeping at night down the hall once more, the man Nathaniel would no longer have a need for a strange, night-spirit creature to be hanging in a woven cocoon from the ceiling in his room.

She knew all of this, and it filled her with a wilting sadness, but she tried to stay strong in her heart, clinging to the idea that she had this one good thing in her life.

"I'll tell you the way home from here," Willa said. "The journey is long and difficult, but just keep following this creek until it meets the river, and then follow the river down into the valley."

"But we don't know the way," Iska said with a sudden firmness that surprised her.

"If you follow the river, you won't get lost," Willa said.

She knew she couldn't go with them. The pain would be too great. It was *their* home, not hers. The man Nathaniel was *their* father, not her father. She knew she couldn't bear to see them together as a family as she had once been with Nathaniel. And she couldn't bear to say good-bye to him again.

"But what if someone attacks us along the way?" Hialeah said, seeming to join in with her brother's sudden and bewildering stubbornness.

"The night-spirits have been scattered," Willa said. "I don't think any of the guards and jaetters will be coming down here."

"But they might," Iska said. "They might be scouring the river, looking for easy prey."

"They might be very angry about what happened last night and want revenge on any humans they find," Hialeah joined in.

"If they find us, they'll kill us!" Iska insisted, nodding his head vigorously. "You've got to come with us, Willa."

"I'm sorry, Iska, I can't," Willa said.

The expression on Iska's face dropped in disappointment. "Why not?" he asked, his voice shaking with emotion.

"Your father has been missing all of you terribly . . ." she began uncertainly, looking at Iska, Hialeah, and Inali. "But when he sees the three of you . . ."

Her words dwindled off. She knew she didn't have an answer that she could explain to them. But as they all stared at her with their determined eyes, she could see they weren't going to give up.

"All right," she said finally. "I'll take you down the river into the valley. I'll get you home, and then we'll say good-bye."

It would have normally been a four-hour journey down into the valley, moving along the narrow edge of the river and climbing over the larger rocks, but with the three humans, it took much longer. Despite his initial enthusiasm, Iska struggled to keep up. And although Hialeah did not complain about carrying Inali mile after mile, Willa could see the girl was struggling.

"I'll take him," Willa said, gathering Inali into her arms, and the little human clung to her like a baby possum to his momma's fur. When she moved too fast or leapt to a particularly distant rock, Inali gripped her extra tight and whispered "Don't let me go" in her ear.

The children made too much noise when they traveled. They talked loud. They walked loud. They breathed loud. And their monotone skin stuck out so conspicuously in the forest that it was a wonder that this species had ever survived their journeys through the world. She was sure that every predator in the area was going to hear their heavy, tromping feet and see their bright faces and arms.

But on the other side of it, she liked how as soon as she took Inali into her arms, Hialeah began helping Iska up the steeper climbs, and sometimes Iska helped her in return, brother and sister, making their way home. Humans weren't always born as twins like Faeran were, but the bond was there. She could see it.

As they traveled home, they came upon a pack of jaetters with sharpened spears scavenging along the bank of the river. Willa ducked down behind a rock with Inali and pulled Iska toward her. "Shh," she whispered to Inali, touching his lips with her finger. Hialeah quickly pinned herself behind a pine tree. *Smart girl,* Willa thought. *She's learning quick.*

Another time they saw a group of six loggers with axes and picks trudging along a path through the forest. *Just keep walking,* Willa told the men in her mind, as she and the children hunkered down in the bushes beside the trail.

Working together over the next few hours, they hid and they snuck, they ran and they climbed, until the spruce and firs of the mountain slopes began to give way to the leafy trees of the valley.

Finally, she and the three children came to the pools of reflecting water that lay in the stones along the bank of the river. Willa remembered looking into these pools and seeing her face turn to stars on the night she was shot.

"We're here," she said softly to the others, not quite able to keep the sadness from creeping into her voice.

"She's right, this is our part of the river!" Iska said excitedly, seeming not to notice her solemn tone. "These are our rocks! We're almost home!"

As he said these words, Willa's heart filled with a slow and quiet sorrow. She knew she would soon be parting from her companions and on her own again.

They approached the house from the same direction Willa had that first night she came to fill her satchel. She remembered worrying about the possibility of a vicious dog and violent men with killing-sticks. And she remembered studying the day-folk lair made from murdered trees and stones broken from the bones of the river.

It felt so different now.

Other than the den she had shared with her mamaw, this was the only place where she had ever felt like she belonged.

She knew she shouldn't approach the house. She knew that it was going to hurt. But she kept walking, Iska on one side and Hialeah on the other, and Inali in her arms.

The house came into view.

She just wanted to get one last glimpse of the man named Nathaniel, and then she would go.

But as she scanned the house and the barn and the mill, she did not see him. He didn't appear to be outside. And the house looked quiet and still.

*Too quiet and too still.*

The empty porch.

The closed door.

The shut-up windows.

The dark rooms.

There was something about it that made her certain that the house was empty, and that he wasn't just gone. He was gone for good.

Iska and Hialeah didn't seem to notice any of this. Willa set Inali down. Then the three children ran together happily and noisily across the grass, up the steps, and banged through the front door into the house.

Willa watched and listened.

"He's not here!" Iska said as he ran through the house, looking in the kitchen and the other rooms.

"He's gone," Hialeah said, her voice filled with confusion and disappointment.

As Willa stepped through the front door into the main room of the house, she glanced at the spot where Nathaniel kept his rifle. The rifle was gone, along with the knapsack he used for long journeys.

Iska dashed up the stairs, ran from room to room, and then called down to them. "He's not up here either! It looks like he's taken his clothes."

Willa looked at the mantel over the fireplace. The photograph of the family that had been there was gone.

He hadn't just gone hunting. And he hadn't gone into town for supplies. He had left for good.

"Why did he leave?" Hialeah said, her voice on the edge of breaking down.

Willa shook her head. *This can't be,* she thought. *He can't be gone. I can still smell him.*

"Where did he go?" Iska asked.

"He hasn't been gone long," Willa said. "I think we just missed him."

"We need to go after him," Hialeah said. Willa could tell that she was exhausted, but she wasn't going to give up.

"But we don't even know which way he went!" Iska cried in despair. Willa knew that it wasn't like him to lose hope, but the disappearance of his father after all this time was more than he could bear.

"Don't worry," Willa said, touching his arm. "He can't have gotten far. There's one place I know he'll stop before he leaves here. We'll pick up his scent there and track him. And don't worry—he leaves big footprints."

Willa led them outside and across the grass of the front yard. Hialeah walked stoically beside her, carrying Inali in her arms, but Willa could tell by her quietness and the stern look on her face that she was worried. She was the older sister, the protector, the one who knew what to do, but she was seconds from tears.

As they walked through the sourwood trees and entered the meadow, Willa saw Nathaniel at the far end.

He was standing over the graves, his gun and his knapsack slung over his shoulder, his head hanging low, saying his last prayers and his last good-bye. It appeared he was leaving what was once his life, and setting out on a new journey, perhaps never to return. There had been too much loss here, too much pain. He had given up hope. And now he was going to leave the world, the mountains, the forests, all that he had once loved.

"Papa!" Iska shouted as he ran toward his father.

Hialeah ran quickly behind him, still carrying her little brother.

Hearing Iska's shouts, Nathaniel closed his eyes very hard, as if he could not believe what he was hearing. It was as if he thought his mind was playing cruel tricks on him. He clenched his eyes shut, blocking out the pain.

But as Iska ran toward him and kept shouting, Nathaniel finally opened his eyes and turned.

A look of shock covered his face. His face shifted as if he wouldn't allow himself to believe what he was seeing. He was standing on the graves of his children, but his children were running toward him.

And then, all at once, he seemed to give way. Nathaniel set down his rifle and supplies, and fell to his knees as his children dove into his arms, shouting and talking and carrying on. He wrapped himself around them and pulled them close. The children were ragged, dirty, scratched, and bruised, but they were here, and they were full of joy.

The man Nathaniel began to sob with tears of relief and gratitude. He held his children tight as he cried and kissed them, quickly and repeatedly, one after another, cupping their faces in his hands and looking at them, then pulling them close again.

"You're alive! I can't believe it!" he was muttering. "Thank God, you're alive!"

Iska talked rapidly and excitedly, telling his father about everything they'd been through, how he was captured, how he had survived in the prison, how Willa had fed him cookies, and how they had worked together to escape. The stoic Hialeah didn't say a word at first, but as soon as her father looked at her and gently asked how she was doing, she broke down and wept in his arms.

Through all of this, Willa remained standing where she was. In the forest at the edge of the meadow. Very still. Her eyes watching it all. Her heart beating hard in her chest. She did not step into the meadow. The meadow was not hers anymore. The meadow was Nathaniel's and his family's. It was the resting place of family lost and the embraces of family found, but it was not hers.

She looked up at the Great Mountain, with the mist clearing from its rounded peak. *The mountain knew.* The mountain had been watching all along, and it was still watching, still with her, and the mountain knew.

As she turned and looked at the humans again, she saw that

Nathaniel finally had what he most wanted in the world. He had finally found his children.

She breathed in long, slow, deep breaths, ragged and unsteady, waves of emotion pouring through her, churning up inside her, but as she watched them, she couldn't help but feel something building inside her, just seeing them together, filled with such happiness and joy. She felt a great swelling in her heart, almost a sense of pride, a sense that she had done something worthwhile. And that was all she could cling to: that she had done what she had set out to do.

Finally, she turned and walked away, silent and invisible, into the forest in the same way she had come.

As she walked back to the river, she said good-bye to everyone in her mind.

She said good-bye to Gredic and the other jaetters, and the survivors of her clan who would find a new way without her.

She said good-bye to her mother and her father, who had passed away so long ago.

She said good-bye to her little twin sister, Alliw, who she'd played with as a child and lived now in the ancient stone of Dead Hollow.

She said good-bye to her mamaw, who had given her all that she had become and all that she would ever be, who had nurtured her and cared for her, from a seed into a tree.

She said good-bye to the boy Iska, who had spoken to her through the door of his prison cell; and his little brother, Inali, whom she had carried in her arms; and his bold sister, Hialeah, who had led her brothers down through the valley during the night to their hiding spot in the cave beside the river.

And, wiping tears from her eyes as she walked away, she said good-bye to the man Nathaniel, who on a frightening night, after losing everything he cared for, had shown her a single moment of kindness. And started it all.

Suddenly a large hand gripped her shoulder and turned her around quite forcefully.

Startled, Willa looked up to see Nathaniel's bright blue eyes staring down at her. He and the three children surrounded her, all looking at her.

"Where do you think you're going?" Nathaniel asked.

"I—I—" she stuttered.

"How is all this possible, Willa?" he demanded in amazement. "How did you do all this?"

Willa thought about the how and the when and the why she had done what she had done.

Then she looked up at Nathaniel and said, "I just wanted to do one kind thing."

As Nathaniel looked at her, his brows furrowed, his eyes narrowed, and he pursed his lips, as if he was struggling to understand her. "But where are you going now?" he asked, his voice filled with sadness.

"I don't know," she said softly.

Nathaniel shook his head as if he was frustrated with her answer. He knelt down on one knee in front of her, held her gently by the shoulders, and looked into her eyes. "Do you understand what happened, Willa? You just vanished. After the loggers attacked, you just left. I thought you had gone for good. I thought you left me. I couldn't stand it anymore. There was nothing left here for me but memories and pain."

Willa listened to his story in shock. She could hear the strain in his voice. She had no idea what he had been going through since she had left.

"But now," Nathaniel continued, his voice softening, "with the children back . . . and with you . . . Willa, please don't leave. You're part of my family. I love you."

"We all love you!" Iska said, touching her shoulders.

"Stay with us," Hialeah said, grasping her hand. "You can sleep in my room if you want."

"Or you can sleep in the tree if you want. You can sleep wherever you want to," Nathaniel said. "It doesn't matter. Just stay."

Too stunned to talk, Willa gazed around at their expectant faces. Was this actually happening? Or had she fallen asleep under the log after being scorned by her clan, and all this was a dream?

She had always thought of love as the rarest and most delicate of things, and that there must be a limit to the amount of love that a human or a Faeran could give or feel, a limit to how much love there could be in the world. She had thought that once the man Nathaniel had reunited with his real children there would be no place for her. But love wasn't the stone. It was the river. Love was like the glistening stars in the midnight sky, like the sun that always rises, and the water that always flows.

A part of her deep down inside feared that the more she

loved the day-folk, the less she would love the forest, that her memory of her forest ways would fade and her powers dwindle. But here with Nathaniel and his children, it didn't feel as if her world was diminishing. It felt as if it was expanding, growing, changing. Love was infinite in so many ways. It felt as if she could keep opening her heart to the magic in the world, and the magic in the world would keep filling it.

The only way she could live and grow into the girl her mamaw worked so hard for her to become was with the nutrients of a family's earth and the warmth of a family's sunlight.

Finally, unable to find the words she needed in a language they could understand, she slowly leaned forward and put her head against Nathaniel's chest. Tears welled up in her eyes, and she wrapped her arms around him.

The three children cheered and hollered, for they knew what it meant, and Nathaniel whispered, "This is your home now, Willa."

*Move without a sound. Steal without a trace,* Willa thought, remembering what she'd been thinking that first night she crept up toward the house.

"I think I may have stolen your hearts," Willa said. "And you've stolen mine."

THE END

# Acknowledgments

*Willa of the Wood* takes place in the Great Smoky Mountains, straddling the border between North Carolina and Tennessee. As one of the oldest mountain ranges on Earth, the Great Smokies is not only the most visited national park in America, it is also the most biologically diverse, with over 1,600 species of flowering plants, 100 species of native trees, 30 species of salamanders, 50 species of ferns, and much more.

I would like to thank the Friends of the Great Smoky Mountains National Park, the Great Smoky Mountains Association, and the US National Park Service for all the important work they do to manage and preserve this cherished region of our country.

Special thanks to Steve Kemp for working with me on the manuscript. He was a wonderful resource and constant stream of knowledge on the Great Smoky Mountains.

Special thanks to Esther and Bo Taylor—respected members of the Eastern Band of Cherokee Indians and valiant guardians of the Cherokee language. Among the many important roles they play in the community, Esther is the media coordinator at Cherokee Elementary School and Bo is a storyteller and archivist, as well as the Executive Director at the Museum of the Cherokee Indian in Cherokee, North Carolina. Thank you for your guidance and assistance on the *Willa of the Wood* manuscript.

And special thanks to Sara Snyder, PhD, Director of the Cherokee Language Program at Western Carolina University.

I would also like to thank my editor, Laura Schreiber, and editor-in-chief, Emily Meehan, and the whole Disney Hyperion team for their ongoing support and insight. I feel honored every day to be part of the Disney Hyperion family.

My deepest appreciation to my wife, Jennifer, who worked closely and diligently with me on this novel through the entire process to help shape the story to what it became.

Special thanks to my daughter Camille for our early morning treks into Willa's world, our long walks along the river, our climbs through the moss-covered rocks, and for all the story notes we took together along the way. May you always see the many colors of green, Camille. And thank you to my daughters Genevieve and Elizabeth for their feedback and ideas on Willa's story.

Thank you to the team of freelance editors who provided input on the story: Sam Severn, Jenny Bowman, Kira Freed, and Jodi Renner.

Thank you to my publicists and managers, Scott Fowler and Lydia Carrington, for everything they do, and to my literary agent, Bill Contardi, who started it all.

Finally, I would like to thank the good people of western North Carolina and eastern Tennessee for your continued support, encouragement, and enthusiasm.

Robert Beatty
Asheville, North Carolina

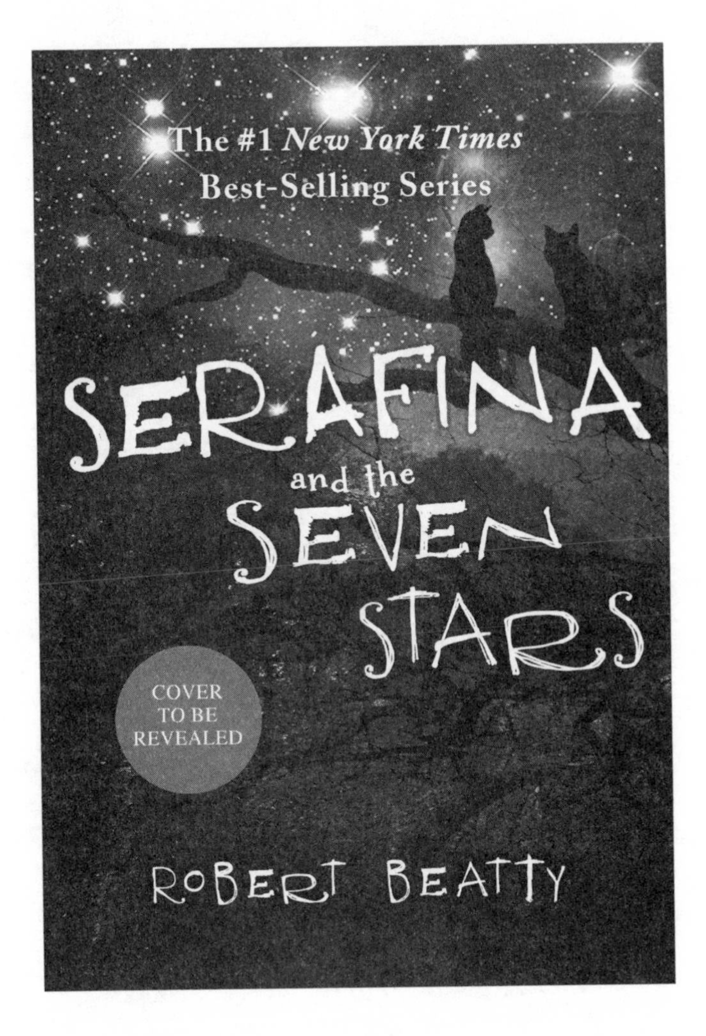


Turn the page to start reading a
brand-new book in the Serafina series!

**Biltmore Estate**

Asheville, North Carolina

1900

Serafina raced through the forest, her sharp panther claws ripping into the leafy autumn ground, propelling her long, black-furred body through the underbrush. She scrambled up moss-covered rocky slopes and dashed through shaded meadows of swaying ferns, making her way swiftly home.

The sound of rapid footfalls charged up behind her.

She burst forward with new speed, leaping over the trunk of a fallen tree, then tearing through an open field.

But now two of them were on her, snarling as they lunged at her sides.

The first mountain lion pounced on her back with a ferocious growl and tumbled her to the ground. The second slammed into her head.

She spun on them with a hissing bite, pushing them away

with her legs and swatting them repeatedly with her claws retracted, then broke free and ran.

*You silly cats need to get out of here,* she thought as she leapt the stream that marked the backside of Diana Hill. *We're getting too close to the house. You've got to go back.*

She surged forward, trying to put enough distance between her and her young half sister and half brother that they would finally return to the depths of the forest. But seeing her attempts to outrun them, they became more invigorated than ever. Her sister bounded ahead of her, growling playfully as she looked back at Serafina over her shoulder, challenging Serafina to chase her.

*Slow down,* Serafina thought as they reached the top of the hill. *You need to be careful here.*

But in that instant, the air exploded with the loud wrenching sound of twisting metal, bending wire, and a mountain lion yowling in pain. Her sister had been running so fast that she never saw the wire fence in her path, didn't even know what a fence was, and slammed right into it. The terrified lion kicked and clawed, trying desperately to fight this strange, coiling attacker.

The other mountain lion circled his sister's flailing, wire-entangled body in agitation, but was utterly unable to help her.

Serafina's heart lurched in panic. She quickly shifted into human form and moved toward her struggling sister.

The more the young mountain lion fought against the wire, the more entangled she became.

Serafina grabbed the rat's nest of metal with her bare hands and tried to tear it away. But the lion kept fighting, pulling against the wires, scratching and biting and growling.

"Just stay still, cat. You're wigglier than a pollywog in a pond. Just stay still. I'm trying to help you!" Serafina told her sister in exasperation, but as the entwined lion stared up at her with her golden eyes, Serafina knew her sister couldn't understand her.

"I told you we were done playing for the day," she said as she pulled and pried at the wire. "You shouldn't try to follow me home. We're too close to the house."

As she worked to free her sister, she glanced around to get her bearings. A short distance away, surrounded by the vine-wrapped stone columns of a small gazebo, stood Biltmore's Roman statue of Diana, Goddess of the Hunt, with a bow in one hand, a quiver of arrows on her back, and a deer standing at her side.

*We're far too close,* Serafina thought again, as she struggled with a length of wire that had ensnared her sister's legs. Her brother and sister might get themselves into all sorts of trouble if they passed into the grounds of the mansion; the last thing she needed was for someone to spot a mountain lion running across Biltmore's lawn.

From this high position atop Diana Hill, Serafina could see Biltmore House below her, with its pale-gray limestone walls and leaded-glass windows gleaming in the light of the setting sun, the steeply slanted slate-blue rooftops piercing the sky, and the misty ranges of the Blue Ridge Mountains rising in the distance.

The house was a beautiful sight, tranquil and serene. But

she didn't trust pleasant feelings. Or beauty. And she definitely couldn't cotton to the nerve-wracking peace and quiet that had been slithering around the estate for the last several months. This mishap with her sister aside, nothing sinister had happened at Biltmore in a long time, but she hadn't been able to shake the feeling that it soon would.

She finally managed to get her sister out of most of the wires, but there was still a bad one wrapped around her front leg. The lion kept yanking her paw away at the worst possible moment, anxious to get free, but hindering Serafina's efforts.

"Just hold on, girl," Serafina said, stroking the lion's head. "I'm almost done."

There were small cuts on her sister's shoulders and legs, but Serafina wasn't sure how she could help her. She didn't have any bandages, and even if she did, there wasn't any way to keep them in place.

*I need Braeden,* she thought in frustration. *He would know what to do. He would calm the lion and heal her wounds.*

But Braeden was gone. And the shock of it still throbbed in Serafina's heart. After all their struggles, fighting to stay together and to stay alive, they had been undone by a few words on a wretched piece of paper in a city far away. She had wanted him to stand up, to fight, to slash at his uncle's words.

But he couldn't fight it. He knew he *shouldn't* fight it.

And now she was once again alone.

As she wrenched the last of the twisted wire from her sister's leg, the lion rose to her feet and rubbed her whiskered face appreciatively against Serafina's cheek. And their brother came over and rubbed his shoulders against them as well.

It seemed as if maybe they were a little sorry for their rambunctiousness, and she was sorry, too. She should have stopped running sooner than she did and warned them of the dangers of the man-made world. Biltmore's groundskeepers must have put up the wire fence to protect the stand of small maple trees they had planted at the top of Diana Hill. The cubs were full-grown now, but they were still young and inexperienced.

But as she was hugging her brother and sister, a shift in the breeze touched the bare skin on the back of her neck, and put a chill down her spine.

Startled, she turned and scanned the line of trees surrounding the distant house, looking for any sort of danger: a mysterious figure or encroaching enemy—anything that might signal that trouble was a-prowl.

She studied the balconies and towers of the house for unusual movement, and then the gate, the road, and the paths leading into the gardens.

Over the last few months, she had patrolled the grounds day and night, sleeping only when she had to, for her memories of her past battles never slept.

*No,* she told herself as she gazed down at the house and out across the mountains, she wasn't going to let any of this beauty and pleasantness fool her.

Something was wrong.

Something was *always* wrong at Biltmore.

Black cloaks and twisted staffs, shadowed sorcerers in the murky night—she didn't know in what form it would come, but she was the Guardian of Biltmore Estate, and she knew she had to stay alert, or people were going to die.

When she heard a sound drifting through the forest from the north, goose bumps rose on her arms.

She tilted her head and listened.

The whispers of the wind moved through the boughs of the trees.

She didn't trust wind. Or trees.

In the months since her past battles, the slightest creak of a distant stick or the faint rustling of leaves had sent her into a twitch and a shifting glance. And now, as she stood on the hill and heard the sound of the whispering wind coming toward her, she wasn't sure whether it was truth or lie, but a crawling sensation crept up her sides.

Pulling a long breath in through her nose, she smelled something on the breeze, a trace of sulfur and charcoal that she hadn't smelled in a long time. It reminded her of death.

And then she began to hear the sound more clearly: the clip-clop of trotting hooves, a carriage coming up the Approach Road toward Biltmore.

The logical part of her human mind told her that not all carriages were filled with demons and murderers. But her lungs started sucking in air, as if they knew they would soon be needed.

*This could be nothing,* she tried to tell herself. *It could be a carriage full of kind and gracious gentlefolk coming for a pleasant visit.*

But her heart pounded in her chest.

*The beauty. The forest. The wind.*

She quickly turned to her brother and sister. "Now listen—get on out of here, right away! Run!"

For once, the two big cats did exactly what she told them, hightailing it into the cover of the forest.

Serafina ran to protect Biltmore even as a carriage and its team of horses came barreling through the main gate into the courtyard. Before she could even see who was inside, a second carriage came rolling in behind it, and then a third, until there were thirteen carriages in all, their drivers steering them straight toward the front doors of the house.